Praise for *Blood of the Dead*

"*Blood of the Dead* isn't what you think it is. Sure, it starts out as a zombie jamboree that drags you through hell on Earth, but then it goes further . . . a *lot* further . . . and takes you straight to hell and back again. This is the stuff of nightmares, boys and girls, with some unnerving and frightening action scenes that will have you on the edge of your seat and haunt your dreams."

- Rick Hautala, author of *The Wildman* and *Occasional Demons*

"A satisfying addition to the ever-growing zombie subgenre . . . non-stop action and flesh-eating mayhem . . . *Blood of the Dead* will be enjoyed by any zombie fan."

- *The Horror Fiction Review*

"Frantically paced and never predictable, *Blood of the Dead* takes the usual staples of the zombie-genre—blood, guts, guns and action—and mixes them with the bizarre to create a unique story. It's a formidable mix— think *Night of the Living Dead* with a healthy dash of *Dante's Inferno*! Fuchs leads his cast through a nightmare world filled with relentless pain, constant fear and never-ending waves of dead flesh, then takes them some place worse . . . . You've never read a zombie story like this before!"

- David Moody, author of the *Autumn* series

"Talented author A.P. Fuchs has woven a bloody tapestry out of human flesh, the dark ruins of a decimated earth and the raw fear and uncertainty of the few remaining survivors. Richly drawn characters face loss, isolation, hunger and, of course, hordes of the living dead in this post-apocalyptic gem. Zombie fans will do themselves well by picking up a copy of *Blood of the Dead*. Scary, heartbreaking and imaginative, this book sits near the top of my very short list of zombie favorites. An absolute blast!"

- Gina Ranalli, author of *Chemical Gardens* and *Wall of Kiss*

"Fuchs presents a hellish apocalypse underneath poisoned skies in *Blood of the Dead*. Well-drawn characters navigate the very edge of a meat grinder powered by Fuchs's twisted imagination. The *Undead World Trilogy* looks to be a promising addition to the genre."

- Gregory Solis, author of *Rise and Walk*

"Unrelenting and unnerving, Fuchs crafts an apocalyptic tale of empty humanity among a world overrun by the living dead. A world uniquely envisioned and vividly crafted by the imagination of A.P Fuchs. *Blood of the Dead* offers a rich blend of guns and gore that is sure to please the most diehard of zombie fans."

- Geoff Bough, Editor of *Revenant Magazine*

Book One of the *Undead World Trilogy*

BLOOD
OF THE
DEAD

by

A.P. FUCHS

COSCOM ENTERTAINMENT
WINNIPEG

COSCOM ENTERTAINMENT
130 Stanier Street
Winnipeg, MB R2L 1N3 Canada

ISBN - 10 1-897217-80-3
ISBN - 13 978-1-897217-80-1

PUBLISHED BY COSCOM ENTERTAINMENT
www.coscomentertainment.com
Text set in Garamond; Printed and bound in the USA
COVER PENCILS AND INKS BY ROLAND BIRD
COVER COLORS BY SPLASH!
EDITED BY RYAN C. THOMAS
INTERIOR AUTHOR PHOTO BY ROXANNE FUCHS

Library and Archives Canada Cataloguing in Publication

Fuchs, A. P. (Adam Peter), 1980-
    Blood of the dead / by A.P. Fuchs.

(Undead world ; bk. 1)
ISBN 978-1-897217-80-1

    I. Title. II. Series : Fuchs, A. P. (Adam Peter), 1980-
Undead world ; bk. 1.
PS8611.U34B59 2008   C813'.6   C2008-902786-8

This is for my kids, Gabriel and Lewis.

Special thanks, as always, to my wife, Roxanne, for putting up with all the late nights and endless hours in front of the computer.

A thank you to my best friend, Bruce Hoadley, for being my "come with" guy when I went on my research trip for this book. (Nobody takes down zombies like he does.)

Thanks goes out to Brian Tanner, M.S.C., for answering some physics questions I had regarding a scene in this story, and likewise to Ian Sunderland, M.D., for being the wonderful body part specialist that he is.

Lastly, to Mari Adkins and T.L. Trevaskis for all the translation help. Thank you.

Book One of the *Undead World Trilogy*

BLOOD
OF THE
DEAD

GUTS

JOE BAILEY
ZOMBIE HUNTER

"Whattsa matter, baby? Never made love to a zombie before?"

The man's voice was filled with sarcasm but, looking on from the shadows, Joe Bailey couldn't help but think the guy meant every word and that he truly did want the girl to mess around with the dead man in front of her.

The girl, a blonde of probably seventeen or eighteen, frantically tugged at the iron collar around her neck. Joe knew that getting it off would be impossible. The collar was attached to a long iron rod. On the other end was the guy who wanted to see her come apart at the prospect of defiling herself with the undead.

Who knew what they had already done to her before now. What was once an off-yellow dress was mere tatters sagging off her frame like a torn shower curtain. Her cries were muffled by the band of silver duct tape across her mouth. From where Joe lurked off to the side, he could see how her long blonde hair had been pulled forward across her cheeks and stuffed into her mouth to help keep her quiet.

The air stank with booze and dope and the funk of the dead.

The man holding the rod jerked it to the right and left, whipping the girl side to side as he steered her toward the dead man across the basement floor. Four of his friends looked on, yipping and cheering. All five men were eager for what was about to happen. Three were on one side of the room, including the man holding the pole; two were across the way, both gripping a similar iron pole. This one was attached to another collar, one clamped around the neck of an overweight gray-skinned man with a blood-stained white shirt, brown dress pants and only one shoe. The fat man, Joe supposed, had probably been a hard worker when he was alive. Though he was now dead but somehow back to life, he still carried a look of innocence in his eyes, a look of pleading behind the rage and mindless hunger that consumed him.

The jerks cackled and cheered and stepped closer as their buddy forced the girl toward the monster, the dead man trying to step forward with arms outstretched, wanting to grab her. The two guys holding the zombie at bay fought with each tug against the pole. It was a wonder the zombie didn't spin around and take those guys out in an effort to break free. Then again, intelligence was never in a zombie's favor. Joe had been around them long enough to know that much.

Joe remained in the shadows behind an old furnace off to the side. The creeps holding the girl hadn't heard him break in through the first floor window of the house and sneak down the stairs into the shadows, each too consumed with the idea of bringing this girl to the edge of torment and despair before, finally, shoving her off the edge.

"Oh come on, girlie-girlie. It ain't so bad," her captor said. "The dude's just hungry, that's all. You know as well as I do that they need to eat now and then, just like anyone else."

The girl's muffled screams, grunts and heavy breathing through her nose sent a shockwave of apprehension through the air.

The guy holding the iron rod shook off his beaten leather jacket, first his right arm then, after switching his hold on the rod to the other hand, his left. He wore a blue T-shirt, one which reminded Joe of what the sky used to look like before it had permanently clouded over in a sickly mix of gray and brown.

"Whoo-hoo-hoo-hoo-hoo!" Blue T-shirt sang. "One, two, the dead's coming for you!"

The girl screeched behind her gag. Blue's friends howled. They shoved each other playfully like drunks.

"Ready, Betty?" Blue asked.

If "Betty" was the girl's real name or not, Joe didn't know nor, right now, care.

He cursed himself for sitting in the shadows so long, having to watch as Betty inched toward her doom, but if he didn't time this just right, neither he nor she would make it out of here alive. You didn't have to be paranoid to know that each of the men were packing heat, something that had become commonplace once the dead had taken over.

The zombie snarled and a gob of bloody-spit spilled from the corner of its mouth. It violently lurched forward, catching the men holding the iron rod off guard. A muffled *pop* came from the zombie's neck. It had broken it from the force of the pull.

And it still kept moving.

The men holding it at bay yanked back on the rod, jerking the dead man back a step. The zombie grunted, but kept its feet firmly planted so it only leaned back against the air at an impossible angle before tugging

2

itself upright again. The dudes holding the rod lost their grip and the second the iron rod clanged against the concrete floor, the girl screamed, muffled and scared.

"You idiots!" Blue shouted. Indecisiveness flashed across his eyes. He wasn't sure what to do.

Joe pulled the large X-09 to shoulder height, cocked the enormous hammer, and got ready. As was his custom, he counted to three then kissed the tip of the thick barrel before settling his finger around the trigger. One cock of the hammer was good for two shots. He had designed the X-09 himself, a large handgun, black and smooth with a Western flare that packed more punch than a double-barreled shotgun. He could have made a fortune off it if the world was the way it used to be.

But those days were gone.

The zombie scrambled toward the girl. She veered to the side and breathed a shrill wheeze when the collar stopped her stride.

Blue yanked her back then threw her and the pole into the zombie. He and his buddies spun around and ran for the long flight of basement stairs.

Joe jumped out from behind the furnace, aimed at the two yahoos scrambling up the steps in front of Blue and sent a bullet into each of their backs. The sounds of the double gunshot froze Blue in his tracks and by the time he turned around to see the source of fire, Joe had already cocked the hammer again and had the barrel aimed between Blue's eyes.

"What the—" Blue started. He was cut off when the girl shrieked and the zombie, who was now on top of her, growled. "Me or her. What's it gonna be, hero man?"

"Both," Joe said and pulled the trigger.

A blood-red hole the size of a quarter sprang to life at the center of Blue's forehead, the back of his head spraying outward in a rain of flesh and bone. Eyes still gazing at Joe, the dude dropped to his knees then toppled face first onto the floor.

Joe turned and dove to the side as the two guys who had earlier held the zombie at bay aimed their pistols at him and fired. He pulled the trigger in mid air, sending a bullet into the zombie's back, the impact forceful enough to send the dead man rolling off the girl and to the side.

A numby *bang* rocked Joe's shoulder when he hit the ground. Fortunately the long, brown rain-ruined suede trench coat he wore was padded top to bottom so the pain wasn't as sharp as it should have been. He cocked the hammer.

The girl rolled onto her side and tried to get up, but the awkwardness of the neck collar and attached pole screwed up her balance and she fell back down, landing on her stomach and face.

The two men with the pistols opened fire.

Joe sent off two shots, tagging each of them in the heart. Their chests exploded almost simultaneously in a burst of blood and they hit the floor.

The zombie rushed on all fours and tackled the girl, slamming its forehead into the back of her skull. She lay there, still.

Joe got to his feet, cocked the hammer, and took three huge strides over to it. He yanked the dead man up by the collar. The creature turned its head toward him, its bloodshot eyes filled with malice. It reached for Joe's arm.

Joe pulled the trigger.

The shot took off the top of the dead man's head, everything from the eyebrows up. The syrupy splash of brain matter and the soft sound of bone hitting the concrete followed right behind.

Now no longer moving, the dead man's body suddenly weighed a ton and Joe needed both hands to dump it off to the side.

He got down on his knees beside the girl and checked her neck for a pulse. It was there, still frantic from the ordeal.

He turned her over and grimaced at the sight of her bloody face, a deep gouge caused by teeth on her left cheekbone.

"Crap," he muttered.

Her tearstained eyes opened slowly then rolled back in their sockets. When they rolled forward again, a soft smile rose on her face.

"Thanks," she whispered.

Joe stood, sighed, and aimed the gun between her eyes. "You're welcome."

BILLIE FRIDAY
PUNK GIRL

Where were you when it all began?

The words had sat on Billie Friday's computer screen for the better part of an hour and, try as she might, she couldn't quite figure out what to say next. How could she? How could anyone describe the transition between blue skies and sunny days to a world of perpetual gray and a moon that never shone? How could someone describe graduating from high school with hope and promise, a planned life of being a veterinarian by day and DJ by night, to going into hiding and secreting yourself away from legions of the walking dead?

"This is pointless," Billie said and shoved her thick-framed glasses further up her nose.

The goal had been to write a letter, a short one, something she could print then copy and distribute to the lingering survivors of the human race, a letter asking them to stop and reflect on where they had been before the devastation began, the hope being to urge them to continue living—continue *surviving*—in a world gone awry and where the notion of a normal life was nothing more than a farfetched dream.

If she was to do only one thing with her life, one thing that made a difference, this would be it.

"Face it, girl, you got no class. No style." *If you did, you'd be able to write this thing no problem.*

She glanced over to the small, standing mirror beside her computer monitor. The girl staring back was but a shadow of the one she'd known in a life that ended a year ago. Her bob-cut pink hair, normally a perfect sphere around her head, sat in disarray. The bags under her eyes were so big that they hung below the frames of her glasses. Yet, she supposed, she *shouldn't* look any different. Anybody stuck hiding out in the bottom corner suite of an abandoned apartment building would look the same.

Fortunately, for her, the power was still up in this part of Winnipeg. The suburb, North Kildonan, dubbed by those who lived there as the "Haven," had become a secret safe area for those trying to piece together

5

some semblance of a regular life. She only knew of a handful of living souls in this part of the city and they had a rule about not interacting with one another, each person to their own abode, unless there was an emergency. If they had joined together and formed some kind of communal living arrangement, and if they were discovered by the undead, they'd most likely be wiped out. This way, being scattered, if something did happen, the losses would be minimal, hopefully only a single casualty, and therefore only a single person added to the undead's number. Given the rate of the undead's multiplication, that was a good thing.

From what she could tell from the bits she caught on the Internet, the situation was similar worldwide. Pockets of people hid out here and there, communicating via message boards and news lists and email. Thankfully, the zombies were, frankly, idiots, so there was no fear they'd learn of the survivors' whereabouts or what plans were in motion to try and overcome the army of the dead.

Where were you when it all began?

There were those words again.

Billie remembered exactly where she was. It had been the last day of high school, the excitement of prom night hovering on the air. The only damper to the feeling was the thought of squeezing into a formal dress, something she'd hated since as far back as she could remember. No date, just her and some friends, ones she'd known since elementary school.

It had been late afternoon and school had just let out. The sudden relief of having made it through twelve years of schooling—fifteen, if she counted her two years of preschool and one of kindergarten—lifted her heart and melted the stress and weight that had plagued her all year as she studied her butt off so she'd one day be accepted one province over into the University of Saskatchewan's Western College of Veterinary Medicine.

As always, she made her way home alone, a walk she looked forward to every day, a chance to unwind and plan her evening. And, as always, the plan was to get home, make a tall glass of chocolate milk and hide in her room so she wouldn't have to face her parents when they returned from work. It wasn't that she hated them, but she was tired of hearing from them day in and day out that she should quit dying her hair (though during the school year as per school rules she had to dye it "natural" colors, which then led to her dying her hair white and raising a ruckus with the principal and teachers; "Hey, white *is* a natural color!" she told Mr. Landon. "Only if you're eighty!" he shot back), stop listening to

Green Day and that "devil music," and for once, just once, tie her shoelaces before leaving the house.

She also wanted to avoid her geeky sister, who always sided with her parents. Audrey took this same path home, but whether her sister was ahead of her or behind, she didn't know.

Taking a deep breath, she stopped her stride when the air shifted and suddenly grew *heavier*.

"Now it's gonna rain and guess who's going to be stuck in it?" she muttered.

With each step, the air grew thicker and thicker, the smell no longer that of clean earth and green trees and grass, but something . . . off . . . like the kind of smell that surfaced when you swore you just passed a BFI bin but there was nothing there.

That's when the clouds rolled in, dark and gray, thick and dense, threatening to dump blinding sheets of rain.

For a long time, the clouds hovered there, taunting the earth.

On the opposite sidewalk, others walking home kept glancing up as well, everyone bracing for a storm.

Then a drop fell and landed on Billie's hand. The droplet was warm and gray, like paint mixed with water.

"What the—" she said, glancing up.

The rain was a drizzle at first, spiky, tiny gray pellets falling from above.

Those across the way squealed and stopped walking, checking themselves over as the rain dyed their clothes dark gray.

Panicking, Billie ran and shoved her way through a group of kids further up the sidewalk.

The rain picked up and soon thick, sticky drops of gray doused her clothes and blanketed the street and sidewalk, hindering all visibility.

Keep going straight, she told herself, mouth clamped shut for fear of accidentally imbibing whatever this gross liquid was.

A group of teenagers was running down the sidewalk up ahead. Sprinting, she quickly caught up to them. They must have heard her coming from behind because when she veered to the right to avoid crashing into them, they tried moving out of the way and went to the right as well. Billie smashed into a heavyset redhead. Instead of banging shoulders and running past her like she expected, the redhead went limp on impact and toppled to the ground. One of the redhead's friends stopped to try and help her up. Billie and the others kept running, but guilt quickly smacked Billie's heart. She knew the right thing to do would be to turn around and see if the redhead was all right. When she spun around, she could no longer see them, the sheet of odiferous gray rain coming down so thick that it was like trying to find your way around in a steam room.

Great, now they're gone and I—

Boomp! Her feet smacked into something and she tumbled over, her elbows skidding across the grass as she broke her fall, her skin stinging.

Soaked to the bone in this funky gray substance, Billie looked over her shoulder and saw the bodies of the redhead and her friend lying there.

"Hey, are you okay?" she asked.

No answer.

She crawled over to them and shook them. "Hey! Wake up! Let's go!"

Nothing.

The redhead lay face down; the other was face down, too.

She rolled the redhead's friend over.

Her breath caught in her throat.

It was her sister.

"Audrey!" she screamed and with slippery hands pawed at her sister's face, trying to wipe away the gray slick covering it. She hadn't recognized her earlier, not with the liquid gray coming down.

Audrey lay there, unmoving.

Crying, Billie scooped her hands under her sister's small body and, squatting beside her, set her feet up against Audrey's side, ready to lift her.

Audrey coughed.

"Audrey! Thank God!" Billie shouted.

Her sister coughed again, then belched and threw up a pasty mix of puke and blood. It splashed onto Billie's hand and arm but she didn't care. Her sister was all right!

"Come on, I'm getting you to a hospital." She pulled her hands out from under her sister and stood. "Help! Somebody help!"

Screams broke through the sound of pouring rain in reply. Others called out for help as well.

"Help! Please! Somebody!" To her sister: "It's going to be okay, Audge. It's going to be—"

Her sister remained on the ground, eyes wide and white, the pupils and irises gone.

"Audge?"

8

Audrey, unblinking despite the fierce rain, stood slowly and started ambling toward her.

Billie took a step back. Then another. Then another.

The redhead convulsed once, coughed, and puked up a similar wad of blood and mucus. She, too, slowly got to her feet and started moving toward Billie. The redhead bumped into Audrey. Audrey didn't flinch as the redhead walked past.

"What's . . . what's happening? What's happening?" Billie kept moving back and stopped when she bumped into something. Turning around, she saw that that *something* was another student, a black guy around six feet tall. His eyes were solid white.

The gray rain poured down.

Billie darted away from him and tore through the thick, gray droplets, not caring where she'd end up other than away from whatever had become of her sister, the redhead and that guy.

Home. She had to get home.

The ground went uneven beneath her and she knew she was running on grass. Then the ground dropped as she ran over the curb. Her foot folded beneath her and she hit the slick pavement.

"Ow!"

She scrambled to her feet and tried running again but had to settle for a limpy jog as her left foot refused to land flat on the ground, the pain in her ankle simultaneously sharp and hollow.

"Someone . . . help . . ." she managed between rain-soaked gasps.

Shadows in the rain, just up ahead.

"Hey! Over here!" she screamed.

The shadows turned to face her but didn't run toward her like she had hoped.

She kept on toward them, wondering what she'd say once she met up with whoever that was and how she'd describe the sudden change in appearance of her sister and the others.

With each footfall, she chanted her sister's name, a part of her wanting to go back to try and save her, another scared to death of going near her.

The shadows grew larger and soon five people appeared: two adults and three kids, all gray and wet. The adult woman walked toward her and raised a hand, reaching out to her. The man walking beside her did the same. Then the kids followed their parents' example and stumbled toward Billie, their arms raised, some shoulder height, others only up to their folks' stomachs.

A sharp ache in her lungs, Billie skidded to a stop when she noticed these people had white eyes, too.

Breaking down, she forced herself to wipe the tears from her eyes, turned to the left and ran away.

She ran forever.

She didn't know how much time had passed until three shadows appeared against the rain.

Wheezing, she stopped, put her hands on her knees, and tried to catch her breath. Only now was she able to taste the salt of this bizarre rain on her tongue. Spitting it out, hoping it wouldn't make her sick or do to her what it had done to her sister, she tried calling out to the three shadows. Only a small squeak escaped her lips.

Audrey emerged from the rain, as did the redhead and the tall black guy.

The three walked at the same pace toward her, their footing weak and unsure.

Head dizzy from the exertion, Billie knew she was supposed to be doing something right now but wasn't sure what. It involved movement, but what kind? What was she supposed to do? Her head ached from the crying, the running, the frantic breaths of fear.

Run!

But it was too late.

Audrey picked up speed and grabbed hold of her while the other two kids with white eyes looked on.

Her sister held her in a bear hug.

With rubbery arms, Billie tried to push her away but Audrey was too strong. Her sister's steps were feeble and at one point in the struggle, Billie tripped over Audrey's feet. A spike of pain shot through her already-tender ankle. She fell to the pavement. Audrey jumped on top of her, her weight uncontrolled. Dead weight.

"What are you doing? What are you doing? Get off!" Billie shouted.

Audrey reached for Billie's neck. It was impossible to shove her sister's hands and arms away; her hands kept sliding off Audrey's rain-slicked skin.

Thunder boomed and for a moment Audrey seemed distracted. Billie torqued her body to the side but Audrey quickly snapped her back into place on her back, helpless.

Tears distorted Billie's vision, turning Audrey's gray face with red lips and blood dripping down her chin into some kind of funhouse mosaic.

Her sister dipped forward and set a pair of blood-soaked lips on her neck.

Billie tried to push her off but couldn't.

Teeth. Audrey's teeth pressed against her skin.

Something hard poked Billie's leg. She reached into her pocket and pulled out a pen.

She'd never forget the sound of the pen's tip puncturing the back of Audrey's neck.

She'd never forget the block of ice that settled in her stomach when she withdrew it then jammed it into Audrey's ear.

She'd never forget the look on her sister's face when she managed to push the head far enough away from her neck then off to the side: anger.

Billie couldn't remember what happened next, just the sense of freedom from being out from under the weight of her sister's body and the joy of leaving the other two white-eyed people behind.

But she'd never forget that rain.

It lasted for a week.

DES NOTTINGHAM
ZOMBIE WRANGLER

"Ha! And they said I couldn't stand up for myself," Des shouted, thinking back to the kids of four years ago who stuffed him in a locker at school. "Now I'm king and all you bozos are gonna pay!"

He hid just inside the mouth of an alley and peered out onto the dark street. It was littered with dismantled cars, each stripped for anything that might be useful or of value. The surrounding buildings were all dark. It was night, just the way he liked it.

Just him and the undead.

Several blocks down the street, four members of the dead ambled down the sidewalk, their bodies swaying awkwardly side to side as they planted decrepit feet down one in front of the other. It was because of them and those like them that the world was in the state it was in.

Des Nottingham waited, careful to remain out of sight. When the time was right, he would pounce and take the suckers down.

Just like at school: sneak up on ol' Des and snuff him out. Ha! Now it's my *turn to have my way!*

He admired his well-muscled arms, as rippled as sandbars. His body was a far cry from what it used to be and from what people remembered.

For a moment, he thought he should have had a gun then thought better of it, remembering that, for him, he just simply preferred to smash heads. Most folks just settled for popping a bullet between the creatures' eyes and left it at that. Des preferred to plow their skull into the pavement whenever he could, cracking the bone and smearing sweet goo and brain matter across the concrete.

"Can't live without yer brains, can you?" he said.

The dead men drew nearer. Each had been middle-aged when they'd died. Now they were mere shells of their former selves, all pasty gray skin and bulging eyes.

Leaning up against the wall inside the alley, Des went over the game plan in his mind. This was his favorite part, the few seconds before the kill (if killing something that was already dead counted as killing, that was).

He peered around the corner.

The zombies stopped, as if sensing his presence.

"Uh oh," Des breathed. *Don't say "uh oh," you idiot! You knew you were going to face them. What's the difference if they saw you first?* He smirked. *Hmph. Life or death. That's the difference. Just don't let them bite you and you won't come back as one of them.*

The creatures drew nearer, arranging themselves single file, each hugging the wall of the building beside them.

Sure, make it easier for me. Figures. No challenges left in life, it seems. Bummer.

He waited a moment longer and the second the shadow of one of the undead materialized at the mouth of the alley, Des jumped out, Black Sabbath's "Iron Man" playing in his head. He wrapped his fingers around the zombie's neck. Using the momentum from the jump, he swung on the zombie's neck to the side, yanking the creature down and taking it to the pavement. He landed on top of it then quickly got to his feet and sent the heel of his heavy, steel-toed boot into the back of the zombie's skull, cracking it like an egg. He brought his knee up and mashed his foot down again, further splitting the bone. A splash of black blood and mooshy brain burst from its housing and splattered onto the pavement. Des leapt into the air and landed on the zombie's head with both feet, squashing it like a melon.

The other three creatures came toward him, two of them with their arms raised, trying to grab him.

He took the closest one's wrist in his hands, spun on his heels so his back was facing it, then brought the creature's elbow down on his shoulder, breaking it against the joint. A sharp shard of bone popped through the remains of the creature's dust-covered navy blue suit jacket. The break didn't faze the dead man, not that Des expected it to, but at least this way the creature was with one less useful appendage.

Des kicked the creature in the gut, the force of the blow making it double over. He then grabbed the zombie by the ears, jumped up and sent a knee into the dead man's nose. The creature fell off to the side just as the other two came at him and worked together, each taking one of Des's arms.

"This the best you got?" Des said and chuckled.

He ran for the wall in front of him, dragging the zombies with him. He kicked out his right leg and ran up the wall, flipped over and freed himself from their grasp. He landed behind them.

The creature with the broken arm moved for him.

Des ran around it, jumped on its back, and slammed his elbow down into the top of the dead man's skull. The blow was enough to daze the creature. Des dismounted, grabbed the creature by the scruff of the neck and ran it into the building wall, smashing its face against the brick in a dark smear of black blood and scraped skin. He jerked the creature's head back then launched it forward again, breaking the creature's face and skull against the building like a water balloon. The corpse fell and hit the sidewalk and moved no more.

There were still the other two to take down and they were on him fast. He usually wasn't this slow.

Don't get distracted, he told himself.

"You punks ready for some more?" he said as they grabbed him, one with its arms around his chest, the other scooping him up by the legs.

They hoisted him off the ground then tossed him several feet in the air, sending him flying into the frame of an Oldsmobile that had smashed into a streetlight long ago.

Des lay there against the 'mobile, unable to move. *Come on, get up.* He still lay there. *Let's go already!* Slowly, he managed to right himself, then planted his feet on the ground.

"Okay, how about a little" —and he raised his arms, palms up, curling his index fingers toward himself a few times— "huh?"

The zombies moved toward him.

"Yeah, that's what I thought."

Des took off his boot, drew out the lace so there was some slack, then spun it around and around like nunchaku.

The buzz of the boot spinning through the air sent a wave of excitement through him. He let the nearest creature have it, whacking the steel-tip of the boot into the side of its head. It stumbled off to the side. The other came closer. Des let him have one, too.

"You really think you're gonna take me, don't you?" He socked each of the creatures once more with the boot.

Dazed, the creatures stopped moving for a second before redoubling their efforts. One grabbed him, holding him tight, while the other moved in for the kill. Des whipped up his left boot and nailed the zombie between the legs just as it was about to bite. The blow didn't faze it. Like kicking a heavy pillow.

As the creature's mouth opened near Des's neck, he realized he'd be done for if he didn't act immediately.

With a violent jerk, he swung his head into the zombie's, skull smacking against skull. The zombie teetered to the side, giving Des more room to maneuver.

He stomped on the foot of the one that held him, elbowed it in the stomach then yanked his arms free. Though he knew mashing down on its toe and hitting in the gut didn't do anything, it still felt good to do it.

Des grabbed his boot off the pavement and threw it at them, not caring which one he hit. The boot smacked the zombie he'd headbutted. Des pounced on its back and tackled it to the ground. He landed on top of it, straddled its back, then picked up its head by the back of the hair and plowed its face into the pavement over and over, breaking its head open. Wet brain and black blood splashed all over him. He didn't care.

Lost in the moment, he had forgotten about the last zombie until it grabbed his shoulders from behind, dragged him off its kin, and went to sink its teeth into his face.

Des punched it in the head square on then came in from the side and hook-punched its jaw, dislocating it.

"That'll teach ya not to French me, you slimy goober!" *Sheesh. "Goober"? What a loser.*

He wrestled out from underneath it, scrambled on all fours until he was behind it, stood, then grabbed the zombie by the shins and yanked the creature's legs out from under it. The corpse hit the pavement with a sickening smack.

Quickly, Des made for the body of the zombie with the broken arm, tore the broken arm off at the elbow, then returned to the last of the creatures and beat it with the arm, using it as a club to the creature's skull. He whacked it over and over until the zombie stirred no more.

He threw the arm to the side, stood and dusted himself off.

Black Sabbath still rang in his ears.

"I am Des Nottingham: Zombie Wrangler!" he shouted, fists clenched and arms raised above his head in victory.

Just then everything went black and Des was sucked off the street and back into the living room of his tiny bachelor apartment, reclining on his La-Z-Boy.

That was twice this week the power went out while he was in the middle of a game.

AUGUST NORTON
RECLUSE CHRISTIAN DUDE

This wasn't the way the world was supposed to end.

No matter which way August Norton approached it, nothing—*nothing*—that had happened was *supposed* to have happened.

The dead were not supposed to rise. Ever.

The only Biblical prophecy that stated the dead would appear was Revelation 20:12-13, which spoke of the sea and death and Hades giving up the dead that was in them to face the White Throne Judgment at the feet of Christ. Then, and only then, would the dead rise and, even when that event occurred, the dead wouldn't be on the earth because the earth and sky would flee from the presence of Jesus.

But these weren't the "dead," he reminded himself. They were the *undead.* And they were on Earth and Planet Earth was still here.

Since the dead began to rise and transform any people unfortunate enough to be in their path, August had locked himself and his family away at his cabin an hour's drive out of town, at first for safety, then for answers.

Over the past year he had read the Bible three times. Read every Bible commentary he had in his library—four, all told—poured over the ancient End of Days prophecies countless times, sought the Lord earnestly in prayer—and was met with a dead end at every turn.

For well over two hundred days he promised his wife, two sons, their wives, and his five grandchildren that the Lord Christ was in control and that what happened the world over wasn't beyond God's remedy. Even when his family's faith began to falter he remained strong. Each morning they met in prayer. Each night they met again. Day in and day out.

Until the last day, the one that made him question God for the first time since being saved as a young man back in '62.

He had thought despite all the pain the dead had caused, despite being forced from his home, God would come to the rescue. It had been a hard life even before he became a Christian. Growing up with little to eat, not many friends in school, fighting in Nam, watching his friends being shot or blown to pieces from behind that helicopter window. . . . Even now he still dreamed about them once in awhile. He thought that after settling down and having a family everything would be fine. Peaceful. But life was seldom peaceful and especially not now with the dead roaming around.

His son, Jonathan, had gone outside for a midnight cigarette. He'd never came back in.

Jonathan's wife, Lydia, after lying in bed alone for over an hour, had gone out to look for him. She, too, never returned.

In the morning, August's other son, David, had gone looking for his brother. He couldn't go far. The rule was not to exceed the invisible, hundred-yard self-imposed boundary the Norton family had put around the property. Not long after he had gone out, David's wife, Jan, had wanted to join her husband. August permitted it, much to his later regret, and Jan, like the three before her, never returned.

That night, sitting around the kitchen table, August, his wife, Eleanor, and the five children ate dinner in silence, August's mind half in prayer, the other going over scenario after scenario as to what might have become of Jonathan, Lydia, David and Jan. Every scenario kept drawing the same conclusion: they had been taken and, most likely, transformed into the hell-birthed creatures that roamed the earth.

Eleanor looked up at him from her canned beans with blue, earnest eyes. She didn't need to say anything. The question was: what now? They were both too old to manage safety *and* the children on their own. August was sixty-seven; she was sixty-four. The kids, Jon junior, Bella, Finch, Katie and Stewart were nine, seven, seven, five and four, respectively. Jon, Bella and Finch, though kids, were old enough to handle themselves well enough, but Katie and Stewart needed a mom and dad.

August shook his head—*I don't know*—and poked at his own beans with his fork.

They finished dinner.

During cleanup, August peered through the window above the sink and saw four shadows off in the field across the way. They moved slowly toward the cabin.

"E, you better get over here," he said as calmly as he could despite the urgent tone that forced itself through.

Eleanor finished drying her old hands, set down the dishtowel and joined him.

"What is it?"

"Straight across, there."

She pulled up her bifocals from the chain around her neck, set them on her nose and leaned closer to the window so she could see. "Oh no," she whispered.

"Get the kids."

She nodded and left his side. As she proceeded to the living room, she said, "Kids, why don't we go play a game in the bedroom?"

Jon junior held up the Superman action figure he had been flying around. "It's okay. Me and Supes're gonna save Bella and Katie from the evil Finch and his stupid sidekick, Stewboy."

"Not stupid!" Stewart shouted at him.

"I was only kidding, doofus."

"What your mouth, J.J.," Eleanor said. "Stewart is not stupid and you don't call people . . . I forget what you said. Now bring Superman and we'll go to the next room. I want to show you kids something."

"A surprise?" Katie asked.

"Come and see."

The little girl was on her feet in a jiff and joined her grandma's side. After a moment, the others, with a huff, stood and followed Eleanor and Katie into the bedroom.

"Now this is what I wanted to show you," Eleanor said as she closed the bedroom door.

Keeping one ear on their muffled voices, the other listening attentively for activity out front, August went to the closet near the door and pulled down his .22. It wasn't much of a weapon, but it was all he had and all he ever wanted to have.

"Oh, Lord, is it murder if they're already dead?" He tugged down the box of bullets from between the stack of gloves and old hats lining the top shelf.

He brought the rifle and bullets to the kitchen table and checked the ammo. Only about twenty shots, and the bullets were faded and worn. He couldn't think of how long they'd been sitting up there, probably since sometime in the '80s.

After loading the rifle, he snuck back over to the window and looked outside. The four shadows were closer now and, sure enough, they belonged to Jonathan, Lydia, David and Jan.

Whistling the first line of "How Great Thou Art" as loud as he could, he waited for Eleanor to whistle back the next line. She did. It was an agreed upon signal between the adults that something was wrong and the person beginning the tune had to leave the cabin. The response of the second line was affirmation that the departure would be okay.

August smiled to himself, proud of his wife. He knew her heart was breaking inside, but at the same time each were strong enough in their faith to know that, should something happen, it wasn't good-bye forever. It was "See ya till we meet again."

He checked the window.

Jonathan and Lydia were on the front lawn, ambling toward the door. David and Jan were no longer with them.

"Be with me, Lord," he whispered. He slipped on his old, brown boots.

Rifle at the ready, he took a deep breath, and unlocked the door. Once outside on the front steps, a chill swept through him. He should have put on a jacket over his brown-and-red-checkered shirt.

Jonathan and Lydia were not far away, maybe twenty feet, maybe less.

August locked the door, pounded on it twice, letting Eleanor within know he was still all right. She tapped twice on the glass of the bedroom window at the front of the property in reply. It was also another code, one that said "I love you."

He glanced toward the window. Eleanor had already closed the curtain.

August faced his son and daughter-in-law. Even in the dark, he could see the color was bleached from their faces, their eyes white, their expression cold and heartless and not just from being dead. A portion of Jonathan's cheek was missing and was a mess of red and black tissue. Lydia only had her brown hair on one side her head, the other side ripped away along with her ear. The damage to her head hadn't been enough to kill her though. Only change her.

August shuddered at the thought of what might have happened. But that didn't matter now. His family was inside and he had to protect them.

He stepped down the three front steps and set his feet firmly on the grass.

Jonathan and Lydia stepped toward them, their footfalls feeble yet strangely sure at the same time. He knew that if they could, they'd run at him and take him down.

Not tonight.

August raised the rifle. "Jonathan," he called. "You know I love you so I'm going to ask you once, if you can hear me somehow." Tears pooled at the bottom of his eyes and his voice cracked when he spoke next. "Turn around and walk away."

Jonathan's expression did not change nor did he give any sign that he understood his father.

"I love you, son," August said and lined up his shot.

BANG!

The shot hit him in the heart. Jonathan stopped, and then, as if nothing happened, kept advancing.

Shocked it didn't faze his son, August felt the corners of his eyes pinch with tears as he aligned his next shot.

BANG!

A hole appeared in the center of Jonathan's forehead and he dropped to the ground.

Tears leaked out of August's eyes and through blurry vision he watched as Lydia kept moving toward him, her arms raised, about to grab him.

"Good night, darling," he said and sent a bullet through her eye and into her brain. She hit the ground, as well.

Muffled banging came from the rear of the property.

The back door, August thought, eyes wide.

He propelled his old legs as quickly as possible around the cabin with the hope of catching David and Jan still outside.

The muffled thudding continued all the while he rounded the cabin and just as he arrived at the rear, a loud *crackle-crack* signaled the door had been broken. He got there just in time to see Jan squeezing her way through the three-foot hole in the door. David was already inside.

August got the rifle ready and got as close to her as he could. With her body half fallen over the hole in the door, her rubbery legs kicking at the ground as she tried to crawl her way in, sending a bullet into the back of her head was easy.

"David!" August shouted. As if David could hear him, and even if his oldest son did, he wouldn't listen to him.

The back door had been locked ever since the Nortons arrived at the cabin about nine months ago so August reached in through the hole and fumbled around until he found the deadbolt. He tried opening the door. It opened a few inches then hit something. He tugged again. It wouldn't budge. He glanced down. Jan's weight on the door was enough to put pressure on the wood, causing the bottom corner to scrape along the floorboards and catch against one of them that had warped a long time ago. August had forgotten about that board and cursed himself now for having put off fixing it.

Grunting, he yanked on the door over and over.

Foomp, foomp, foomp. Banging from within.

Foomboom!

The children screamed.

"E!" August shouted. "Kids!"

"August!" Eleanor shrieked.

The kids squealed. Tiny footfalls echoed through the cabin. For a moment August expected a pair of them or more to find him. Instead, the screams were cut off one by one until silence reigned.

Shaking, tears running from his eyes, August turned and ran down the back steps and was about to go to the van out front and hightail it back to the city, when he stopped himself.

"I can't," he whispered. "They're . . . they're going to . . ."

He checked to see how many bullets he had left. Seven. He wished he had taken more. The rest were still on the table inside.

Sobbing, he walked to the front, expecting David and the others to appear and charge him. For a moment he entertained the idea of letting them. Why not. The world was going to end anyway.

But if they do, I have no idea if I will be truly dead or not. Will I still be alive or aware in some way? I refuse to let myself or, even, my spirit go over to them. He prayed, asking God to preserve the spirits of his family, that somehow his family was indeed dead and the creatures were nothing but demonically-possessed human shells.

David was the first to appear at the front door. He pushed it open, took the first step fine then stumbled down the rest. As he straightened, the others appeared, the kids first, then Eleanor. Each had a similarly hard time coming down the steps.

August jogged a good distance away, turned and aimed.

I love my sons the same. "David. You know I love you so I'm only going to ask this once. Turn around and walk away."

David, his body rocking side to side, a piece of his hip missing, kept coming toward him.

"I love you, son," August said.

Déjà vu flooding him, he pulled the trigger and knocked out the middle of David's face. His son's body dropped.

The kids stepped side by side, each with a hole in their necks, syrupy blood still oozing out.

"God, I am so sorry." He shot each of the little ones down.

Eleanor moved toward him, her beautiful face untouched. Her white eyes looked through him and even though he knew she was dead, he thought she could understand him somehow, understand what he was about to do.

He didn't know where David had bit her and if not for those white eyes, he could believe she hadn't been bitten at all and this was all some kind of act she was putting on to fool the undead around her.

Eleanor raised the fingers of her left hand. Two of them were missing.

"My darling," he said. "Forgive me."

He wiped his running nose with thumb and forefinger then caressed the trigger. He squeezed but the slickness from the snot was enough to make his finger slide off and tug the barrel down.

The bullet pierced his wife's neck and a stream of dark blood squirted out in a fast arc.

"No!" he gasped.

He was out of bullets.

Hand to his face, his heart raced, not knowing what to do. The strength drained from his legs, the adrenaline coursing through him too much for his old body to bear.

Eleanor neared and had both hands held out toward him. She grabbed hold of his neck and pushed, landing on top of him. He had never known her to be so strong. The notion of demonic-possession flashed across his mind again.

He wanted to speak, to ask the name of the spirit that had her, but the pressure around his neck was too much and he couldn't get a sound out.

God, help me! Jesus, help me! Over and over he pleaded for the Most High to intervene. Over and over he was met with silence.

He pushed against her arms. They wouldn't budge. Her face drew near to his, mouth open, teeth at the ready.

He took the rifle by the butt, stretched out his arm so the tip of the barrel was pointed at the side of Eleanor's head . . . and plunged it into her temple.

She stopped her charge, her dead weight settling on him. He let the blood oozing from the wound wash over them both and laid with her for several minutes, catching his breath and absorbing what he'd just done seemingly without thinking.

Now, three months later, August wondered if God had abandoned him that night.

Maybe God had abandoned the world.

Sucking back a shot of Tequila, August reclined in the chair in the living room and stared at his bare feet. The nails were long and curling. Same with those on his hands. He hadn't shaved nor cut his hair since that night his family died.

He glanced to the floor and in his mind's eye looked through it to the crawlspace beneath to where he had buried his family.

I'll be with you soon.

The food was almost gone. They had gotten a six-month supply originally but had made it stretch. It stretched even more once there was only his mouth to feed.

Let's see. I can probably make it a couple weeks without food. If I want to go sooner, I just won't drink anything for a few days. Either that or . . . He looked to the rifle leaning up against the door. There was one bullet in the chamber.

It was for him.

i
APRIL

Joe Bailey entered his apartment just after dawn. He closed the door behind him, locked the knob, the two deadbolts and chained the top.

His dog, April, a white and brown Springer Spaniel-Collie cross he had rescued shortly after beginning his crusade to hunt the undead, came bounding from the living room.

"Hey, April," he said.

Sitting at forty-five pounds, she wasn't the fiercest animal in the world, but she knew what to do if anybody but him entered the apartment. For a long while, after he first got her, she'd bark and growl each time he came home. Now, she was able to recognize his footfalls in the hallway.

Joe made his way to the kitchen, opened the fridge, and pulled out a beer. Popping the cap off and letting it fall to join the others, he took off his trench coat and dumped it on the table. He hit the front room, not bothering to turn the lights on. The sickly gray sky brought enough light into the place and even that was more than he cared for.

Flopping down on the aged blue and gray sofa, he sat with legs out, fatigue filling his eyes and fuzzying his head. Staying up all night shouldn't be taking the toll that it was, but his body said otherwise. He should be used to it. He'd always had trouble sleeping and used to fill the late-night hours writing comic books. Those days were gone, writing funny books, but he still should have been able to weather the night and catch what zees he could during the day.

But things were different now, and the rise of the undead was only a part of it.

April hopped on the sofa beside him and plopped her head in his lap. He scratched her behind the ears between each sip of beer.

"What'd you do tonight?" he asked.

April didn't reply but only let out a deep sigh, as if saying, "More, more, more."

"I killed people," he said. "Lots of them."

24

He gulped a mouthful of beer, belched, then drank a little more. He'd need at least four more to get a buzz going and he only had three left in the fridge. For a time, he took what he could get from the vendors and liquor stores. Once those supplies were all looted, he began brewing his own. And now, even doing that was getting difficult because others, it seemed, had the same idea and raided every store that carried brew-it-yourself kits.

It was at home that things caught up to him, not when he was outside. Out there, prowling the streets, taking out the dead where and when he could—out there, there was freedom. In here, his place was swimming with memories.

Memories filled with April, the *girl* that he knew for only a weekend.

It had been a three-day blip on the radar, three days that changed his life.

He had never been in love before, and who would have thought the girl with the rich black hair and liquid-smooth gray eyes who'd plunked herself down across from him while he was scribbling in his notebook at Second Cup would change everything? At the time, she had only wanted to get away from her controlling boyfriend, Dan.

Joe—Joseph then—and April were never an item.

That weekend had been a one-off thing, but one that nailed him so deeply that he couldn't help but write it all down and record every moment.

She had got to him that weekend, dug deep in a way no one else had. For a time afterward he thought he'd let her work out some of things she had going on, then, at some point, wait outside her apartment to see how she was doing. But that day never came. Each time he had thought of it, the fear of possible rejection consumed him. Instead, he found himself rereading the manuscript detailing their weekend together, a poetic memory that ripped his heart out each time.

When the dead began to rise and hell opened its gates, she was the first person he thought of. Not his family. Not his friends. Her.

Joseph had run through the rain from his place all the way to hers, the streets too cluttered with crashed cars and panicking people for him to get there by bus. The front glass door to her apartment building had been locked so, using his elbow, he smashed the glass, went in, and did the same to the second glass door beyond. He hadn't known her apartment number, she never told him, so he shouted her name up and down the halls only to be met by screams, growls and the sick, sloppy sound of the dead feasting on flesh.

At the top floor, a little Spanish girl no more than six in a green and blue flower-patterned dress sat crying up against a wall in the hallway.

Joseph ran over to her. "It's okay, it's okay," he said softly. "Where's your mom and dad?"

The girl kept balling.

The door to the suite just beside her was open. When Joseph peered in, a pair of dismembered legs lay strewn on the floor in an L shape.

He picked up the girl. "I've got to get you out of here."

The girl still cried as he carried her.

"What's your name?" he asked.

After a few sobs, she said, "Lila."

"Lila. Hi, I'm Joseph." A pause, then, "I'm looking for someone. Do you know where a lady named April lives?"

Lila nodded and pointed to the suite at the front corner of the hallway.

Joseph smiled, but he wondered how he was going to manage carrying Lila and checking up on April at the same time.

A low and gurgled wheeze rose up behind him.

He turned around and a long arm with a gray hand reached out and gripped the girl around the skull, snatching her from him.

"Hey!" Joseph screamed.

The dead Hispanic before him, probably the girl's father, stared back with a pair of eyes that were fogged over white. The man snapped the child's neck then bit into her throat.

"NO!" Joseph screamed.

The man sunk to his knees and feasted on Lila's tiny body.

April . . .

He looked at Lila, her broken body limp in the man's arms, blood running over her dress.

I'm sorry.

Joseph ran to the end of the hallway and kicked open April's door.

His heart stopped in his chest and time stood still. This couldn't be happening. Not her. Not like this. Girls like her grew up to be princesses. Girls like her deserved a fairy tale.

They didn't deserve to die.

Sitting cross-legged on the floor in the landing was April. Her head was bowed; her normally wavy and shiny black hair was slicked with blood and goopy flesh. It hung like a beaded curtain over the corpse of an old woman in her lap.

26

The wet slurping sound of meat and skin being sucked on like noodles became Joseph's only consciousness.

"April . . ." he whispered.

She looked up, a piece of trachea dangling from her mouth, blood dripping from her chin. Her white eyes softened, as if she recognized him, then she went back to her meal.

Heart pounding, sharp aches threatening to steal his soul away, Joseph just stood there, one dead man devouring his daughter in the hallway, the love of his life sitting before him eating another.

He didn't know how long he stood there staring at her, but was soon drawn out of the bizarre mesmeric hold she had on him by a shadow in his right peripheral.

A dead man with white eyes walked slowly toward him.

It was Dan.

April must have gone back to him and worked things out.

Joseph would recognize him anywhere, recognize the fellow who had caused April so much grief.

At first the bullet hole at the top of Dan's forehead didn't register. Neither did the blown-out portion of the front of his mouth. How Dan wound up like that, Joseph didn't know and the fleeting thought of it being self-imposed before the dead began to rise crossed his mind.

Eyes glazed over, lower lip quivering, Joseph cursed himself and clenched his fists.

His heart broke then, the shards from its bursting apart spiraling out in a blast of glassy pain, stabbing him everywhere within.

Dan had killed April. Had turned her into one of *them*.

Limbs trembling, Joseph squeezed his eyes shut and let the tears leak out. There was nothing left for him. The hope of a future with April was gone.

He envisioned himself walking over to Dan and letting April's boyfriend take him.

"I love you," he whispered to her.

He opened his eyes, half expecting April to be normal again and for her to have heard him. Instead she sat there, still eating.

Dan was only a few feet away, his beefy arms held out, about to grab him.

Joseph let himself die inside.

His expression hardened and he turned and faced Dan. A stream of profanities raced through his mind and nearly spewed out of his lips. But Dan wasn't worth it. Not even worth cursing at.

The second Dan moved to grab him, Joseph swatted his arms away, ran to April's kitchen and ripped out each of the drawers in the hopes of finding a knife. Something hard dropped and smacked the linoleum with a loud *thunk!*

A rolling pin.

Dan appeared in the kitchen doorway.

Joseph lunged at him and brought the rolling pin down on his head. Dan stumbled back a step and before he could regain his balance, Joseph struck him again. On the third blow, the skull split, and on the fourth, brain and blood began spattering out. Even after Dan's body hit the floor, Joseph still wailed on him until his head was nothing more than a mishmash of bone, blood and brain.

Hard fingers grabbed him by the forearm and yanked him partway off Dan's body. Instinctively, Joseph swung out with everything he had and it was only when his eyes made contact with the tip of the rolling pin did he watch its end strike April in the side of the head, sending her skull flying into the wall beside them. It hit with a wet *smack*, stuck there a moment, then slid off with a smear of blood. April's body crumpled to the ground, a pool of dark blood gathering around her head.

"April! No! Please, no. Not her. Not you. No!"

He scrambled over to her body and grabbed her by the shoulders. When he picked her up and turned her over in his lap, her head lolled back, eyes open, blood gushing ever more from the side of her head and out the corners of her mouth.

Rage burst out of him in a stream of terror and he screamed at the top of his lungs until his voice went hoarse and he started to cough.

Then he screamed again, over and over, until his voice went raw and he could no longer breathe.

Joseph remained in April's apartment well into the night, listening to the sirens outside and panicked screams from those in the building as they watched their loved ones butchered by the walking dead before they themselves were consumed.

It took him two days to finally come home. Two days of walking the city streets, lost in a haze of pain and confusion and fear. Two days of not eating but witnessing from afar the undead feasting on anyone they could get their hands on.

Two whole days in the rain.

When he finally arrived home, he locked the door, took a baseball bat to bed and cried himself to sleep, dreaming of killing April, waking, dreaming of killing her again.

Joe awoke the next evening, leaving *Joseph* behind in that place of nightmares.

Dead, like everyone else.

2

MIDNIGHT MEETING

The only thing Billie had to go on to distinguish night from day was the clock. Long gone was the time when day and night were divided by sunny skies and a moonlit black quilt.

It was 11:40 P.M.

Billie pulled her cereal bowl from the sink, gave it a quick rinse, then poured the last bit of Cap'n Crunch into it. She opened the fridge and pulled out the milk carton and began to pour it into the bowl. Only a drop came out.

She grunted. "Great. Just great." She eyed the bowl of cereal and debated eating it dry, but this was Cap'n Crunch she was talking about. Without milk, it was like trying to crunch through tiny razor-edged blocks of wood.

She tossed the empty carton into the garbage bin by the door and went to her computer and logged onto a chat program, hoping her buddy was online. ZW1 was. She right-clicked on his name and sent him a private message:

i'm coming over. out of moo juice. be there in 15.

A moment later, ZW1 replied: *yep. knock 4 times. 2 stomps.*

She typed: *gimme 3 stomps back and a slap.*

ZW1: *k.*

Billie padded her jean pockets and made sure she had her keys.

She left her apartment, locked up, and headed outside.

Before the plague hit—if a "plague" was what it was; the creatures just appeared the day of the gray rain—she used to go for late-night walks all the time. It was part of her pre-bed ritual, a time to clear her head and just have some alone time before coming back home and falling asleep. Nowadays, late-night walks were done only out of necessity and though, right now, she couldn't call a milk run a matter of life or death, she could really use the company. It had been at least a month if not longer since she last saw anybody. All her communication was done online. And it'd been equally long since she heard another human's voice, seeing as how the phone lines were no longer in service. She didn't have a mike or headset for her computer.

The night air chilled her, the canopy of gray clouds that had covered the earth having completely thrown the planet's climate into a state of perpetual fall. It should be winter right now, but instead the grass, though dead and withered from lack of sunlight and water, was still out. The trees were mere skeletons of their previous forms; bushes and shrubs cold and lifeless, just dry, crooked branches crisscrossing this way and that. The clouds above blocked everything. No rain. No snow. The air dry and always cool. Billie often wondered what might happen should the clouds either dissipate or give way. Had the rain or snow gathered on top of them and lay there dormant, waiting to fall and blanket the earth? And if it did fall, what kind of storm would it be? Surely nothing could be worse than what was happening right now. Then again, what moisture that could be up there could be enough to wipe the remnant of humanity off the planet.

There was no one alive to give answers. Not anymore. For a time each country's military rose to fight off the dead, and for a time, each one fell at the hands of the creatures roaming the earth.

Billie stopped walking down the sidewalk as a thought hit her, one that she was surprised she hadn't thought of till now. *They need to eat human flesh to survive. They outnumber us at least a hundred to one. There's not enough of us to go around. You'd think most of them would have starved to death by now.* Then again, she couldn't claim to know how the undead's biology worked and how frequently they needed to feed despite the ravenous appetites they exhibited. They could very well be like bears going into hibernation or camels about to wander in the desert and store the sustenance they needed somewhere in their bodies, rationing it until their stores could be refilled.

The thought made her shudder.

She kept her eyes peeled in the dark. The dead suckers were silent. You had to be very quiet in order to hear them approach. The way they dragged their feet, the lack of *weight* on their footfalls, made them almost impossible to detect if you weren't paying attention.

Nothing but the rush of the wind blowing past her ears made any sound. Like many other things, the days of hearing sirens whirr up in the distance were gone. Same with the screams that used to launch into the air by the minute.

She glanced behind her. The sidewalk was clear. All seemed to be well up front and on the sides, too.

Soon she was at ZW1's apartment building. All the windows to the red-bricked building were boarded up, same with the glass of the front door and the window panes that ran up on either side of it.

Billie approached the front door. ZW1 should be just on the other side unless the idiot got sidetracked again. She hoped not. To wait out here in the dark . . .

She leaned over the railing next to the front door and pulled out the one-foot-square piece of pressboard hiding behind the branches of the skeletal bush alongside it. She dropped the board onto the stone step, knocked on the boarded-up door four times then pounded her heels twice on the pressboard. *Thwack thwack!*

From inside: *Foombph foombph foombph*, then against the inside of the wooden door, *SLAK!*

After the metallic jiggling of chains from inside, the door opened a crack. Then all the way.

Des Nottingham stood before her, a hatchet at the ready.

"I don't know why you do that," she said as she dumped the pressboard back in the bush and went in.

"What?"

"Open the stupid door just a skosh then all the way. You think those brain-dead idiots know what we write to each other as our secret code? We change it every time, Des."

He lowered the hatchet and rested it against his scrawny leg as, with his other hand, he locked and chained the front door once she was in. "Yeah, but . . ."

"Yeah, but nothing," she said and moved past him to the stairs leading to the basement.

"Hey, you think you can just come here for some milk then treat me like puke?"

Billie kept walking and didn't reply. She stopped in front of the door to his suite, crossed her arms and tapped her foot impatiently.

Des's thin and pasty face was hard as he neared her, but the closer he got, the more his expression lightened and that dorky smile of his crept up onto his face.

"You're impossible, Billie. Anyone ever told you that?"

"Just my boyfriend before he died."

"Nice," Des said and let her in.

Billie went immediately to the refrigerator, opened it, and scanned the shelves. They were bare save for an old container of mustard, a couple soft-looking carrots, a bag of crackers and a thin, one-litre carton of milk.

She stomped her foot.

"What?" Des asked and came up beside her, his chest bumping into her arm.

"Do you mind?" she said and shoved him back.

A wisp of messy brown hair spilled over his eyes. He pushed it away. "No."

She pulled out the milk.

"What do you need that for?" he asked.

"Was gonna have a bowl of cereal. Barely eaten anything today."

"I can tell."

She turned to face him just as he was finishing eyeing her up and down.

He raised his hands, palms out. "Hey, you look like you've lost at least ten pounds, probably fifteen, since I last seen you. You managing okay in that cyberworld planet thing you got going down over there?"

The truth was, she *wasn't* managing, at least in terms of having enough supplies on hand. Baths had been reduced to just soaking in water, the soap and shampoo just finished the other week. Food supply was down except for a few nonperishables and a few packs of noodles; nothing to drink but water which, based on the way it'd been tasting lately, probably wouldn't last that much longer either. The power was going out now and then. Eventually the water would, too.

Billie had friends she could go to, those she met online who offered time and again to help one another out if someone was short on this or that. But it was leaving the apartment that was getting to be a chore. The thought of going outside . . . . The zombies only played a part in her choice to remain secluded. It was just that she didn't *feel* like going out anymore. Try as she might to fight it, her heart had already begun to give up hope of coming out of this alive. Reason had begun to override the notion of someone coming to the world's rescue. She, along with everyone else, was fighting a losing battle.

"I'll be fine," she said softly.

"Doesn't sound like it. Face it, Billie, you're beginning to look like one of *them*."

"And you're not?"

Des's face paled, his already pallid complexion getting whiter. He was getting thin, too, and probably weighed no more than a hundred thirty pounds sopping wet. His arms, exposed by the white tank top he was wearing, were rail-thin. The black jeans he wore hung off his waist like a pair of balloon pants. "Touché."

"I should have brought my bowl over," she said. "Mind must have gone blank. Didn't remember."

"Want me to go get it for you?" he asked.

She considered his offer then shook her head. "Thanks anyway, but no. It's too dangerous and you know it."

"Bah," he said with a wave of his hand. "Them guys out there don't bother me." Then with a grin, "They're as good as dead anyway, right?"

She couldn't help but smile. With a subtle nod, she quietly said, "Yeah."

He came over to her and wrapped her in his arms. His skin was cool, his hands even cooler. "Come on, here. I got a pack of mac-and-cheese we can make."

"That all?"

"Pretty much. And we might as well use that milk up, too. It'll go bad if we don't." He sighed. "Also heard from Mr. Shank that he hadn't seen Milk Guy for a couple of weeks now. M.G. came out here in that red truck of his every week. Shank says he thinks the creatures got him."

"We're running out of time, aren't we?" she said.

Des squeezed her even tighter. "Yeah. I think we are."

3
OFF TO THE PROMISED LAND

August stood over the oven, eyeing the dial; it was set at four hundred degrees.

Tears ran from his eyes and in his sweaty palms he held an old, worn black Bible, with some of the pages loose from its binding. It was the one his father gave him back when he was a kid. It had been years before August read it, but once he did, he had made a point of taking his dad aside and thanking him for it.

The pages of the old book crinkled each time he wrung it like a towel. Subconsciously he hoped by his twisting and turning the pages, God would get a sense of his own internal twisting and turning.

His family was gone.

He was out here all alone.

It would only be a matter of time before the creatures came for him.

Each sob-soaked syllable reminded him he was at the end of himself.

"You swore You wouldn't leave me," he said. A couple of tears fell to the Bible's cover. "I am with you always, even until the very end of the age, You said." He sniffled. "Where are You? Was it all a lie? Are You a lie?"

For the millionth time since he'd been out here, he thought about how the world *should* have ended, how a ruler would rise in Europe, would befriend then betray Israel, would persecute Christians worldwide, would kill those who didn't fall in line with the new monetary system, would slaughter those who didn't revere him as a god, would lead a revolt against God's people at Armageddon and would fall at the hands of Christ when the Lord returned in glory on the clouds of heaven.

Instead, August was stuck in a world where the dead walked the earth, where countless lives had already been lost.

Where his own family had been murdered.

Even though the undead had killed his family first, he still took the blame upon himself. It was him, after all, who had pulled the trigger and ended their existence on this planet.

Salty tears dribbled onto his lips. He licked them away. "I can't believe You'd abandon me. I can't believe You'd steal my family. Can't believe You'd let hell prevail like it has."

He picked up the Bible in his right hand then set it down again. He repeated the motion several times, something to keep his mind distracted even if it was just a simple up-and-down motion like this one.

"Dead. They're all dead. And You don't care. I've asked, I've prayed and You've just sat there doing nothing." Fresh tears welled in his eyes. He hadn't slept at all last night and had trouble napping earlier in the day. He hadn't felt like eating even though hunger floated somewhere in the back of his gut the whole day through. Fatigue beat against his eye sockets, its pulse adding to the confusion and weight that was already crushing his tired brain and resolve.

He'd never talked like this to God before. The image of the man he was a year ago flashed before his eyes, the man of yesteryear glowing with the love of the Lord, a twinkle in his eye, an enthusiasm for service. Now he was just the shell of the man he once was, broken and beaten, with a heart turning to stone.

I can't do this anymore, he thought. *No one can.*

August set the Bible down and got on his knees.

"Last chance," he whispered. "Either tell me where You want me or what You want me to do right now or we're done, You and me." A sharp pang struck his heart. To walk away from God after all these years . . . . He couldn't believe he even considered doing it. "I'm sorry," he said. "Forgive me. Just angry, hurt and . . . I don't even know what the word is. I'd kill myself right now if I didn't know what the consequence might be. Your Word doesn't say specifically, just hints at it."

August wiped his eyes then squeezed his nostrils. He wiped his fingers on his pants.

Gazing upward, he said, "I'm listening."

The sallow ceiling stared back at him, blank and silent. He closed his eyes and waited for some kind of pressing on his heart or some strong thought that couldn't possibly be his own. Even a booming voice from heaven would be fine. It'd be ideal, actually.

But there was nothing.

God was silent.

His head fell into his hands and he sat kneeling in front of his oven for a long time, crying, too hurt and too much at a loss for words to even shout out a plea for help. When the tears finally ceased, he reached for the Bible on top of the oven, took it down and opened the oven door.

Opening it to the front page, his eyes settled on the message his father had written him sixty years ago. Even to this day he remembered the way his father had gotten down on one knee and handed him the Bible he himself had used for countless years. Seeing the old handwriting made his heart long for his father.

June 26, 1948.

August,

This is for you.

May Jesus be real to you as you read through these pages.

Love,

Dad

He stared at the text for a long time before closing the book.

Taking one last look at the cover and the words HOLY BIBLE written in faded gold lettering on its front, he said, "Good-bye," and tossed it on the oven rack.

He closed the door.

It wasn't long before the scent of burning paper filled the air.

August wept before the oven, unable to believe what he was doing. How could God ever forgive him for doing that?

If You're real . . . if You're real, forgive me, he thought. *Stop me.*

Heart heavy, he remained on his knees. The heavy stench of smoke hung over him and sat in his nostrils. A dance of flame sprang to life behind the small, dark glass window of the oven door.

August's mouth fell open as the seriousness of what he was doing hit him, like a stern finger poking at his heart.

"No!" he grunted and slammed his hand down on top of the oven, using the edge to help him up.

His old knees creaked as he stood and his head swooned from rising so quickly. The room tilted to the side then righted itself again. Once steady, he sprang for the drawer nearest the oven and yanked it open, pulling out the oven mitts.

Quickly, he shoved his hands into them and opened the oven door. A thick cloud of dark gray smoke billowed out.

Coughing, August turned his head away. He took a deep breath, held it, and squinted his eyes before reaching in and grabbing the book and pulling it out. He faced away from the oven and with a big puff of breath he blew out the flame on its top and sides, then ran the book over to the sink where he patted the bright red hot lines rimming some of the pages.

He reached back to the oven, closed the door and turned it off.

Back at the sink, he stared at the still-smoldering book, some of the pages partly missing, others black with soot, others black and brown altogether.

Taking off the mitts, he was about to ask for forgiveness when his eyes caught sight of the header on the open page.

It read EXODUS.

The following morning, August loaded up the blue Ford minivan with what was left of the food—not much, just a few cans of beans, some Tequila and a few just-add-water noodle soups that he had forgotten about on the top shelf—and whatever else he could find around the cabin that might be of use: an axe, hammer, a few pairs of jackets and boots, pillows and blankets, a half-roll of toilet paper, and, of course, his .22 and bullets.

This was it. It was time to return to the world. What else could it have meant when the Bible opened to Exodus? Maybe God finally did speak up after all this time?

But before he would leave, there was still one matter to attend to.

Rifle in hand, August stood before the front of the cabin, envisioning the bodies of his family buried beneath.

He said good-bye to each one, then paused before he said good-bye to Eleanor.

He licked his lips. "I don't know what's going to happen, darling. I truly don't. Just know I'll do my best to honor you and, perhaps, save a few folks along the way." He frowned. "Ah, what am I doing? You can't hear me anyway. I'll just pass a message up to the Big Guy and He'll do all the talking for me." Then, "Hopefully."

August turned and went to the Ford. He opened the door and, resting his left forearm on the frame, set the rifle up for one last shot. He had debated if he should do this or not. Every bullet counted and he only had ten left, but the thought of his family's cabin falling into the hands of the creatures, the idea of them breaking in and roaming the rooms and contaminating it sickened him.

The front door to the place stood open. A can of propane sat on the matt in the landing. It was old, partly rusted, but August thought it would still do the trick.

August closed his eyes a moment and said good-bye to the old place. When he opened his eyes, he aligned the shot . . . and pulled the trigger.

4
BACK INTO THE GRAY

April licked Joe's hand as he laced up his boots. They were army issue, a pair he got back in his mid teens when he was enrolled in air cadets for a short time. Fortunately for him, he had maintained the same shoe size since the ninth grade so the scuffed, black boots fit even now. Steel-toed, they had saved his life on more than one occasion when the undead tried to turn him into one of their own, a kick to their skulls rescuing him from a life imprisoned inside the shell of a human corpse.

"Sorry, pal. You can't come with me," he told his dog and strapped on his kneepads.

He stroked the patch of brown hair on her head then kissed her on the nose. She licked his nose in return, their little exchange before he went out each night. Though April was only a dog, she was the closest thing he had to a friend and, he supposed, she'd be the closest he'd ever have to someone to come home to. Killing the undead was easy emotionally, but leaving the dog behind each evening was always hard. To lose his buddy . . . . Joe didn't want to think about it. He'd already lost enough loved ones as it was. April, the girl from a life when things were normal, his friends and his family.

He gave his pet one final scratch behind the ears then exited his apartment and locked it.

"I'll be back soon," he called through the door.

Opting not to use its holster, he held the X-09 through his trench coat as he headed outside, prepared to make the transition between the safety of his home to the uncertainty of the streets.

He lived in the Haven. The only question that hung over him each day was, for how much longer? The power lines would inevitably go down and he, like the others who lived in the area, would be in the dark, just like everywhere else in the city.

Walking down the sidewalk, Joe glanced up at the gray, cloudy sky. Tonight the gray was blotched deep brown in parts like someone had splashed coffee against it. He remembered the days when the area used to be teeming with people, cars, kids on bikes zipping down the sidewalk—the area he grew up in. His parents' place had been seven streets down and theirs was the first place he hit after coming home from the days of walking the streets after being at April's. Even now, a year later, he remembered walking up his folks' driveway, the houselights off, both outside and in. He didn't need to be a pessimist to know his mom, dad, brother and sister were already dead. The question at that point had been *how* dead?

He remembered it clearly:

Armed with a knife from his kitchen and a baseball bat, he cautiously approached the front door. After taking a deep breath, he pressed down on the tab above the handle and pushed. The door moved slightly, but no further. Locked.

Maybe they're all right?

He dug in his jean pocket and pulled out his keys. He still had a key to the place even though he no longer lived there. Joe unlocked the door, pressed down on the tab above the handle again and pushed. The old door swung open with a creak.

Listening carefully for any sign of life, he stood there, knife at the ready, his other hand tightly gripping the bat.

It was quiet within.

"Hello?"

No reply.

Exhaling slowly, he went in, scanned the front landing to make sure the coast was clear, then proceeded into the living room. Everything seemed fine. The black leather couches on the white carpet sat untouched, just as his mom liked it. (Those couches were off-limits the moment his parents got them; Joe never understood the point in having them if you couldn't sit on them.) The dining room beside it was also empty and intact, his mom's fake fruit centerpiece still in the middle of the large oak table, a few pieces of mail on a nearby chair. He went over to the envelopes and checked the postmarks. Days old. They were still sealed and it wasn't like his parents to leave mail unread for longer than a day.

"Mom? Dad? Hello?"

Silence.

A pinch at the back of his throat; he swallowed twice, one not being enough to suppress the itch that surfaced back there.

Heart beating quickly and steadily, he went to the kitchen. At the entrance, his jaw slackened and a flush of heat came over him. The dual-windowed kitchen door that led out onto the patio was in pieces. Murky red blood coated the jagged pieces of glass still in its frame and a streak of dark red painted the white-and-gray-squared linoleum floor, as if something or someone had been dragged across it.

The creeping feeling that someone might still be in the house tugged at Joe as he went for the kitchen door. He just hoped that if someone was inside, they were alive and not dead.

Joe peered through the broken glass. The backyard looked the same as the last time he visited except everything was muddied over with that awful gray stuff that had fallen from the sky. Pools of blood and smears of meat blotched the patio in hideous red, the smell of it having sat out in the open so long sending his stomach into twists and twirls.

He swallowed again, a lump forcing its way down his throat.

"Anybo—" His voice squeaked. He cleared his throat. "Anybody?" The word was so quiet that he doubted that anyone would have heard him.

"Mom? Dad?"

Tears pooling at the bottom of his eyes, he stepped outside and tried to avoid stepping in the patches of blood.

He dropped the knife and bat. The edge of the bat struck his toe through his shoe but he didn't care. To his left, on the patio table, were the heads of his family, his father's and sister's sitting side by side, his mother's and brother's lying on their ears, eyes locked onto each other, frozen terror on their faces. Blood coated the table and rimmed it by its legs.

Mind blank, Joe numbly walked toward them. Unable to think, he glanced to his feet, his shaking hands, then finally, to the yard. There were no bodies, just a few patches of intestines, a blood-soaked arm and a sheet of skin.

Joe couldn't breathe.

His heart banged so hard inside his chest he thought he was going to faint.

Green stars rimmed his vision and a shadow crept in along the edges of his sight. He felt lighter than air. The last sound he heard was his head hitting the patio wood.

Now, walking down the sidewalk in the Haven, Joe still couldn't believe he had gotten out of there alive, that the zombies hadn't come for him. If any had entered his parents' yard while he was unconscious, they might have left him alone, somehow thinking he was already dead and not worth their time. He'd never know if that was the case or not.

Joe pulled out the X-09 and held it tight with his right hand. He no longer teared up at the memory of losing his family. For this he felt shame. Either he had accepted their deaths or had grown so cold and bitter that he didn't care.

But if I feel bad about not caring, then I have to care, right?

"Whatever," he said softly and pulled out a Old Port cigar from the inner pocket of his coat. From the side pocket he produced a box of wooden matches, stopped walking, lit the tobacco, then continued.

The smell of the smoke sometimes drew out the dead.

He hoped he'd run into one or two. Each time he blew one away, he felt a little better about himself and reclaimed a little piece of the lives the undead had stolen from him and everyone else.

Many nights he had wandered around, thinking about what he was doing. And many nights he realized how stupid it was when he stepped back and took a hard look at it. He was playing vigilante, trying be like the superheroes he had written about before the world fell to hell. But at the same time, he also gained a keen understanding of the catharsis this brought and the amazing feeling of trying to set something right when everything had been set so wrong. He didn't care if others noticed. So far as he knew, no one did. There were others like him anyway, guys and girls who went around with guns and killed as many of the undead as they could. Without them, the city would be in far worse shape. The military that been dispatched to each city nationwide after the rain fell had lasted only a short time before the undead bulldozed them like a pack of raptors hungry for the kill. The cops were all dead. Even those like him, well, there weren't as many out there as there used to be but, thankfully, they were still out there.

Hopefully they'd still be able to make a difference before it was too late.

5

THE RAT

Billie spent the night at Des's place. She was going to go home with the milk, but after hearing several gunshots echo outside, Des insisted she stay with him and go home in the morning. But when morning came, they ended up getting caught up in a world of playful conversation and video games. Besides, both had enjoyed spending time together after being so far removed from another living soul for so long.

This evening, Billie had fallen asleep on Des's La-Z-Boy. She said she just wanted to close her eyes for a minute and take the edge off a budding headache, but Des knew better. Not eating properly slowly took you down and now it was finally catching up to her. He'd make sure she got some food in that stomach of hers before she left.

Des stood over her sleeping form, hands at his sides, mouth closed, eyes fixated on her face. Seeing her like this, so peaceful, so at ease, made him wish he was someone else, someone who wasn't such a geek. He didn't know for sure if a "geek" was how she viewed him, but he'd seen other girls roll their eyes at him the way she sometimes did, seen other girls not look him square in the eye when he spoke to them. It was a role he was used to playing, though. His sister, Jante, who died the day the rain came while waiting for his parents to pick her up from a college class, had a friend, Shelly. Shelly was dead, too, but Des would never forget her.

Shelly came over to the Nottingham residence regularly, and while she and Jante would sit around the kitchen table nibbling on chips and popcorn talking about their latest crush, Des would always eavesdrop from downstairs, one ear listening to them, the other listening for Xbox monsters.

It drove him nuts that he was attracted to her, and he knew full well it was just a high school crush because only high school crushes were of the kind where you fell head over heels for someone without really knowing them. Each night, lying in bed and waiting to fall asleep, he thought about her. He imagined her wearing a white T-shirt with black, form-fitting pants with bell-bottom legs and bringing her into his arms. Imagined running his hand up her back and his fingers through her shiny red hair. Imagined her closing her perfect blue eyes as he leaned in to kiss her.

Imagined her embracing him and returning his affection.

But that was only a dream.

One night, while everyone was out except him, Shelly came over, looking for Jante. At first, it appeared Shelly was going to leave when he told her that her friend wasn't home, but after seeing the look of heartbreak on her face, he invited her in for iced tea. Shelly accepted and the two talked, mostly about Jante, and each time he tried to probe for the source of her sadness, she'd look away and turn her glass on the table, the look on her face that of impatience as she waited for him to stop talking.

Shelly left that night. She didn't even thank him for the iced tea.

It was the last time he saw her alive.

And now it was happening all over again with Billie. He'd only known her for about six months, having met her online while folks gathered on the Haven message board to get organized and figure out what their next move would be and who would help who. At first they only exchanged a few words on the board, mostly business, but when they found out how close they lived to one another, the few words on the board turned to private messages. Then the private messages turned to a few emails before they decided to meet one evening just to say hi and see a human being face to face. Even though they never really hung out all that much—as most people hated going outside unless they absolutely had to—they got to know each other well through emailing and, as the months passed, the deep feeling of his having known her all his life crept in. Before he could stop it, he realized he had given a piece of his heart away.

Billie sighed in her sleep.

Should he wake her? It was already getting late. Maybe he should just let her sleep and he'd walk her back to her place in the morning?

"Sleep good," he said softly, placing a hand on her shoulder.

Billie stirred and blinked open her eyes. "Oh. What time is it?"

"Quarter to twelve."

She reached her slender arms passed her head and stretched. "Yeah? Man, slept too long. You were supposed to wake me after twenty minutes or so."

He smiled. "You didn't say that."

"Did too."

"Did not."

She brought her arms down, adjusted her glasses and lowered the foot rest. She paused a moment to gather herself before standing. She ran her palms down and over her hips, straightening her jeans.

"Be back in a second," she said and headed for the bathroom.

"Don't forget to flush!" he called after.

She glanced back over her shoulder. "Ha, ha." She turned the bathroom light on, went in and closed the door behind her.

Des plopped himself down on the La-Z-Boy and tapped the armrests with his fingers as he waited. He closed his eyes.

Billie screeched from the bathroom.

His eyes popped open and he bounded from the chair and ran down the hallway. He nearly fell into her when she opened the door just as he approached it. "What? What's wrong?" He looked past her and scanned the bathroom, half expecting an undead to be in there. The coast was clear.

"Why don't you fix this?" she demanded.

"What?"

She grabbed him by the arm and dragged him, pointing to a half-foot-tall-half-foot-wide hole in the drywall just below the sink.

"That's where the pipes are," he said.

"No, you jerk." She tugged him closer and shoved him toward the hole. "That's where the rats are. I swear I just saw one. It poked its ugly little head out, looked at me, then disappeared."

"What are you talking about? Are you stoned?"

"Are you? You live in an apartment with rats!"

He crouched down. "Billie, there have never been rats in this building."

"Well, there's one now."

He smirked. "Get outta here." Des got down on all fours and peered at the shadowy hole in the wall. "There's nothing there."

But what if there was?

Des got down lower, leaned close to the hole, a small shudder running through him at the thought of really getting close and peering in and glancing side to side inside the wall. "I need a flashlight."

"Do you have one?"

"Yeah, but no batteries."

"Great."

He got closer, took a deep breath then exhaled hard through pursed lips.

He brought his face close to the hole, listening carefully for any sign of life. A foul smell wafted from the hole, the stench from the neighboring apartments finally having seeped into the walls despite the previous owners' body parts having been removed about ten months ago.

Holding his breath, he put his face up against the hole and did a quick glance side to side into the dark of the wall.

"See anything?" Billie asked.

"Nothing. Don't hear anything either." He paused. "Wait."

There was movement behind him. "What?"

He snapped his arm back and scurried his fingers up her foot. Billie shrieked and leaped back.

Laughing, Des looked up to see sheer terror on her face.

"Don't ever do that!" she shouted.

"Come on, don't be such a chicken. It was just—" Something tickled his fingers. When he looked down, a large brown rat with goop-slicked hair and stark white eyes lunged at him.

Screaming, Des doubled backward. The rat got flipped up in the tumble then landed squarely on his chest.

"It's on you!" Billie screamed.

"No—" Its tiny sharp claws dug into his chest through the tank top then jumped for his face. Des blocked its attacked with his palms, striking it backward. The rat flew through the air and hit the wall with a dull *thud*. It fell to the ground and got to its feet just as Des did the same.

"Get out, get out!" He shoved Billie toward the hallway.

The second they were out, he grabbed the handle to close the door, but the rat jumped out before he could and landed some distance away.

Man, that sucker's fast, Des thought absentmindedly. If it was an undead rat, he expected it should move slowly like its human counterparts.

"In there!" Billie shouted, pointing to the bedroom.

The two went in and closed the door behind them just as the rat smashed into it hard on the other side.

Silence.

"Do you think it's dead?" Billie asked.

"Don't know. Maybe, but I think it's already dead, if you know what I mean." He flicked on the bedroom light.

She nodded. "Then it's affecting animals now, too."

"Yeah," he breathed.

"We can't stay here."

"I know."

"We have to go."

"I know."

"We can't get out."

"Okay, Billie, I get it. I know that, too."

"What?" She looked at him, brow furrowed.

"Nothing. Never mind."

THUD!

They looked at each other, eyes wide.

THUD!

"Okay, let's go," she said.

"How?" He pointed to the bedroom window. "They're all boarded up and my hammer's in the hallway closet."

She ran to the boards over the window and tugged at their edges with her finger tips. She couldn't get a solid grip.

"See?" he said. "They're on there tight. And they're doubled up, too, so they're as thick as steel. Well, not steel, but you know what I mean."

"So we're trapped."

THUD!

"Yup," he said. "Unless . . ."

"What? You gonna go out there and kill that thing?"

"Got any better ideas?"

Billie didn't reply.

"Okay, then away we go, right?" he said.

"What? What're you talking about, 'away we go'?"

"I go out there, kill it, then we leave, yeah?"

"Okay, fine." She crossed her arms. "Do it."

"You don't want to help me?"

She threw up her arms in frustration. "How?"

He thought for a moment. "Okay, how's this. You be in charge of the door."

THUD!

"In charge of the door?"

"Just open it when I say, okay? Sheesh."

THUD!

"Fine." She stomped over to it.

"Thank you."

"You gonna go now?"

"Yeah, unarmed. That's real smart. Wait a sec." Des went to the closet, slid the door open and began pulling the hangers off the bar. "If there's one thing I hate about this place, it's the super small closets. I mean" —*THUD!*— "how is anyone supposed to fit anything in here? They're, like, four feet wide!"

"Maybe they were meant for little old ladies who don't have many clothes," she said sarcastically.

"Yeah or a place to hold their cats. Maybe." He finished taking the clothes off the bar then popped the bar itself off the supports. The long, wooden bar was a little over an inch thick, solid wood straight through.

He hefted its weight. Probably around fifteen pounds. Good enough.

THUD!

He joined Billie by the door; his heart kicked into overgear. "When I say 'now,' you open it, okay?"

She didn't reply.

He put his face close to hers. "Okay?"

She nodded. "Be careful, all right?"

"Don't really have a choice."

THUD!

"I'm serious."

He took a step back and held the bar like a baseball bat. "Me, too."

Okay, deep breath. One, two, three. "Now!"

Billie yanked open the door.

The rat jumped into the air.

Des swung hard and swift.

With a skooshy smack the wood made contact, knocking the rat back into the hallway wall. A burst of dark red splattered on the wall on impact. The rat dropped to the floor.

"There, that was easy," Des said, chuckling.

Sqweesqweesqweesqweesqweesqweesqweesqweesqwee . . .

A horde of rats scurried into view of the door.

Billie shrieked and ran over to him.

For a split second he debated the two of them getting up on the bed, but a lot of good that would do them. The rats would jump up anyway and . . .

The rats dove into the air and came at them like a swarm of bees.

"Come on!" Des grabbed her by the hand. He waved the bar in front of him like a windshield wiper, knocking the rats away each time some jumped up and tried to take a piece out of his face.

Billie crashed into him, jumping and skipping as they ran down the hallway to the door.

Des grabbed the doorknob and pulled. The door didn't open.

"It's locked, you idiot!" Billie shouted.

What're you giving me—*No time!* He unlocked the chain, the deadbolts and ran out with her in tow and slammed the door behind them.

Thudthudthunkthunkthudthudthunk. The rats plowed into the door.

Breathing hard, he was about to put his head between his knees when Billie took him by the hand and pulled him down the hallway and up the stairs. The two worked frantically to unchain and unlock the front door of the building and then headed outside.

They finally stopped to catch their breath once they reached the sidewalk.

"Did you see that?" he said, glancing toward the building.

"Yeah. I can't . . . believe . . . they just . . ." She took another deep breath.

"What now?" he said.

"We'll go to my place. Let's just get inside and we'll talk there."

"Good idea." He grinned. *Des Nottingham: Rat Wrangler.*

"Let's go."

The two walked briskly down the sidewalk, each glancing over their shoulder every few seconds to see if the rats escaped and they were being followed.

The sidewalk remained bare for most of the walk home.

Until a shadow lurked in the distance.

It was coming toward them.

6
MR. SHANK

Billie stopped walking and grabbed Des's arm. "You see that?"

Des squinted, eyes forward. "Yeah."

"Do you think—?"

"Maybe."

"We can't turn around either." She looked over her shoulder, checking for the rats. There were none. However, though she couldn't be sure, she thought she might have heard a soft thudding on the air, possibly the rats having escaped Des's apartment and now banging on the entrance door.

"Can't see anything. He's too dark, too far away. Let's cross to the other side. That way, if it is one of them, we should have a bit of an edge, some distance, and can run," Des said.

"Okay."

The two crossed the street, neither one taking their eyes off the shadowy figure on the sidewalk. They walked cautiously along the sidewalk, eyeing the dark figure across the way. It kept walking down the sidewalk, slowly. There was still a chance it was someone out for a late-night stroll but not likely.

They kept a steady pace, neither speaking but both thinking the same thing: get ready to run in case it was one of the dead.

As the figure across the way drew closer and came into clearer view, Billie asked, pointing, "It's an old guy. Do you know him?"

Des surveyed the old fella before answering. "I think so." He leaned his head forward on his shoulders, as if the few inches gained from doing so made it easier to see. "Hey, it's Mr. Shank."

"Yeah?"

"Pretty sure."

A load of weight melted off Billie's chest. "Oh, good. For a second there I thought we were in trouble."

"Well, even if it was one of them" —Des's voice suddenly took on a more confident tone— "we'd still be okay, I think. Those things move slow, remember? We could have outrun it no problem."

"But the rats. Those guys were fast."

"But still rats. So far, none of the dead have exhibited any sort of speed. All walk as if they have dumbbells strapped to their ankles."

"I suppose."

They kept walking, hoping Mr. Shank would look up from the sidewalk and see them. He never did and kept his eyes to the ground as if he was verifying his feet were in fact touching the pavement with each step.

Shank was about forty feet ahead of them, still on the other side.

"Hey!" Des called out, waving his hand in the air.

Billie grabbed him by the wrist and yanked his hand down. "What are you doing?"

"What? It's Mr. Shank. What's to worry?"

"Are you blind? There's something wrong with him."

"Get outta here. Shank's always been a little weird, for starters. And if you think just because he's walking slow that he's a zombie, that doesn't prove anything. The guy lost a foot in World War Two. He's got one of them prosthetic things and always walks slow with a bit of a limp. He uses his ca—" Des stopped talking then stopped walking.

"What?"

"Shank always has a cane. Now he doesn't."

Her heart sank then tripled its beat. "Oh."

Des's brow furrowed. "Hey! Mr. Shank! Yo!"

Shank kept walking, eyes to the ground.

Des hollered again. "Hey, you dead or something!"

"Idiot! What kind of a question is that? He's not hard of hearing, is he?"

"A little. Usually have to talk a bit louder when talking to him, but I don't have to shout or anything not unlike my dad, who couldn't hear a gun go off even if you put the barrel right up to his ear."

"Okay, anyway . . ."

Shank's legs dragged beneath him, most notably his left foot, as if it were giving him extra trouble today. He was almost right across from them.

"Should I call out again?" Des asked.

Billie focused her eyes and took a good hard look at Shank's face, checking for any sign of death. From what she could see from about

52

twenty feet away, his skin was worn and weathered like any old man's, his eyes shadowed by the brim of a gray fedora. Bright spikes of gray-white hair jutted out from beneath the hat. The gray dated suit he wore didn't show any signs of tear or blood from where she was standing.

"Okay, just one more time. If he doesn't hear us, let's just move on and if he is all right, you can tell him we passed by him next time you see him," she said.

"'Kay." Des cleared his throat, whistled, then shouted, "Mr. Shank!" He waved his hand. "Yoohoo!"

Nothing.

"Okay, let's move it, then," Billie said.

No sooner did they get going than Mr. Shank faltered on the sidewalk across the way, stumbled a step, and dropped to his knees.

"Des . . ." she started.

"Oh great. Maybe he is alive. Zombies don't do that." Des bolted across the street.

"Des! Wait!" She pushed her glasses up the bridge of her nose. "Moron," she muttered and took off after him.

Mr. Shank had fallen face first just before Des got to him. Des was already on all fours and had his head to the old man's when Billie caught up to him.

"Is he . . . ?" she asked.

Des shook his head. "Can't tell. He might be breathing, but with the way his arm is, blocking his face, I can't get close enough to be sure."

Koom! Something fell over in the distance, making Billie jump. Sounded like a garbage can had been toppled over.

"Here." She knelt down beside Shank's body. She thought that with all the death and *undeath* she'd seen over the past year, she'd be used to the idea of being around the sick or dead. She wasn't. Slowly, she reached out and was about to grab Mr. Shank's wrist so she could move his arm away from his face. When she touched the soft fabric of his suit, she jerked her hand away. If he *was* dead . . . "Move his arm."

"Fine. Here." Des handed her the bar from his bedroom closet, then placed a pair of hands under Shank's forearm and gently adjusted it so he could have access to the old man's face. "You're such a girl, you know that?"

"Sue me for being born this way." She smiled.

Des smiled, too, then leaned in close and put an ear next to Shank's mouth.

"Hear anything?" she asked, squeezing the bar, desperately needing to relieve some stress.

"Hang on a sec. Can't hear nothing with you jabbering."

She stuck her tongue out at him even though he didn't see.

"I can't . . ." he said and got closer to the ground. He turned his head so he was facing her and scooted to the side with his ear closer to Shank's mouth. "The angle . . ."

Billie's mouth was dry. She wriggled her tongue in her mouth, trying to get some spit going. "I don't think he's alive, Des."

Des closed his eyes, brought a finger to his lips, shushing her, and waited.

Putting one palm on her thighs, the other still holding the bar beside her leg, she straightened her back, took a deep breath, then checked the sidewalk for the rats again. The sidewalk was bare.

She looked back at Des. He opened his eyes, his ear still close to Mr. Shank's mouth.

"Can't hear anything," he said.

"Check his pulse."

"Okay."

Mr. Shank's arm snapped up from his side, jerked into the air, then dropped onto Des's head.

Des screamed and tried to pull away but Shank's palm on his skull kept him pinned.

It could have been the sudden movement that did it, but suddenly Billie's eyes were drawn to Shank's other arm, the one she couldn't see when she had studied him from across the street. A moist, dark red patch was on his biceps, the gray material ripped, as if something had bit into it and torn it away.

"Des!" she screamed, dropping the bar. She grabbed him by the shoulders, tugging him back, trying to free him from the old guy's hold. The man wouldn't let go. "Get off him, you . . ." She kicked Shank in the underside of the forearm, sending the arm up and loosening its grip on Des.

Des scrambled backward on his belly then got to his feet. "Did you see, did you see?"

"Run!" she said. She began to run but had to stop abruptly.

She hadn't seen them coming, not with her attention on Des and Mr. Shank.

A dozen undead stepped slowly toward her, some dragging their feet, others managing fairly well considering they had no life in their legs.

She and Des turned around and both stopped short when they were met by fifteen more coming from the other side.

Billie could scarcely breathe.

A soft scraping sound signaled Mr. Shank was getting to his feet. The old man straightened, dropped his shoulders as if they were too heavy for him, and started moving toward them, one arm out, the other trying to extend but not seeming to get past stomach level.

Not far behind the old man's feet was the bar from Des's closet. She was closest to it.

She checked the zombies; she had maybe three seconds before it'd be too hard and too late to move. Carefully, her eyes on Mr. Shank's white ones, she crouched down, and duck-walked closer, reaching for the bar. Shank stumbled a step to the side, blocking it from her. She didn't know if the move was intentional or not.

"Uh, Billie?" Des said, poking her in the back.

She spun around.

They were surrounded, the zombies having formed a ring around them.

There was nowhere to run.

7
IN A SWARM OF DEATH

Des tried to swallow the cotton ball at the back of his throat. The tissue back there was so dry that he coughed and had a hard time catching his breath. Billie, so transfixed on the mass of zombies surrounding them, didn't look his way to see if he was all right.

When he was finally able to breathe, he looked at her with watery eyes.

"We're going to die," he whispered, the words dripping with defeat.

Billie only nodded.

Should he tell her how he felt about her? If this was the end, what could it hurt? It's not like it would matter in a few moments anyway.

I love you, he said to her in his mind.

He wished she could hear his thoughts. He wanted her know, wanted her to understand that despite the world nearly at its end, despite all the loss she'd suffered in the past year, despite the hopelessness that plagued each and every day, there was someone who cared about her.

Deeply.

I can't . . . I can't say anything. Not like this. It'd be selfish of me, if I did. It could also backfire and confuse her and I don't want her last thoughts to be something like, "What do I say back 'cause I don't feel the same?"

The zombies moved closer, their white eyes filled with hate. Their mouths hung slack, eager to taste fresh meat, so raw and still filled with fresh blood.

"I have to try," he said quietly.

"What?" she replied softly, her eyes settling on a middle-aged woman with short blonde hair. A part of the woman's cheek was missing as was a chunk of her right hand. Her pale skin was the same washed-out gray as the rest of the dead.

"I'm going to fight them."

"You are?"

The zombies closed in.

Des screamed and lashed out, swinging his right arm up in a wild arc and bringing it back down on the side of an elderly zombie's face, clubbing him on the cheekbone. The dead man's head angled to the side, lolled for a second, then was brought upright again. Des kicked him in the groin then moved for the undead teenage boy beside him, knocking aside the kid's arms. He brought his forearm across the teen's throat, whacking it in the neck. The kid fell back. The other zombies drew in, their arms swinging out. Billie shrieked and disappeared beneath a mass of smelly flesh, rubbery arms and claw-like fingers.

"Hey!" Des tried moving toward her. He was shoved back as three dead women cut him off and pushed him away into the waiting arms of a large black zombie who, judging by the smell and decay of his skin, must have been dead for the better part of the year. The big fella's blood-caked mouth opened wide, his once-pearly-white teeth now faded to yellow with black marks like burnt corn. Des wriggled himself to the side within the man's grasp just as the guy's teeth were about to take a chunk out of his shoulder.

Tears sprang from the corners of his eyes. He hadn't meant to cry; he just couldn't help it. Panicked instinct and preparation for death took over and no matter how hard he resisted the black guy's hold, the more he found himself entangled within his enormous plaid shirt-covered arms.

Billie's cries went from loud to quiet to loud again as she struggled to get out from under the three undead on top of her. Des couldn't see her; he could only hear her.

"Help!" she screamed.

"Bill—" Des was cut off when a chubby, blood-slicked finger stabbed into his mouth. It tickled the uvula at the back of his throat and he immediately threw up, warm puke gushing out of his mouth like cruddy water out of an overflowing toilet. Gravity took over and the puke splashed back to the rear of his throat, cutting off his air.

Something firm and hard gripped his legs. Someone tugged on his arm and yanked so hard he thought he was going to be torn apart.

BOOM!

Cool liquid splashed on Des's face.

BOOM! Crhk. BOOM! BOOM!

More cool liquid, sticky and grimy.

Crhk. BOOM! BOOM!

"Des!" Billie shouted. "Ah!"

Des fell to the ground, his shoulder blades smacking into the pavement. The stinging impact jolted him and his eyes shot open. Black blood covered his vision. He smeared it away. An old dead lady with bright white hair and olive skin stumbled over and stood over him, her murky white eyes lost in a sea of rage. She jerked out both arms, fingers splayed, and lunged on top of him. Her growls and high-pitched shrieks consumed Des's ears. The funk of the air emanating from the hole in her throat made him gag.

He spat a runny wad of bloody puke in her face. With everything he had, he brought in his fist and clocked her in the temple.

"Get off!"

Crchk.

BOOM! BOOM!

Crchk.

BOOM! BOOM!

The zombies wailed, growled, gurgled. The thud-thud-thud of bodies hitting the ground rumbled along the pavement, Des's ears drinking it up.

Crchk. BOOM! BOOM!

The gun shots rang out and the wall of bodies that had once loomed over him began to thin then, after a few more moments and fire-cracking blasts, were gone altogether.

Des coughed, rolled over onto his stomach and emptied his guts again. Head swimming, he took a trembling breath and slowly got onto his hands and knees.

"Stand up," a voice said off to the side.

"Don't pull so hard," Billie said, though to whom, Des couldn't see.

What sounded like the soles of shoes scraping on pavement made Des turn his head to the side so he could get a better look at what was going on. Just beyond a carpet of five bodies, a young man with a shaved head was pulling Billie to her feet. The guy pulled on her wrist so hard when he helped her up that he nearly tossed her into the air. His large gun was aimed at her head the entire time.

"Get away from her," Des said, his voice hoarse and just above a whisper.

"Quiet," the man said, his green eyes rock hard, his gaze not just penetrating but downright cold.

"Oh, man . . ." Des pushed himself to his feet, teetered a step, then moved toward them. He tripped and fell when his foot caught the underside of a zombie's arm, and he landed on top of another corpse.

58

A strong hand grabbed him by the back of the neck and yanked him to his feet.

A young man with a weathered face that made him look ten years older than he probably was stared at him then gave him a push to the chest.

"Hey, watch it!" Des said.

The man pointed the gun at Des's head. Immediately, Billie lunged at the guy. The man caught her, spun her around, and locked her arm in a chicken wing. Billie, bent over at the waist, her arm forced at an odd angle behind her back, yelped from the pain. She tried to move but each effort seemed to make the pain worse because her face pinched up, her lips pursed, her brow furrowed.

Nearly out of breath, Des stared down the barrel of the gun. "What do you want?"

The man seemed to consider his words, then said, "Take off your clothes."

"What?" Des replied.

"Wh-what . . ." Billie said.

"You, too," he told her.

Des wiped some more blood off his face. "You're kidding."

The man cocked the hammer of the gun. "No. You got four seconds."

"Ju-just listen . . . listen to him . . ." Billie said, her face still contorted in pain.

The man let her go. She stumbled to the side a step. The look of pain never left her face as she moved beside Des.

"One," the man said.

"Grrgh. Fine!" Billie huffed and began removing her shirt.

"What are you doing?" Des said, looking over at her.

"Do you want to get shot?" she asked him.

"Two." The man took a step closer.

"No, but . . ."

Billie's shirt was already off and she was working her belt buckle so she could remove her pants. "You always make things so difficult. Don't blame me if you get a hole blown through your face."

"Three."

"So the guy comes, kills some zombies then wants us naked?"

"Let's go, folks," the man said. "Four."

Des raised his hands. "Okay, okay. Chill out, crackerjack. I'll—"

"Now's not a good time for wisecracks, Des," Billie said.

"All right. Whatever." He quickly kicked off his shoes and took off his tank top and pants and let them drop by his feet. *Don't blame me if in a few minutes we're walking around like the rest of the creatures, gray and naked.* "Do you want our gitch, too?"

The man shook his head. Billie looked relieved as she stood there huddled with her thighs pressed together and arms covering her chest.

"Take off your socks. Both of you," the guy said, gun still aimed at them.

They did.

The man moved over to Billie, put a hand on her shoulder and squeezed hard, keeping her in place. Gun pointed at Des, he told him to turn around.

No, this isn't awkward at all, he thought and, arms in the air, turned around, moving slowly, still sore. He felt a palm graze his back then wipe off some of the blood that must have gotten back there.

"Okay, now you," the man said.

Billie slowly spun around in her spot. The guy moved her hands away from her chest and looked her over. Des half-expected the man to have some sort of sleazy smile crease his face, but instead the man conveyed zero emotion nor even pleasure in looking at such a beautiful girl wearing nothing but her underwear.

The man lowered the gun. "Get dressed," he said and turned his back to them.

This was it. This was his chance. Grimacing, Des raised his fist and was about to plow it into the back of the guy's head when Billie stopped him.

He must have looked at her incredulously because she quietly said, "Don't. If he was after us or wanted something, he would have killed us. His turning around is a sign of trust."

"So, what, we're supposed to trust him, now?"

"What's the matter with you? He just saved our lives. Stop acting like such a guy. The dude was checking us over for bites."

"Then why didn't he say so?"

With a smile that Des thought was completely inappropriate given the circumstance, she said, "Where's the fun in that?"

Rolling his eyes, he scooped up his clothes and got dressed as quickly as possible, minding himself not to let his eyes wander over to Billie lest she should see him and lay into him later. She was the only friend he had and the last thing he wanted was to blow that friendship never mind anything else that might—*might*—transpire between them.

60

When they finished dressing, Billie cleared her throat, hands on hips. Des crossed his arms.

The man turned around, keeping his eyes locked on theirs.

He pointed his gun at them.

8

MORE

BOOM!

The shot rang out. Joe didn't have to be beside these two to know they heard the bullet whistle by; it zipped between their heads and into the bald, undead fellow who dragged his feet as he came up behind them.

The two ducked at the noise, covering their ears. When they straightened, they followed his gaze to the zombie lying on the pavement behind them, blood pooling out of the dead man's head.

The young man and woman looked at him with wide eyes, jaws slack.

"You're welcome," he said.

"Oh, right. Thanks. Sorry," the young man said.

"Yeah, thanks," the girl said.

"You guys really shouldn't be out here," Joe said.

The girl with pink hair glanced at the bodies around her feet. "We know. We just . . ."

Joe hefted his gun. Still one shot left till he had to cock the hammer again. The chamber held twelve rounds. He still had four twelve-round clips attached to his belt. There were more at home. "Just?"

The scrawny young fellow stepped forward. "We had to get out of my place."

Joe arched an eyebrow.

"Bad case of rats."

"Rats?" Joe said.

"Yeah, dead ones. You know, the kind with white eyes just like" —the guy kicked one of the bodies at his feet— "these suckers right here."

The infection's spread?

"Don't worry. They're still trapped inside his building, just over there." The girl nodded down the street.

"You look surprised," the guy said to Joe.

"Should I be?" It wasn't the best thing to say, but Joe had been so isolated from the rest of the world for so long other than for his nocturnal activities that he forgave himself for this one slip in conduct.

"All I know is something's changed," the girl said. She stepped forward and stood by her friend. "There's been rumors online that things just feel different somehow. It's hard to put into words. But, I think, you and me and those rats just proved that something has changed. So far as we know, the animals hadn't been affected by the rain."

"A rat's an animal? Thought they were rodents," the guy said.

The girl jabbed him in the arm then looked at Joe. "Forgive him. He's an idiot." To the guy: "Yes, doofus, rats are animals, too."

The guy rubbed his arm where she poked him. "What're you calling me 'doofus' for?"

The girl smiled.

Joe was not amused. Perhaps last year he would have found this kind of humor funny. He always had a thing for how people interacted and loved reflecting on it, usually with a bit of wit. It was one of the reasons he loved *Seinfeld* so much in his former life. These days, however . . .

"You should get off the street," he told them.

"You're right," the girl said.

"You two have a place to go?" He wanted them to say yes. He still had work to do tonight.

"Yup," she said.

"Okay, then. We're done."

"Uh huh."

Her friend didn't seem to know what to say. By the looks of things, she was the commander in whatever relationship the two had going.

He eyed them a moment then said, "Bye." And turned to walk away.

"Look, um—" the young man said behind him.

Joe stopped but didn't turn around, only cocked his head toward them.

"Thanks for saving us."

Joe managed a half smile. "You're welcome. Stay safe."

"'Kay."

Joe walked away.

You're such a coward, Des thought as he watched their mysterious rescuer move away from them. *Uh oh.* "Hey, uh, guy in the coat?"

The man stopped walking.

"Those rats are over there, remember? You're headed right—"

The man merely nodded and kept going.

To Billie: "The dude's gonna get himself killed!"

"Not if they don't escape," she said.

"True. Still."

"Okay, it's over. Let's go." She maneuvered around the bodies, arms held out to keep her balance as she tried to find footing.

"Careful, Bill."

"Don't call me that."

"I said 'Billie.'"

"No, you didn't."

The two walked down the street, eyes peeled for any more of the undead. They took turns looking back at the man who had appeared out of nowhere and saved their lives.

It wasn't long before the man turned a corner, and was gone.

Des clicked his tongue. "Great."

"What?"

He stopped walking and gestured with his thumb over his shoulder. "Left my bar back there."

"Do you really want to go back?"

"Do you?"

"No."

"Me neither."

He licked his lips. *Some "zombie wrangler" you turned out to be.* "Wanna just leave it, then?"

She shrugged. "Up to you."

He set his eyes on the mound of bodies in the distance. He *really* didn't want to have to go over there and pick through them. Even more, he didn't want to get their blood on his hands and accidentally imbibe it. He thought of the big black zombie that nearly killed him and how the dude had put a blood-covered finger down his throat. What kind of blood that was, he didn't know. Hopefully the kind that wasn't contaminated. Already feeling ashamed over his lack of courage, he decided to keep it to himself for now and only tell Billie if he absolutely had to.

"We'll be all right. There's more of the undead back there than we've ever seen all at once in this area. That's probably all of them and even if there are a few more out there, they're probably not on this street," he said.

"Okay. Your call."

They kept walking.

A few minutes later they came to a four-way stop. As they crossed the street, Des felt the strength run from his legs when he caught sight of moving shadows flanking them.

The undead were coming in from either side, droves of them.

"Run!" he shouted and pulled Billie by the hand.

The second Billie caught sight of the zombies she hopped into a sprint and the two bolted down the street.

It wasn't long till they left the four-way and walking dead behind and were almost at her place. The two halted when a fresh pack of zombies were making their way toward them, several already looming around her apartment building, rocking side to side on their heels to a tune only they could hear.

Des threw his hands into the air. "What's going on?"

"I don't know. This is new. And we're trapped."

"Not necessarily. We can cut through the houses, you know, hop fences and zip through a few backyards. Maybe the neighboring streets aren't as crowded and we can come back later."

"Which way?"

"Right."

"I'm asking which way to go?"

Didn't she understand him? "I said 'right.'"

They took off across the street. As they ran, Billie said, "Thought you were being sarcastic."

"Now's not the time, Bill."

"Don't call me that!"

They reached a five-foot-tall brown-slatted fence.

"Here," Des said and cupped his hands together. "I'll boost you over."

"Thanks."

Billie raised her knee, put her foot in his hands and placed her palms on the top of the fence.

"On three," he said. "One, two, three." And boosted her up.

Billie was straddling the top beam on her stomach when she suddenly stopped.

"Come on, hurry," he said.

She hopped back down. "Not this way."

"Why?"

She didn't need to answer.

Groaning and wheezing filled the air.

Des peered over the fence then shot back with a jolt when a pair of white dead eyes popped up to greet him.

With a shout, he turned and ran, Billie behind him.

They reached the street and were greeted by a row of undead men, women and children.

The deceased came toward them.

The strong, hinting feeling that this could be a new chance to prove himself struck him hard and quick. But who was he kidding? There had to be at least thirty walking dead in front of him and who knew how many behind.

He could only think of one thing to say: "Run!"

They made a beeline to the right, zipping past the row of zombies as fast as they could. Des pressed his heels hard into the ground, creating a deep burn in his thighs. Billie ran beside him and he realized that she could have easily outrun him but was holding back for his sake.

Does she have to be that *good?* he wondered. *Man, beautiful* and *fast.*

He glanced over at her, watching her pink hair swing in the wind as she gunned it forward.

A large shadow appeared in his peripheral and *WHAM!* a dull smack plowed into his skull as a massive arm and meaty hand crashed down on his forehead, cutting off his sprint and sending him backside first to the ground. The world spun. Billie was somewhere ahead. Dizziness kicked in and for a second Des forgot where his legs were. Then, remembering they were splayed out in front of him, he tucked his knees into his chest, went to stand, and was struck down again.

An enormous dead man stood over him, three or four hundred pounds of rotted and gray flesh with skin peeling in places. The putrid stench of BO mixed with rotten fish made his stomach lurch. He swallowed the gulp of puke that rose at the back of his throat; its sharp orange-juice-like taste only added to the discomfort wreaking havoc on his insides.

The mammoth zombie grunted.

Dragging footsteps scraped along the ground behind him. He dared not look back to see how close they were. He could only imagine sneaking a peek and finding them so close he'd be a goner anyway.

Where was Billie?

66

From somewhere behind the wall of the dead gathering around him: "Des! Where are you?"

"Here," he croaked. He doubted she heard him.

The fat man's dead hand crashed down again, swatting him in the side of the head. His whole body swayed with the blow and he was face to face with the grass in no time. The grass's boggy scent was utter relief compared to the foul stench that clouded the air. A part of him didn't want to get up but lie on his side and drink it all in. But he had to get up. He *had* to. He couldn't die. Not without telling Billie . . .

"Haaaaaiii yaaaaaah!"

Des glanced up.

Billie was on the fat man's back, legs wrapped around his sides, her small, feminine fists raining blow upon blow on the dead man's head and the tops of his shoulders.

"No . . ." Des said and cursed himself for not being able to speak properly. Was he that out of it?

The fat man growled, reached a flabby arm over his shoulder and grabbed Billie by the back of the neck. With one clunky swing forward, he whipped her off his back and sent her in a flip on top of Des. Her skull collided with his and ringing sounded in his ears as green and black fuzzies raced across his vision.

He might have said "Ow." He wasn't sure. His eyes hurt. A sharp pain throbbed at the top left side of his head. Billie was beside him, holding the side of her head, face down to the ground.

"You okay?" he whispered.

She hid her face from him, crying.

"It's okay, Billie. I'm—"

The fat zombie called out a hoarse cry, as if announcing to the others that it was time to feast.

"Billie?"

She huddled into a ball.

"Billie, listen to me." Des cleared his throat. Was he really going to do this? *Might as well. Gonna die anyway. Can't get mad at me if she's de—She can't get mad at me.* "I'm sorry, Billie. I wish I could have saved us."

Growls, grunts and wet slurps filled the air above them. Des only half-noticed that the creatures were actually waiting a few moments before eating. Usually they just grabbed their prey and dove right in. Something was happening with them. He just didn't know what it was or what to call it.

Sobbing, Billie finally turned her head on the grass and faced him. Her wide blue eyes were rimmed red from the tears. Hopelessness filled her gaze and blanketed her face.

"I want to say—" he began, whispering. "What I want to tell you is—" Why couldn't he say it? Was he *that much* of a coward? "What I'm trying to tell you is . . . you see, I—"

BOOM!

A bucket of blood splashed onto them, stealing Billie from his sight.

BOOM!

More blood, like a tidal wave.

The ground shook as something huge and heavy fell to the ground.

The dead around them growled.

Des wiped the sticky blood from his eyes, trying not to gag from its stench.

Billie was now on her back, doing the same.

The fat dead man lay still at their feet. The others looming over them had their gaze set forward, some, Des thought, with disbelief written on their faces though he wasn't sure they were smart enough to even be in a state of disbelief.

Many dipped their heads and settled their eyes on them.

Crchk.

BOOM! BOOM!

Two dropped dead. One toppled across his and Billie's chests.

Billie shrieked and more shots rang out above them.

"Come on, get it off!" she yelled at him.

He stared at her for a moment, half his mind still wanting to tell her he loved her, the other half coming to grips with the fact that if they didn't get off the ground, they *would* die.

"Des, you idiot, let's go!"

Grimacing, he said, "Fine. Wanna be tough with me? Fine. Let's get this sucker off then I'm gonna throw you to them. Got it?"

BOOM!

She chuckled despite her tears and with one push they rolled the corpse off them.

He got to his feet first then helped her up.

Dead hands reached for them from all sides.

BOOM!

A dead child fell.

BOOM!

So did a young woman with a hole in her chest. Half her head suddenly went missing in a spray of brain and dark blood.

Des punched the first zombie he saw in the face then kicked another in the knee.

"Don't let them grab you!" he told her.

"Duh!" And she slapped a stooped-over old man across the cheek.

"You hit like a girl!"

"I am a girl!"

BOOM!

BOOM!

With two palms, Des shoved an obese woman away then brought his foot down on a smaller one. He realized after the fact that it was a zombified little girl with her eye missing.

His heart ached for her despite her being the reanimated shell of a cute four-year-old with brown pigtails. That girl, probably in love with dolls and tea parties, could never have known that one day she'd be dead, walking, and stomped on by some gamer who didn't have the guts to tell the girl he adored how he felt about her.

BOOM!

Des found a heavy branch a few feet away from the little girl's body and tossed it to Billie, who immediately began swinging it into the skulls of any of the dead who came near her.

Des scanned the ground for another branch but couldn't see anything, nothing but the—

"Come on," he breathed. "Can't I get a real weapon? Always some dude's body part." He remembered the dismembered arm from his video game. With renewed determination, he added, "All right." And ran and picked up a dismembered leg from the ground, cut off at the knee, a piece of bone sticking out of it.

He swung it around like a baseball bat, socking anything that moved in the side of the head.

As the throng of zombies began to clear, he was finally able to locate the source of the gunshots: the dude with the long trench coat and big gun.

He glanced over at the man, hoping the guy would see him and he could give him a nod of acknowledgement. Instead, the fellow, lost in a trance of trigger-pulling mayhem, blasted shot after shot into the dead, bringing them down one, sometimes two, at a time.

Privately, Des was impressed with the "double kill," the way the guy was able to fire off one bullet through one zombie's skull, the same bullet embedding itself in the brain of another behind it.

A strong hand grabbed Des's ankle. He brought the leg in a downward swing and knocked out the teeth of dead man who was mostly just torso. The half-body flopped around on the ground as the zombie tried to grab Des's leg again. Des beat the guy in the back of the head with the dismembered leg then dragged the dazed zombie to the curb and slammed its face down on the curb's edge. With one hard kick, he plowed his heel into the back of the dead man's head, curb-stomping the sucker down so hard that the jagged edge of the curb ripped straight through and removed the top of the guy's head from the rest of his body.

Only then did the man in the trench coat seem to notice and give Des a nod of approval.

Billie had noticed, too, but looked away as if in disgust when Des set eyes on her.

Nothing works in my favor. Ever.

A few more shots and the undead finally stopped moving.

The three stood at different points amidst the field of bodies.

Des couldn't believe how many there were. It was more than what had just been on the street. All those from the other side of the fence must have somehow gotten over it and joined their kin.

Still, three taking out fifty or more wasn't bad at all.

He stepped around and over the bodies and went over to Billie.

"Are you okay?"

She wiped a splatter of blood from the side of her face and cleaned the lenses of her glasses on her shirt. "I'll live." She put her glasses back on and glanced down to his lower right.

He followed her gaze. "Oh." And dropped the leg.

The two looked at the guy in the trench coat, who stood among the dead like some kind of beacon, smoke trickling out the barrel of his enormous gun.

The man hefted the weapon. "Shouldn't have left you alone."

Des put his hands on his hips. "We could have handled it."

The guy smirked. "Didn't look like it."

"Always have to say something, don't you?" Billie quietly said to Des.

"Usually."

The three moved off to the side, away from the bodies.

"This isn't normal," the man said.

"No, it's not," Billie replied.

70

The man scanned the bodies. "Seventy-two."

"Seventy—" Des started but his voice squeaked. He cleared his throat. "Seventy-two?"

"Fast counter," Billie said.

"Necessary habit," the man said.

Billie and the man stared at one another for a moment then finally broke away when Des coughed.

"Sorry," she said and offered her hand out to the man. "I'm Billie." Then with a nod to her right, "This is Des."

The man didn't say anything but only took her hand. Was it Des's imagination or did the two hold hands longer than a normal handshake?

"Hey, how ya doin'?" Des said and offered his hand, hoping the dude would let go of Billie's.

The two men shook hands.

"And you are?" Billie asked.

The man seemed to consider her words carefully before he spoke. "Name's Joe." It sounded like he didn't want to reveal his real name. Did "Joe" have something to hide?

They all stood in awkward silence. Joe was clearly not used to talking much or, probably, hanging around anyone. Most people looked at you straight in the eye when they spoke. Joe kept his gaze downward or over your shoulder.

Billie nodded toward Joe's gun. "You seem to know what you're doing with that thing."

"I try," Joe said.

"Have you, I don't know, had to use it a lot recently?"

"Today, yeah. I can't tell you what's going on, but I think they've discovered the Haven or at least realized that this is the least dead place in the city."

"Seems that way," Des said, trying to contribute something. All of the sudden, it seemed like Joe was the star and Billie was his biggest fan. *Don't sweat it, man. You got tenure.*

"Where were you headed?" Joe asked.

"My place," Billie said. "Now I'm not so sure that's a good idea. Who knows how many more are out there?"

Joe nodded.

"I don't know, what do you think? Think we should go back that way and risk it?" Billie said.

"We can go to my—Wait, never mind. Rats," Des said. The drone of flies filled the air as they began buzzing around the dead. "We have to get moving." To Billie: "Know anyone around here?"

"A few, but I don't know their specific addresses and I'm not in the mood to go banging on each and every door."

Low moaning in the distance, a street or two over.

"They're coming," Joe said. "Let's go."

"Where?" Des asked.

Joe walked past them, bending his elbow and resting the barrel of his gun on his shoulder. He didn't look back when he spoke. "My place."

9
GHOST TOWN

The TransCanada Highway led straight into Winnipeg, becoming Portage Avenue once it hit the outskirts of the city. August had hoped he would have been able to take his van right in, but when he drove into town, he was greeted by a clogged street filled with abandoned vehicles. Even the turn-offs he could have taken for an alternate route into the city were packed with driverless cars, trucks, vans.

Even now, as he neared Portage and Main on foot, the hub of downtown, he remembered standing at the door to the Ford, one hand on the doorframe, looking out onto a ghost town. Not a sign of life anywhere. A part of him had expected it, for there not to be anyone left, but a greater part had held out hope and wanted to see a few folks wandering the streets, helping each other out, maybe even a person or two who could have told him that the undead had left the city and they were in the process of rebuilding. Not in Winnipeg and, August suspected, probably not anywhere else in the world, either.

He wasn't sure what he was going to do once he made it to the city, whether his own plans or ones from above. A few times during the trip he muttered a few words to the Big Guy upstairs. The lines to heaven must have been down, because he hadn't heard a peep, only static. It was either that or God wasn't picking up the phone.

The radio had been filled with static, too. No news, no music, no emergency broadcast of any kind. Nothing.

Talk about wandering in the wilderness, August had thought more than once.

Rifle in hand, he had hoofed it down Portage Avenue, his old legs enjoying the walk after sitting for so long, but also crying out every now and then with a cramp or tired muscles. Quite a few times he had sat on a bench or at a bus stop to catch his breath and give himself a break. And more than a few times he had yearned for a drink, something stiff and solid, preferably Tequila.

He had already downed the little that was in the bottle he brought from the cabin. And to bring everything else he took from there and lug it all the way down Portage, he might as well set up an antique stand and invite the dead for a coupon day.

He had hit up a few of the bars on the way downtown and each one was the same: empty, with toppled over chairs and tables, blood spattered on the bar tops and walls and pool tables. The only plus was that he did find one bar with a half dozen or so empty liquor bottles lying on the floor, probably having fallen there during a struggle. An old Jack Daniels still had a bit of whiskey in it. But only a sip. He sloshed the teaspoon's worth of alcohol around in his mouth a few times before swallowing. It was enough to take the edge off, but that was it. Nothing to really calm him down and put his mind at ease.

He checked a couple of gun shops along the way for bullets. Most were cleaned out, just barren shelves that cried out to him, saying, "Wish you'd been here." Only one had a bit of ammo left and he scored a couple of boxes of .22s.

Sometimes it was better to proactively pick off the dead lest he cross paths with them later.

He could have taken on a number of them, that would have been fine, but it was this empty city that got to him right now, the utter barrenness a constant reminder of his lonely time at the cabin, the heavy weight of being in complete solitude when he should have been with his family. Their deaths hung over him the entire walk down Portage, the painful memory of their demise switching between the fore and back of his mind, depending on what he was doing. But they were always there, sometimes alive, sometimes dead, all of it overshadowed by the looping images of putting holes in their heads.

August arrived at Portage and Main.

This was not the city he left behind.

The looming towers of the Richardson building, CanWest Global, the Scotiabank building and the Bank of Montreal building were no longer the pillars of beauty they once were. Broken windows checkered the facades. Here and there, bodies lay bent over the broken glass, half in and half out on the higher floors as if the jumpers had chickened out and decided falling on broken glass was the best option. August wondered if some were still alive—undead alive—and would start walking soon. Then again, the bodies probably had a portion of their heads missing but he couldn't tell for sure from this far down. Those creatures didn't stay dormant, so far as he knew.

Cars cluttered the intersection, many with their doors open, echoes of panicked screams from their former drivers still lingering on the air. Many looked as if they had been on fire at one point, portions of some of the hoods black with soot.

Overturned military vehicles sat here and there—a few jeeps, a tank—a testament to the city's last stand before the zombies took them, too.

One part of the street had water pooled in the gutters, a black car smashed up against a no longer-running fire hydrant just beyond.

Blood stained the concrete in several places and August could clearly imagine the undead dragging half-eaten, still-breathing people up and down the street, taking them into the shadows to be devoured.

A lone tricycle sat off to the side, its tiny young owner long gone.

A few rapid shots fired in the distance.

August got his rifle ready in case any creatures wandered out of the alleys and side streets, looking for someone new to gnaw on.

Through the dark glass looking into the Scotiabank lobby across the way, August made out a few humanoid shadows, unmoving, lying in a heap.

He glanced around at some of the neighboring buildings and squinted, seeing what was behind other windows. He made out a few more bodies, but that was it. Most of the windows were too dark or too far away for him to make out anything else.

"What are you doing here, old man?" he whispered. "There's nothing." *There's no one.* He felt fresh tears building up, rising to the brim of his eyes but refusing to spill out.

The deep gray sky overhead seemed to grow darker, as if it, too, was pointing out his predicament and telling him he was too late for . . . for . . . . And that was the problem. He didn't know *what* he was too late for. He hadn't had a plan when coming here. He just knew he should make his way back and that was all.

Using his rifle as a makeshift cane, August slowly walked over to the shoulder-high cement wall in front of the Richardson building and leaned with his back against it.

Once more he glanced around. To his left was the Fairmont Hotel, the only one in the city that changed its names more times than any of the others. Sticking out from one of the top windows was a small, light blue biplane. He could only imagine the scene the day it crashed, its pilot at first happy to escape this place only to be thwarted in the end and plowed into the building's side. Judging by the way it was situated, it appeared the doors to it were still closed, whoever had been in it probably still dead inside. Maybe *undead.*

He thought about firing a shot into the plane's side window to see if anything within moved but thought better of it because he knew he'd have to conserve ammo for *when*, not if, the time came.

The drive into the city, the long walk down Portage, the stress of being alone—it caught up to him and he slumped against the wall. He needed to rest but he couldn't stay out here in the open.

Maybe the hotel will have an unspoiled room and I can catch some sleep for a little while? he thought.

He started to make his way over there but stopped himself when he remembered the small plane lodged in one of its windows. If something *was* still inside the plane . . . . No, he didn't want to risk it.

He looked around. Nothing but office buildings. Yet there had to be a secure place he could go and rest in. Some place away from all this death, some place fortified enough so that should the dead come a'knockin', he'd be safe.

The bodies behind the lower window of the Scotiabank seemed to look at him.

The Scotiabank.

The bank.

A bank!

August rounded the cement wall and found the set of stairs that led down to the entrance to Winnipeg Square. There were six banks down here: Scotiabank, Royal Bank, Bank of Montreal, TD, CIBC and a Credit Union.

Surely one of them had their safe open. If he remembered correctly, it was still business hours when the rain came.

August went downstairs and through the doorframe with its glass missing, and walked down the motionless escalator.

One of the banks was almost straight across from where he entered.

As he crossed the wide hallway, he kept his ears open and listened intently for any sign of life. He considered shouting hello, but decided against it.

Rifle at the ready, he cautiously approached the bank, a part of him eager to fire and work off the anger that had built up within. These creatures took everything from him. These creatures weren't even supposed to be here.

The world wasn't supposed to end this way.

The thought of how the apocalypse was *supposed* to happen constantly filled his mind, years of Bible study forming the backbone to all he believed about the End of Days. He still couldn't get over the fact that the undead walking the earth wasn't mentioned anywhere in the Scriptures and now that they were here, it brought a lifetime of faith into question. Even for a time, at the cabin, his belief in God melted to nothing, whatever lump that constituted his belief no more than a small pile of residue and it was only that *residue* that still made him hang onto God when everything else inside him said He didn't exist. No matter how long he thought about it or how much he tried to shake it, his belief wouldn't falter. It only dimmed, faded to the back of his mind and heart, then resurfaced now and then, depending on how he was feeling or what was going on.

The enormous wall-to-wall glass doors to the bank were shattered, jagged pieces of glass lining the frame like shark teeth.

The lights were off except for a faint yellow glow from somewhere in the bank's corner. He didn't know what was causing it other than whatever it was was on the floor.

Ensuring his rifle was ready to fire, August glanced behind himself, didn't see or hear anything, then stepped over a sharp triangle of glass in the frame and went in. He scanned the dimly lit room side to side as he moved, already his mind imagining one of the dead jumping out at him and him firing.

Palms sweaty, face hot with anxiety, he slowed his breathing, cutting back on the sound his frantic exhaling emitted.

The row of teller stations in front of him were covered with scattered papers, those stupid pens attached to chains dangling off their corners, hanging above the floor.

He took another step and a foul smell greeted him. Immediately he got his eye behind the site at the end of the barrel and pointed it toward where he thought the smell was coming from. The stench grew thicker the nearer he came to the teller counter and when he was right up against it, he scanned the carpeted floor on the other side. Nothing. Just a few swivel chairs, a couple still upright, three more on their sides on the floor.

His eyes immediately drew to the source of the light.

A flashlight. It was still on, barely shining, in the far right corner next to the cash dispenser.

There's probably a heap of dough still in there. For a second he wondered if the .22 had enough gusto to blast it open. Not a chance. Then he felt ashamed at the thought and was about to raise eyes to the ceiling to say sorry when a foul waft of something sharp and thick pierced his nostrils.

He exhaled through his nose, blowing the smell out and decided to breathe through his mouth from here on in.

Rounding the teller counter, he went straight for the flashlight in the corner. Crouching down, his old knees creaking, he picked it up, straightened, then checked the bulb. The light wouldn't last the night, he suspected. It was more orange than yellow.

"Who dropped you?" he wondered. *And how long ago? A day or two at most. Probably a day.*

He slowly shone the light around the room, listening carefully.

Quiet.

That smell.

The flashlight's beam settled on a lump of something on one of the chairs.

That wasn't there before unless I missed it.

The chair was on a three-quarter angle so he couldn't see what it was. He placed the end of the flashlight in his mouth, held the rifle tight in both hands, and approached the chair. Even at a couple of feet away, the shape was still difficult to make out. It looked soft, like a black cat curled up. A dead cat, maybe? Whatever it was, its funk made him want to throw up.

Slowly, he reached out a hand, grabbed the backrest and spun the chair around.

The flashlight dropped from his lips when a gaunt face stared back at him.

With a shout, he hopped back, his heart going from zero to a hundred in half a second.

Hands shaking, he bent down, picked up the flashlight and shone it again at the chair.

A woman's head sat on the chair, her eyes open and rolled so far back that the irises were half circles at the top of her eyeballs. The mouth hung slack, rimmed with black and red. The skin, though he couldn't be sure in the light available, seemed a dark, dark gray, with small black craters spotting the cheeks. Buckets of blood soaked the chair and the floor beneath it.

It took a second for it to register that the light glimmered off the blood; it was still wet.

Scccrpt. Scccrpt. Scccrpt.

August shone the light higher. "Who is it? Who's there?"

Nothing but a dark room answered him.

Scccrpt.

"I mean it! Answer me!"

He put the light back in his mouth and aimed his rifle high, ready to blast the head off anything that approached him whether it was alive, dying or dead.

Silence.

Five long minutes of it.

Legs trembling, August resolved that whatever it was, it was now gone.

He panned the light around the room. The safe was embedded in the wall behind him to his right. The door was open.

He sidestepped over there, listening for that scraping sound.

When his back bumped up against the safe door, which was sitting flush against the wall, he shone the light into the safe.

A body lay at his feet.

Bang!

The fabric of the man's white collared shirt burst and blood sprayed with the pieces.

August's hands still vibrated from the instinctive pull of the trigger. He shone the light on the man and discovered the fellow's legs were eaten away, his arms and his head.

He closed his eyes, pressed his lips together, then opened his eyes again.

Man, could he use a drink.

As quickly as he could, he pushed the torso out of the safe with his feet then grabbed the large, steel bar on the inside of the safe's door and tried pulling it closed. The door weighed a ton. He set his rifle down and this time used both hands. It was slow-going and he shuddered to think it was because he was too old and weak.

You're tired, that's all, just tired. This'll be easy come morning.

August closed the door and left it open a crack so he could get out. He wasn't sure if it'd lock itself automatically if he closed it all the way, and with next to no light, he didn't want to be trapped in there in the dark.

The place smelled of rot, the torso having fouled the air. August wondered if there were more bodies in the dark. Or had they already been eaten or, worse, only partially eaten and were now walking around again?

Slowly, he lowered himself next to the door, mindful to keep his feet away from the crack in the opening, and leaned sideways against it. If something did try to open it, he'd surely feel the door pressing against him and he'd awake.

Lying there in the dark, rifle across his chest, hands folded on top of it, August listened for movement outside.

Silence was his only friend.

August's eyes shot open, his heart drumming a good one. Throat dry, he discovered he had slid flat against the floor. Body aching from being in such an uncomfortable position, he walked himself backward on his elbows and leaned up against the corner near where the safe door's hinges met the wall. He swallowed, the spit moistening the back of his throat a little. He thought about going out into the main area to check for water. He was too tired. His body and mind begged for sleep.

He closed his eyes again and let his mind drift. He thought about praying but just before the words came, he was gone again, until later, when something stirred outside just beyond the door.

Scccrpt. Scccrpt. Scccrpt.

10
AT JOE'S PLACE

Joe really didn't want Billie and Des in his apartment and the only reason he invited them back was because it was the right thing to do.

But is it really the right thing if my heart isn't in it? April came bounding out of the front room just as they entered the apartment. She bowed and barked and growled at the newcomers.

Des took a step back.

"Don't worry," Joe said. "She's friendly." Then added, "To me, anyway." He locked the door and chained the top.

April's lips curled way back, showing her teeth. She barked, the sound echoing off the walls.

"April, quiet!" he told her.

She barked again.

Joe stepped up to her and put his hand on her head. "Quiet. It's okay." The dog stood straight up on all fours. "Don't mind her. She'll get used to you in a moment."

Billie nodded. Des had taken another step back.

The three stood just inside the door, Billie and Des looking at him as if waiting for him to say something.

"If your shoes stink like the dead, take them off otherwise don't worry about it. April'll trail you around if she thinks you're one of them. Might even jump on you."

Des made a face then took off his shoes. Billie took hers off, as well.

Joe kicked off his boots and took April by the collar and led her into the front room. The other two didn't follow and it wasn't until he stood in the middle of the room without them did he add, "You can come in, if you want. Or you can stand there. Up to you guys."

Billie and Des came in but didn't sit. They were a mess, each covered head to toe in sticky zombie blood.

"You should get cleaned up. As said, April'll go nuts if you don't," Joe told them.

Billie shrugged. "How?"

"Got running water?" Des asked.

"No. But I have water. Bathroom's at the end of the hallway. Why don't you guys go down there and clean up. There're a few jugs in there that you can use, same with a tub."

"What about our clothes?" Billie asked.

Good point, Joe thought. He had a few things Des could wear but nothing for girls. "I got some extra. You can use them."

"Where?" Des asked.

"The bedroom. I'll get them."

Joe led them down the hallway, Billie and Des following behind, April behind them. A low rumble emitted from April's throat as she trailed Des's heels.

The two visitors remained outside the bedroom door as Joe and April went in to find them something to wear. A few moments later he came out with a couple of T-shirts, some pants and socks. April remained at his feet.

"Here. This should do it. It's nothing fancy," he said and handed the stack to Des.

Des took it between his palms. "Thanks."

"No problem," he said even though a part of him was having a hard time letting the clothes go. He didn't have much as it was and he'd feel especially rude if he asked for them back when Des and Billie were done with them. He wasn't even sure if he'd see them again after they left.

Des and Billie went into the bathroom and closed the door behind them.

Joe immediately went to the kitchen, pulled off his coat and tossed it on the table. He grabbed a beer from the fridge and shouted down the hallway, "April, come. Now."

The dog remained in front of the bathroom door, gazing up at it as if she could see the two beyond.

Joe whistled. "I said let's go!"

Reluctantly, April obeyed and joined him in the front room.

Muttering came from behind the bathroom door. Joe couldn't make out what was being said but it sounded like Des was speaking.

"Is it just me or does he seem to be a bit of a suck?"

April didn't reply.

"Just me, then."

He took a swig of beer. It was old, the taste sharp and fizzy. Having these two here, in his home, made his heart ache, especially since one of them was a girl. The last person to have been in need had been April. She had slept over, back at his old place. Slept with him. They lay together on his bed and it was there they kissed for the first time. That was all. Just a kiss, but it was one Joe could never forget.

It was the first time he kissed someone he loved.

You gotta get past this, he thought. "Just move on."

But it was impossible.

April's memory lingered in every thought, on every breath, was present all the time. Even though she was dead, even though the stamp of finality had been put on things, he still held out hope that some way, somehow, he'd see her again and this all would have been some big misunderstanding.

"It's hopeless, isn't it?"

The dog looked at him like she did every time he tried to reason out his inability to let April go: a wide, dark-eyed stare, one filled with sympathy and one filled with the hurt of being unable to help. At least, that was how Joe liked to think his dog looked at him every time his heart went for a trip down the gutter.

By the time Billie and Des emerged from the bathroom, his beer had been long gone.

Billie led the way down the hallway, wearing a white T-shirt and black sweatpants. Des followed close behind, wearing jeans and a green T-shirt. Both the socks he had given them were gray.

"Got a place where I can put these?" Billie asked, holding up a wad of rolled-up, blood-covered clothes.

"Yeah," Joe said as he got off the couch and went into the kitchen. He pulled a black garbage bag out from under the sink and had Billie dump the clothes in it. "I'll toss these next time I go outside."

"When is that?" Billie asked, bending her elbows and putting her palms on her lower back.

April barked.

"Quiet!" Joe said. To Billie: "Tomorrow. I go out every night."

"What for?" Des asked.

Joe's mind went blank. He knew why he went out night after night, hunting the undead, but to put it into words . . . . He couldn't even explain it to himself never mind someone else. "Let's put it this way," he said. "The dead are walking the earth. They weren't supposed to. Once you died, that was it. Now, that's no longer the case. It would be one thing if it were a set amount of deceased people walking around. It's quite another when they either eat the rest of us who are still alive or turn us into one of them. This isn't how it's supposed to go, Des. I go out to try and reclaim some of the life that was taken from us. Will I ever get it all back? No. But at least I'm trying. That's more than what most folks are doing. Humanity gave up, remember? We're just pulling through and that's it. Let's try fighting for a change. You never know what might happen."

Billie had a subtle grin on her face. Des's face was blank, as if he couldn't quite compute what he'd just been told.

"So, you're, what, some kind of superhero?" Des said.

Joe smirked. "No, but thanks for the compliment."

"I just don't think it's wise," Billie said, "going out like that, asking for trouble. Look at what just happened. Crazy. And you want to walk into that? You're nuts!"

You just don't know I've got nothing to lose. "Maybe. But you guys also walked into that."

"Yeah, but we didn't know they'd be all over the place."

"Neither did I. This is new. It's been a long while since they've gathered in those kinds of numbers."

"Think they're looking to clean us out, that is, wipe everyone who's left off the map before, I don't know, moving on to the next city or something?"

"Maybe, but I doubt it. They're not *that* smart. Besides, each city is full of the things, remember?"

April came up beside Joe and sat at his feet, never taking her eyes off Billie and Des.

"But they are smarter or at least seem to be functioning at a higher level than before," Des said.

"Yeah," Billie said.

"They seem more feral now, too," Des said.

Billie looked at him, eyes wide. "Feral? Now that's a big word," she said. "One would think you read or something."

"I read."

"Yeah, comics."

"Still reading."

Comics. I used to write those, Joe thought. Des would probably get a kick out of him telling him that, maybe even get all fanboy on him. But that was a lifetime ago.

"We need to learn more," Joe said.

Billie furrowed her brow. "Have a computer? One hooked up to the Net?"

"Computer, yes. Net, no. I got rid of it."

She looked at him incredulously. "Serious?"

"Not everyone's a geek like you, you know," Des said.

"Shut up."

"Pssshh." Des waved her off with his hand.

"I was hooked up, long ago. Not anymore. Didn't need it."

"Surprised you were able to disconnect with the service provider," she said as if she didn't believe him.

Joe flashed back to the night he took a beer bottle to his computer in a drunken rage and tried smashing it to bits. His manuscript detailing his weekend with April was on there and, at the time, he thought that by destroying the computer he'd be able to get away from her and put to rest the torment of losing her. He trashed his modem, but the bottle broke when he went for the processor.

"A lot of surprising things have happened since the rain came, now, haven't they?" he said.

She eyed him coolly. He held her gaze, not giving her an inch. For a guest, she had a lot of guts to talk to him like that.

"Anyway," Des said, "what now?"

"Sleep," Joe said. "We'll talk once we're rested. It's been a long night."

April growled.

"Where do you want us to sleep?" Des asked.

Joe still kept looking at Billie. She hadn't taken her eyes off his.

"Hey, yoohoo?" Des said, waving a hand between them. "I said: 'Where do you want us to sleep?' Didn't you hear me, Joe?"

"I heard you. Take the bedroom. I'll sleep out here."

"Do you mind?" Billie asked.

"It's fine." *No, it's not! That bed hasn't been slept in since . . . since . . . April . . . di*— "There's a sheet and a pillow. Should be good enough."

"*A* pillow?" Des said.

Joe shifted his gaze to him, grimacing. "Is that a problem?"

Des took a step back. "No, not at all. Thanks. Yeah, um, thanks."

Joe turned and sat on the couch. Without looking at them he said, "If there's a problem, holler. April and I are light sleepers."

"Okay," Des said and he and Billie left the room.

Billie didn't say goodnight.

"Arrrgh, that guy!" Billie said as Des picked a side of the bed.

"What?"

"That didn't seem a little strange to you?"

Des glanced side to side, as if looking for a clue as to what she was talking about. "What?"

"He comes out of nowhere, saves our butts—twice!—invites us back here then acts like a jerk!"

"He's giving us a bed, Bill."

She snapped a finger up and pointed at him.

"*Billie,* I mean," he said. He lied down on the bed and threw her the pillow. "I can live without it," he muttered. "Sooo . . . what's going on?"

She glanced toward the bedroom door before joining him. "You know what? Forget it. I'm tired. Upset. Good night."

"Night."

She tossed the pillow on her side of the mattress and plopped her head on it. She closed her eyes but the frustration swirling around in her chest forced her upright. "He's lying to us!"

"About what?"

"About being off the Net, that's for sure. And his whole speech about trying to make the world a better place? As if!"

"He doesn't owe us anything, Billie. He's going out of his way to help us out." He rolled over and leaned on his elbow. "What's really going on?"

She took a deep breath. "This guy's not all he's cracked up to be, Des."

"What do you mean?"

"You know, he says—or tries to come off—as all selfless and noble and heroic. He goes around killing zombies, for crying out loud, all for the greater good and all that."

"And?"

"He's not doing it for us, for the greater good. He thinks he is, but he's not."

"Then what's he doing it for?"

"Himself." She adjusted herself against her pillow. "You can't tell me that he doesn't feel a sense of pride every time he knocks one of them off. You can't tell me that he truly and honestly enjoys it when someone thanks him. You can't tell me that he hates any kind of hero worship. He's as human as you or me, Des. You and I both know that we can sugarcoat our service to others under the guise of 'giving of ourselves' and being 'selfless' and 'humble,' when deep, deep down, even if it's just a small part of us, we enjoy the thought of 'doing the right thing.' It's one thing to feel that whole better-to-give-than-receive satisfaction, but do you know what that saying really means?"

Des looked lost. "No."

"It means that your joy comes out of seeing someone else benefit from your helping them *without* thinking about what it's doing for you, you know? Even if that 'doing for you' is being happy about doing the right thing."

Des clicked his tongue three times, as if counting the seconds until she was done. "Sooo . . . why's this such a big deal, again?"

Billie plopped her head down on the pillow then screwed her lips to the side. "I guess it's just . . . you know I'm not really an open person. I'm—"

"You've always been straightforward with me."

"That's because you need a good kick in the kahoohoos now and then." She smiled. "Anyway, it could just be because I'm tired and maybe I'm on a different wavelength as a result, but this whole 'Joe thing'—and I'm thankful for him saving us, don't get me wrong—but this whole 'Joe thing' bothers me because—"

"Because?"

"Can I finish?"

"Yeah. Sorry."

"It bothers me because . . . I've known guys like him before."

"You have? How many zombie killers do you know?"

She closed her eyes. Des could be really clueless sometimes. "Not that. The kind who put on a mask of 'being a good guy' or 'being the hero' when, really, there's something else beneath all that."

"Who?"

She rolled over onto her side, no longer facing him. A pinch grabbed at her heart. She had resolved not to bring Drake to mind anymore, but right now, sleepy and emotionally drained, she didn't care that Drake's face haunted her memory. "I knew this guy for about seven months prior to the rain." The bed rocked as he scooted closer, presumably so he could hear her better. "We dated, went all hot an' heavy and all that stuff."

"What was his name?"

"Drake. I don't know if I loved him or thought I did or what because even now, when I think about him, I really miss him but not in the way I think I should, you know?"

Des just listened.

She continued. "Anyway, he was always there for me. Listened to me go on and on when I was having problems with my folks. Listened to me complain about some of the garbage going on at school. He even helped me with my homework. Every time we hung out he always picked up the bill, held the door open for me. Drake talked about the volunteer work he did at Winnipeg Harvest, how he worked the prayer lines at Trinity Television, how he went to see his grandma in the nursing home twice a week. The list goes on but you get the idea. I remember thinking, 'Wow, what a guy. Wish I wasn't so selfish that I could donate a handful of hours a week to a soup kitchen or something.' That was another thing on his list, by the way. A soup kitchen. Did it once a month. Point is, after my initial awe of him waned, I started to notice little things, things that, in hindsight, should have been a lot clearer than what they were. But at the time, I only found them kind of odd and that was it. He used the word 'I' a lot when he talked. He mentioned his do-goodings a lot more often than a person really should. He was always quick to step in and offer advice about how *he* dealt with something, say, something similar to what I was going through with my parents."

"What happened? Did the rain . . ."

"I'm assuming so. I really don't know. After the rain fell I thought maybe he was still out there and I should connect with him, you know, the whole 'all-for-one' thing humanity had going there for a while. But the way things worked out and winding up here in the Haven, I didn't see him nor have I bumped into anyone online that I think might be him."

"He would use a handle, like you? The punk girl thing you use?"

"Probably. I don't know."

"So what happened? Between you guys, I mean?"

She closed her eyes, expecting a tear or two to leak out. Instead her heart just ached even more. "What happens to most girls, Des, when they think they've found Mr. Wonderful? He dumped me for someone else. Didn't know who."

"I'm sorry."

"Me, too. Had a real good thing going. Well, I thought so, anyway. What sucks about it was there was no lead-up to it. No time of things going downhill or things getting shaky. Just one day, 'Oh, hey, Billie. I don't think we should see each other anymore.' 'Really, Drake, why?' 'Well, I found someone else. Been seeing her for a while, actually. Sorry I didn't tell you.'"

"Sheesh, he really said that?"

"No, dummy. But something like it. I don't remember his exact words. All I know is he found someone he liked better and blew me off."

"I'm sorry."

"It's all right." A tear *had* rolled down her cheek. She only noticed it now. She wiped it away. "Let's get some sleep. Who knows what time Joe wakes up or how long he'll let us stay here."

"Maybe if he really is Mr. Hero, he'll let us stay for as long as we need."

"Right. And we don't live on a planet of the dead."

Joe stood outside the bedroom door, leaning up against the wall. He had heard everything.

11

IF JUST FOR A GOOD NIGHT'S SLEEP

The scraping had stopped a few minutes ago, but August wasn't convinced that whatever it was was gone. He lay there listening intently, ready to point his gun at a dead-yet-moving target.

Silence.

Dark.

Just him, the safe and his gun.

He dared not shine the flashlight lest whatever might be behind the door see it and be alerted to his presence.

He slowed his breathing and made an effort to lay absolutely still, any little thing he could do to shut off all sound.

The bank was silent just beyond the safe's door. The tiled floor was cold. A shiver ran through him.

It grew even quieter, so much so the thudding of his heart pounded in his ears. He took a deep breath and exhaled slowly to relax, but even now, after all he'd been through, relaxing was something that wouldn't come easy.

I could really use some help right now, he thought, eyes gazing upward. He only hoped the Big Guy upstairs was listening.

The seconds ticked by. He waited, and was sure several minutes had passed, but the more he thought about it, the more he realized that maybe only *one* minute had gone by, if that.

Maybe God *was* listening? If He wasn't, maybe something would have already tried to shove open the vault door, search out the dark, and gorge itself on aged flesh.

The scraping didn't return.

August closed his eyes and stared at the blackness, his ear nearest the door searching for sound.

Darkness prevailed, and August slipped away into sleep.

Drunngg, drunngg, drunngg. The low, monotonous tone jolted him awake. *Drunngg, drunngg, drunngg. Drunngg, drunngg, drunngg.*

He lay still, eyes searching the dark, the hollow sound of the incessant drumming charging his insides with an electric throbbing pulse he last felt the night he slaughtered his family.

August got to his feet, not bothering to check his watch to see what time it was. Odds were he had only slept a few minutes and to verify that with the clock would only make his heavy eyes worse.

Drunngg, drunngg, drunngg.

He stepped up to the safe's door, waited a moment to check for any sound other than the low drumming and, not hearing anything else, slowly pushed it open.

Hesitantly, he pressed the flashlight's button, just knowing he'd see some monstrous form ambling its way toward him. The beam lit up the dark. Nothing but the dead that were already there. He shone the beam around the room. The bank was empty.

Carefully, he made his way to the entrance doors and shone the beam up and down the hallway. Satisfied the coast was clear, he stepped out into the hallway and listened once more.

Drunngg, drunngg, drunngg.

It was coming from upstairs.

If I stay here, whatever it is might come down. If I go up, whatever it is might see me and I'll be dead. He hated moments of indecision. The right choice would be to get back inside the safe, close the door as much as possible without risking locking himself in, and just wait it out.

Drunngg, drunngg, drunngg.

He glanced toward the bank, his eyes settling in the direction of the vault door. Even with the dim light of the flashlight shining on it, it still looked forbiddingly dark, as if suddenly it had become a separate world of endless night and deadly despair.

"Oh, man . . ." he breathed.

His old legs refused to budge.

Drunngg, drunngg, drunngg.

The noise beckoned him.

He was already moving before he realized it and the next thing he knew, he was over by the inactive escalator that led up to the Richardson building's lobby.

He shone the light around, searching for moving shadows. The carpet-rimmed tiled hallway was empty.

Putting the flashlight in his mouth, he got his rifle ready, brought it high, and slowly ascended the escalator, his breathing short and shaky, puffing out on either side of the flashlight. Some drool leaked from a corner of his mouth. He ignored it, too terrified to stop and wipe it.

At the top of the escalator the lobby was charcoal black.

Until he was about three quarters up the escalator did it seem normal it would be so dark, but then he remembered that ever since the rain came, the sky remained washed over in dark gray with brown shadows whether it was day or night. There should be at least *some* light coming through the windows in the lobby, and there wasn't any.

Maybe someone boarded them up while they were stuck here and left it that way when they took off? If they took off. A shiver ran through him at the thought of more dead bodies, ones that died from no food or water, lying around upstairs.

Drunngg, drunngg, drunngg.

The droning beat was louder here on the escalator. Whatever it was that was making that noise, he was getting real close to it.

Drunngg, drunngg, drunngg.

Drunngg, drunngg, drunngg.

He took another few steps up.

Drunngg, drunngg, drunngg.

A few more.

Drunngg, drunngg, DRUNNGG.

Drunngg, drunngg, DRUNNGG.

Almost at the top. One more step and . . .

DRUNNGG, DRUNNGG, DRUNNGG.

It was near deafening and it was coming from his left.

He dropped the rifle. What he saw locked every muscle in his body.

Joe lay on his back on the couch, arms folded behind his head. April slept on his feet, keeping his toes warm.

Billie was right. He was trying to be something he wasn't. The problem was, he couldn't help himself. Ever since losing April, he couldn't seem to get things back on track. No matter how hard he tried to get it together despite the evil the rain brought upon the world, he just simply couldn't. He had tried everything—ignoring his feelings, suppressing them, distractions, denial, chanting things like, "She never existed. She never existed. It's all in your head. It's all in your head"—none of it worked. He even started a new manuscript, something he hoped that would be cathartic and get the frustration and pain and anger and anguish out of him.

Forget it. It was nothing but one step forward and twenty steps back.

For a brief time he thought about suicide, something he never thought he'd consider, but he couldn't bring himself to do it. He imagined it, sure. Even imagined stepping out into a horde of the undead and offering himself to them as some sort of pathetic sacrifice. He watched in his mind's eye as they tore off his limbs, reached their gray fingers into his abdomen and pulled out the long, noodle-like tubes of his intestines, the blood splattering on their faces, his skull being smashed into bits of bone and brain and blood and skin and—but he couldn't bring himself to do that either. He didn't know much about the afterlife and didn't know what the consequences for suicide were, if any. Yet he also thought that if he were to spend eternity in a place called hell that whatever torments it offered would be nothing compared to what he was feeling and the physical agony he'd undergo would be a pleasant relief from the emotional torment within.

But he didn't want to face the possibility of that either.

So he stayed alive, drifting through the motions of living day to day in a world gone mad, hoping that somehow an answer would present itself.

It wasn't until the night he decided to truly end it did everything change. He *would* give himself to the undead. He put on the only suit he ever owned, stepped outside and searched the night for any walking corpse that would have him.

Except he never found any. Not for hours.

He couldn't believe the only dead he found were those who'd already fallen prey to the zombies and were missing their heads.

Close to dawn, he came across an abandoned military vehicle, a soldier's headless and armless corpse half hanging out of the side door. Joe went over to it, studied the body. The nametag read DANE. On the seat beside Dane's body was an automatic. Military issue or not, he didn't know. He'd never been one for war or army movies. He rounded the vehicle, picked up the heavy weapon, then wrapped his fingers around the handle, index finger on the trigger, and aimed the barrel at the ground.

RAT-A-TAT-TAT!

The barrage of bullets jolted his insides as they plowed into the cement, sending up shards of concrete.

Tears running down his face, he was about to press the barrel under his chin when a deep wheezing to the side made him turn his head.

A man, short and stocky, with gray skin and white eyes was limping toward him, one of his feet missing.

Without thinking, Joe fired off an onslaught of bullets, blasting the man's chest and face to smithereens.

The body hit the street with a thud. Black blood ran from its body and head. Joe stood transfixed on the corpse, somehow mesmerized by it.

The pain that had been in his heart for so long went away.

Now, lying on his couch, Joe understood himself in a way that he hadn't in years. Billie was right.

He was living a lie.

He wasn't a killer. Just some guy looking for a way out of misery. Just some pathetic, self-centered miscreant who couldn't deal with the past.

No matter how he painted it, he wasn't acting like the person he'd been all his life.

For a second his heart opened and he thought about living again and letting things go.

Thought about being *Joseph* again.

Then his heart shut and fell into a rocky hole, a boulder rolling into place on top, sealing it within.

Joseph was dead.

Mouth hanging open, August slowly lowered himself and, not taking his eyes off the windows that bordered the lobby, picked up the rifle and removed the flashlight from his mouth.

"Wh-wha—Oh . . ."

The windows were smeared top to bottom in inky red blood, spread on thick in places, thinner in others.

No wonder the light was barely getting through. There were only a few places where it *could* get through.

Each step took several seconds, his feet feeling as if they were filled with sand.

DRUNNGG, DRUNNGG, DRUNNGG.

DRUNNGG, DRUNNGG, DRUNNGG.

The ultra-thick windows shook in their frames.

Mouth dry, his swallowing difficult, August moved for a spot on one of the windows where the blood wasn't so thick. He turned off the flashlight and brought up his rifle.

DRUNNGG, DRUNNGG, DRUNNGG.

At the window, he leaned up sideways against it then jumped back a step when more *DRUNNGG*s shook the glass.

Heart hammering, the pulse so rapid and thick it raced up the side of his neck and into his skull, he forced himself to get close to the window again.

DRUNNGG, DRUNNGG, DRUNNGG.

He kept his body a safe enough distance away, and slowly leaned his head closer to the glass so he could see outside.

The undead surrounded the front of the building and, he assumed, the remaining three sides as well.

Some stood at the glass, banging on it with their palms, smearing the blood from their latest kill over the windows. Others kept walking into it, bouncing off the glass then trying again. Some threw corpses at the building but not hard enough to break through. The bodies, slicked with blood, splat on the glass then slid down, only to be picked up again for another round, usually not before the undead took a fresh bite of flesh for themselves.

DRUNNGG, DRUNNGG, DRUNNGG.

August moved back several paces, rifle aimed at the windows. *They know I'm in here.* "Are their senses really that keen?" His voice was just a whisper. He doubted it. Yet they were displaying otherwise. "Or maybe they're so desperate for food and they haven't gotten in here yet?" *Then why are they tossing the dead at the glass?*

He stood there for a long time, losing himself to the endless din of meat slamming against glass, thinking maybe at some point they'd realize they couldn't get in and give up.

The undead never stopped.

12

PEACHES

Joe always had trouble sleeping. Back before the rain, he had spent his nights writing, both as his job and as a way to exercise the relentless bursts of imagination that stormed his mind. He'd sleep for a few hours shortly after the sun came out, then get on with his day, which usually consisted of watching *Seinfeld* and *Smallville* reruns. Now, sleep was still an issue. As much as the old Joseph was gone, his creativity was not and he'd lie there night after night, formulating stories and watching make-believe scenarios play out in the cinema of his mind. Sometimes April was in them, sometimes not. Usually when she did appear in the tales he spun, he'd either write her out or just simply ignore her. If he didn't, all the stories ended the same way: April, dead, covered in blood and gnawing on the neck of an old woman.

Tonight had been no different, but it wasn't his overactive mind keeping him awake. It was the two strangers he had allowed into his home. Even though they slept in a different room, after having been alone for so long, it still felt as if they were sleeping right next to him, staring at him. And no one who had ever lived was able to sleep knowing someone was looking at them.

He checked his watch. It was 8:49 A.M. He had maybe gotten a little over an hour's sleep.

Whatever. I'll catch up later, after they're gone. Then, whispering, "Whenever that is."

Not long after, the door to the bedroom at the end of the hallway opened and Billie came out. Joe immediately sat up on the couch, knowing that he'd feel too vulnerable if she walked in on him pretending to be asleep. Besides, he didn't trust her. He didn't know her.

As she made her way down the hallway, Joe couldn't help but study her, watch her move, take in her pink hair that was only in a slight tussle atop her head. Her skin was soft, her blue eyes tired yet still vibrant in their own way, her small arms and hands reminding him of April's from long ago.

"Morning," she said when she reached the living room.

Joe nodded. He wasn't much of a talker in the mornings. Had never been much of a talker at all, actually.

Billie came into the room and April barked up a storm.

"Quiet," Joe told the dog firmly. April piped down.

The springs in the old chair opposite to him squeaked when Billie sat on it, leaned forward, and rested her forearms on her knees.

There was silence for a time.

Joe, bored of staring at the carpet between his feet, asked, "Sleep okay? You didn't get much."

"Neither did you," she replied.

"Never been one for sleeping."

"Me neither."

The thought of confronting her crossed his mind, to let her know he had heard her earlier. *No, just keep it to yourself for now. Play that card later, when you need it.* He cringed at his cynicism. *When* he needed it. Had he become that cold? Didn't matter. He liked it.

"Where's Des?" he asked.

"Still sleeping. He'll probably be out for a while. All of us had a late night."

Joe nodded.

Silence again.

His heart picked up speed. It'd been a long time since he'd talked to someone, even longer since he had a one-on-one with a female.

"You don't . . ." she started.

He arched an eyebrow.

"You don't have anything to eat around here, do you?"

Joe shook his head. "Not much. Running low. Haven't been able to hunt around for things."

She leaned back and folded her hands and placed them on her lap.

He stood. "I'll see if I can find you something."

He went to the kitchen and opened the cupboards one at a time, checking to see what was left. There were a few packets of dried noodles, a couple cans of beans, one can of fruit, one of kernel corn.

He cleared his throat so he could raise his voice and call into the next room. "Do you want some—" Billie was already beside him. He hadn't seen her approach. He lowered his voice. "Do you want some peaches?" He showed her the can.

She took it and examined it. "Yeah, these would be fine."

"Spoons are over there," he said, nodding to the drawer behind them. "Can opener's in the one beside it."

"Thanks." She went to the first drawer, got a spoon, then went to the other and got the opener.

She placed the can on the countertop and affixed the opener to the lid. As she turned it and the lid peeled back, she asked, "You don't mind? It's your last one."

"That's fine. Besides, peaches are more breakfasty than beans."

She chuckled. "Suppose so. Something they never prepare you for, huh?"

"What's that?"

"The movies. The end-of-the-world ones. Everyone lives on canned foods but they never show how much it really sucks."

"Guess not."

"I just wish . . ."

"What?" He closed the cupboard door.

"I just wish we weren't here, you know? I mean, I'm thankful that I've gotten by, don't get me wrong. I'm probably making do a lot better than most, but after awhile, it's draining. I'm getting sick of the food, sick of watching my back, sick of living alone, sick of life, actually." She pulled the lid off and put it on the counter beside the can. She picked up the can and spoon, and leaned against the counter and picked at the peaches. Her eyes never left the fruit. "Sorry. Just tired and grumpy, is all."

He nodded, relating to everything she said. There was only so much fried beans a person could take before they'd just simply stop eating.

"So," she said, "what about you? Always lived here?"

He crossed his arms and leaned against the counter. "Nah. Used to live downtown. But after the rain hit, had to go where it was safe. Safe-*er*, anyway."

"That's what most folks did."

"They tried to. I remember the day not long after the rain . . . . So many folks wandered the streets, looking for a safe place to stay. The dead came out in droves. Just completely overtook them. There were so many."

She slurped down a peach and furrowed her brow. "Where were you?"

He shrugged. "I don't know. Probably putting a bullet between their eyes."

She rolled her eyes.

He didn't say anything. *Think what you want.*

"Not gonna eat?" she asked.

"Never been a breakfast person. Well, a 'regular' breakfast person. Mine was usually mid morning. Cereal. Haven't had that in ages."

"It's funny you say that because I had gone to Des's to get some milk. I'm a cereal freak, too."

Freak? "Well, I wouldn't call myself a freak."

"No? Living alone, hunting zombies like some kind of modern day Van Helsing?"

"I meant the cereal part."

"Oh."

It was a few moments before he spoke. "My . . . my mornings were quiet. Used to work all night."

"Doing what?"

"Writing comic books."

She smiled. "Des would love you." A pause. "You know what I mean."

"In the mornings I'd stand on my balcony with a cup of coffee and just think, reflect, absorb the peace that was on the air before folks would come out and the day would get underway." A pang stung his heart. "I really miss those days." What was happening to him? He didn't mean to say that last part.

Don't get carried away. Just 'cause she's a girl doesn't mean you're supposed to get all sensitive again. It had always been his weakness: girls, but not in the way women were usually a man's weakness. Back in the day, he used to be the one who'd listen to a girl as she went on and on about how much she hated being with her boyfriend or how she so badly wished she could find somebody like Joe, one who actually cared about her. His classic internal response was always: *Hey, I'm a guy like me. Choose me!* He was drawn to them and they to him. And that sort of thing finally peaked with April.

Now she was dead, and so was he, the guy who always fell into that sort of thing.

"Sounds nice," Billie said softly. She finished the can of peaches. "Where should I toss this?"

Just then April padded into the kitchen.

"Here," Joe said and took the can from her. He set it on the counter behind him.

Billie dumped her spoon in the sink. "This okay?"

"Yeah. I'll take care of it later."

April pawed at her dish in the corner. There was some water left, but no food. Joe dug out the small bag of dog food from beneath the sink, poured some in her dish, then put the bag back.

Crunching filled the air as April went to town.

"At least she's not complaining about the same old, same old," Billie said.

"Not her and I'm sure she wouldn't object to a lifetime of canned beans." Why was he making a joke?

Billie grinned and her smile, for a second, made him remember the joy he felt when he saw April smile for that first time, all squinty eyes and teeth.

The explosive pop of glass shattering came from outside.

Joe went to the window in the front room and peered out onto the street below.

It was covered in the undead.

13
GOTTA GO

Des Nottingham stood at the bottom of the gold-plated railing, his hand resting on the large golden ball on top of a thick golden post. He'd never been in such an ornate ballroom before—never been in a ballroom *at all*—but this was the perfect place to be with Billie.

She deserved it.

He'd been waiting at the bottom of the long flight of red-carpeted stairs for several minutes, his heart beating anxiously. He ran a hand over his slicked-back hair then checked his black tux one more time for any lint. A small speck of white fuzz dotted his lapel. He pinched it and pulled it off. The leather of his highly-polished black dress shoes squeaked when he adjusted his stance. *Just look casual. Don't want to make her think you're too excited.* But he *was* excited. Who wouldn't be? A huge fancy room all to themselves, a romantic melody being played by the small quartet of musicians off in the corner, the stars sparkling in through the enormous window spanning the entire width of the second level at the top of the stairs. Though he only thought it kind of strange, he dismissed the fact he couldn't see where the second level led to on either side, the hallway just melting away into shadow.

Then she appeared.

Des straightened and took his hand off the post. He folded his hands in front of his thighs.

Her eyes never left his as she passed along the baluster, her gentle smile conveying she was looking forward to this as much as he was. She paused a moment at the top of the stairs. A large smile beyond his control forced his cheeks into his eyes.

Her hair was pulled up and back and sat like a rose on her head, a lily pinned up against the left side. He had never known her to wear makeup before, but the way her lips shone with juicy redness and the way the green mascara accented her blue eyes, he couldn't help himself but fall for her harder.

Billie glided down the stairs like an angel floating down from above, her cream-colored dress seeming to glow even as the skirt swished from side to side. It didn't appear her bright white shoes even touched the steps as she descended. When she reached the bottom step, he held out his hand and led her down to the golden lacquered floor. She greeted him with a gentle smile and allowed him a moment to take in this little piece of heaven that had come down to him.

"They're playing our song," he said.

"I hoped they would," she replied.

Des took a step back, bowed; Billie curtsied.

Their bodies magnetically drew to each other's and a shudder of electricity shot through him the moment her body fell into his. Gently, he took up her hand and placed his other on her waist. Not once did she try to adjust herself or take control. She was all his.

"Ready?" he said softly.

"Always."

With a pull to his left, he spun them around and their feet left the floor, floating on the air that was this perfect moment between them.

A moment made of dreams.

Eyes locked on hers, he couldn't believe this was happening yet at the same time it all felt natural, as if they'd done this a thousand times before.

The chandelier above twinkled and the light of its bulbs glowed brighter each time they passed under it.

They moved to the music, Billie giggling every now and then, Des joining in her joy.

When the music slowed then ended, they floated down to the ballroom floor, both slightly out of breath.

"Thank you," she said.

"My pleasure."

"I've always wanted you, you know that?"

Hearing those words made his heart dance. "Maybe."

"I should have acted sooner."

He smiled. "Maybe." He lowered her hand then placed both of his around her waist. She drew her arms up and wrapped them around his neck.

"I've missed you," she said.

He wasn't really sure what she was referring to other than perhaps she was sorry for almost *missing out* on him.

"I'm not going anywhere," he said.

"Better not."

They smiled. He leaned in close and rubbed his nose up against hers. Then he kissed her.

Her lips were soft, the perfume wafting up from her neck permeating his senses and making him lose himself in her.

She pulled back . . . then shoved him. "You jerk, get up!"

"Wha—?"

"Come on, you stupid idiot! Let's go!"

His temperature dropped and he stood there wearing a green T-shirt and jeans.

Billie, his angel, was gone. So were the musicians.

"Hey, Freakboy, get a move on!"

"Bill—?" His voice was quiet, a lot quieter than he meant it. He spoke louder. "Bill?"

A sharp sting flared up on his cheek and the ballroom dissolved into the plain off-white of a ceiling.

"I told you not to call me that!" Billie shouted at him. She stood by the side of the bed. Her small hand reached down and she dug it underneath his arm and gripped the muscle hard, her tiny fingers digging into his flesh, jolting him out of his sleepy haze.

"The building's surrounded," she said. "We move or we die. Let's go!"

Des bounded out of bed.

Joe had the utility closet door open and was arming himself with two leather straps lined with what Billie thought were packets of bullets when she and Des emerged from the bedroom.

"Whoa . . ." Des said, stopping by Joe and eyeing the ammunition covering his torso.

Joe didn't say anything but instead closed the closet door and went to the kitchen. He was back in the hallway a moment later, his long leather trench coat draped over him like a cape, his large gun in his right hand.

Two quick thuds echoed from somewhere below.

April barked at the disturbance.

Joe opened one side of his coat and slid the gun in, presumably into a holster.

"Can they get in?" Billie asked.

"Probably," Joe said. "The doors and windows are boarded up throughout this place, but with enough force, they'll hammer their way through." He went for the front door and paused with his hand on the knob. He gave the kitchen and front room beyond a final glance before pressing his face up against the door and looking out the peep hole.

A low rumble rose in April's throat.

"She coming with us?" Des asked, putting on his shoes, Billie doing the same.

Joe eyed him coolly. Billie gave him a shot in the ribs.

"Sorry."

When Joe turned to face him, Billie felt her insides go hollow. This wasn't the same guy she had talked with earlier. Here was a man who had seen death up close—more than she and Des put together ever had—a guy with dead, emerald eyes.

"Ready?" Joe said.

Billie and Des nodded.

April barked when another two thuds boomed beneath them.

"Let's go," he said and opened the door.

They walked briskly to the stairwell at the other end of the hallway, Joe leading the way. He was already down the first set of steps, April at his heels, when Des asked, "Is there anyone else here? In this building?"

"There used to be," Joe said, taking the next flight. "He's dead."

"Come on, move," Billie said and gave Des a nudge forward.

They followed Joe and April down the stairs, the thudding at the front of the building growing louder with each step down. By the time they reached the bottom, the banging on the boarded-up front door made Billie blink with each *thwump!*

The back door, gray and made of steel, was chained shut. The small window beside it was boarded over with something resembling pressboard though she wasn't sure what it was really called.

Thwump, thwump, THOOM! Thwump, thwump, THOOM!

Some of the bangs sounded like they were coming from inside the suites at the far end of the first floor, but if they were from the undead banging on the boarded-up windows or if they had already broken through and were banging on the doors from inside the suites, she didn't know.

"Think we should take that board down and look outside?" Des asked, pointing to the one over the window.

Joe put his head to the door, listening before moving to the wood over the window.

"Think we should—" Des said again but was cut off when Joe raised his hand, hushing him.

Thwump, thwump, thwump! Thwump, thwump, thwump!

THOOM!

Joe unchained the door and held the long handle that stretched across it with both hands.

"April?" he said. The dog came up beside him. "Someone there?"

April stared at the door long and hard then shifted her gaze toward him.

"Anyone?"

She didn't give any sign someone was waiting for them on the other side.

Thwump, thwump, thwump, THWACK!

All turned their eyes toward the boards covering the front door on the other end of the hallway. A black crack zigzagged up its flank.

"Okay, that's good. Let's go!" Des said.

"Billie," Joe said, his voice dark, commanding. She couldn't help but step up to him. "Open the door when I say, then hold it open for Des, April and I to come out. Then when I say, come out and join us. Good?"

"Yeah."

"Okay," he said and pulled out his gun. He cocked the hammer. "Des, I want you right behind me, keeping an eye looking back this way." To April: "Wanna go outside?"

April's tail wagged side to side in a blur.

Joe kept his eyes fixed on the door. "Okay, Billie. Now."

She opened the door.

THWACK! THWACK! CRACCCKKK!

The droning growls and grunts of the dead filled the air as several of them tried to pile through the hole in the board at the front all at once. One got through but was shoved over by its comrades and fell face forward so its body was half-in-half-out of the building.

Their mouths were wide open and it sounded as if they were barking, like rabid dogs eager to take a chunk out of a person.

Joe quickly stepped out . . . into an empty parking lot. April padded a few feet past him. The look on Des's face told Billie the coast was clear.

"Billie?" Joe said.

She came out and closed the door behind her, muffling the shrieks and growls of the undead coming into the building. "They'll be here any second!"

The three ran the length of the parking lot to the back alley. April stopped where the lot met the road and the hairs on the back of her neck shot upward. Barking, she turned to face Joe then turned her head side to side, as if she didn't know what to do. Joe was beside her in no time. Billie tugged on the back of Des's shirt as he ran past her.

"Hey!" he said.

"Hang on a sec," she said.

Joe turned around. "We're in big trouble."

Zombies coated the alley, both up and down. Legions of them, filling the alley like blood in an artery.

Joe never expected so many to come to the Haven. He, like everyone, thought they either didn't know about it or were satisfied with what they had everywhere else in the city.

April barked and barked, but soon the groans from the undead horde forced her snapping to a whimper.

"It's okay, April," he said. But it wasn't okay, at least, not in the way he would like. Before, it was just himself he had to look after. April always stayed home and only went out to do her business. Now it was him, April and two others. Billie and Des had done all right holding their own against the creatures, but eventually they needed him to save them. April had never fought off a zombie before. He didn't know if they'd infect her or not, but judging by the news of altered rats, odds were April would become one of them if she got bit or tore out a chunk of them for herself. And for a dog, its teeth and mouth were its main defense.

"April, stay," he said. She remained by his feet.

"Joe?" Billie said from behind.

The house across the way was bordered by a fence. They'd run across the alley, hop the fence and, hopefully, make it clear to safety on the other side.

"One sec," he said and shot across the alley. He peeked over the fence. Four undead were drifting into the yard with a couple others following behind.

Still, six was better than the ninety or so coming toward them from either side.

"Over the fence, the both of you. April!" April bounded toward him. He picked her up and tossed her over the fence before hopping over himself.

Des and Billie were right behind. Billie shrieked.

"No!" Des shouted and disappeared back into the alley. "Get off her!"

Joe blasted the heads off two of the zombies in the yard, cocked the hammer again, then took the heads off two more. He reloaded a third time and took out the remaining two.

Wood creaked and groaned; the old fence wasn't holding from the weight of the bodies pressing against it from the other side.

"Billie!" Joe shouted. *I'm calling her first!* "Des!"

More groaning, at first a singular voice then a choir. The undead began pouring into the yard.

A girl shrieked and Joe turned to see Billie's body dumped over the top of the fence. April ran over to her and began sniffing. Joe ran over to her, too. Before he could check her over, the whole fence began leaning toward him. He grabbed her by the hand and dragged her away just as the fence fell inward.

The undead lined the street beyond.

Des was nowhere to be seen.

Coughing. Someone was cough—Billie!

She spat up a spurt of blood and forced herself into a sitting position. Joe fired off a couple of shots into the faces of two undead that had almost snuck up on them.

"You need to get up," Joe told her.

April growled.

Billie nodded and he helped her to her feet.

She was shaky on her legs once she stood, but Joe thought she'd manage just fine if she had another second or two to collect herself.

"Somethin' chipped a tooth," she said and spat a wad of blood down beside her feet.

BANG! BANG! Joe took out two more.

They were surrounded, the undead coming in from the front and back. Maybe the side yards would . . . . A zombie fell over the top of the fence from the yard to the right.

"That way," Joe said, pointing toward the fence on the left.

They ran toward it, reaching it just as the fence that separated the yard from the alley fell in and a horde of the dead came in like a tidal wave. The others that came from the front end of the house were upon them.

Joe socked one in the face with his gun and kicked another in the head. He reached down, picked up April, and when he straightened, an old and fat man of a zombie stood beside him, hunger in his eyes. He eyed the dog like a fatted calf and ripped April from his arms faster than Joe thought any zombie could ever move. As Joe reached for the dog, the porker of a man plowed his face into April's gut and jerked his head back, taking a huge hunk of fur-covered flesh with it.

"APRRIIIILLLL!" Joe screamed and sent two bullets into the fat man's face.

The dude dropped the dog then fell to his knees. Joe sent a steel-toed boot into the side of the man's head and kicked off the top portion of his already bullet-cracked skull, sending bone and brain matter flying into the air.

April's body lay there, her chest rising slowly up and down, her dark eyes staring forward, her gaze wet and lost.

"Joe!" Billie shouted.

Heart breaking, tears pricking the corners of his eyes, Joe cocked the hammer and fired off as many shots as he could until the X-09 clicked and clicked, and there was nothing left.

Growling, he turned to Billie. "What!"

But Billie was gone.

14

AND THE DEAD KEEP ON COMING

"Oh no," Joe breathed. He scanned the sea of dead heads and couldn't see Billie anywhere.

An undead lady with auburn hair took a swipe at him. The blow connected with his cheekbone and sent him staggering to the side. She thrust both arms toward his shoulders, presumably to take a chunk out of his neck, but Joe dropped, rolled, got to his feet and reloaded the X-09. With a quick cock of the hammer and pull of the trigger, he sent her on a permanent dirt nap.

The dead surrounded him, pawing at him as one, grubby fingers pulling at his arms, his legs, some poking him in the ribs.

He hook punched one, sent a knee into another, kicked the shins out from under another one and fired off a shot into the face of a toddler. Another went into the face of a man he recognized as a former survivor of the rain who had become one of them. He didn't know the guy's name but had seen him around. Cocking the hammer and shoving the creatures off himself, he spun in a circle and put a bullet into anything that moved.

Crrunnch!

Joe looked down and winced when he saw the heel of his boot standing on April's rear paw.

Sorry, girl, he thought, *I didn't mean . . .* He made a mad dash through the horde of the dead, plowing through them like a linebacker making a beeline for the goal.

He cleared through a swarm of them, turned, and fired off as many shots as he could in the little time he had before more came through the broken glass of the sliding door that led onto the patio at the rear of the house.

Far to his left was the gate that led out to the front of the house. From what he could see, none of the dead were on the other side. That could change any moment.

Pulling the trigger of the X-09, he removed the heads off two more dead men then, with another cock of the hammer, took the faces off one woman and one teenage boy.

Joe ran for the gate.

Gray fingers streaked with red scratches pawed at Billie from the far side of the patio deck. She was beneath it, having rolled under there the second the pack of zombies had gotten too thick for her to get to Joe's side.

She lay tightly where the deck met the house. The pebbled ground beneath her smelled of rot and soil that hadn't seen the sun and a real rain in a year.

Some of the undead on the other end of the deck and at the sides merely bent at the waist and tried to reach in, the deck stopping them at the elbows. Others were smart enough to get on their knees and try reaching her that way. Yet others had somehow realized that the only way to get to her was to get on the ground themselves and crawl army-style.

The sides were blocked as was the front, with nothing but stuccoed cement behind.

She was trapped.

A bald zombie with a dent on the left side of his head clawed toward her, its grimy fingers digging into the pebbles; the stones came loose, slowing his advance. It stared at her with droopy, bloodshot eyes, the snarl upon its face enough to produce tears in hers.

Billie screamed.

The groaning of the undead filled the air like an angry wind, the sound so thick that Joe was having a hard time thinking of a plan should more of the creatures be on the other side of the fence.

A high-pitched "something" floated toward his ears but was quickly silenced by the undead advancing toward him.

He fired off a couple more shots; two bodies dropped, acting as speed bumps for the rest following behind. It'd buy him a few extra moments and a few extra feet of distance.

Once at the fence, he peeked over the top and was relieved to see only a few zombies on either side, far enough down the street to not pose any immediate threat. He was about to hop over, but stopped himself.

Coward. You just lost three people. Two, but April . . . . April. A picture of his dead dog lying there, insides ripped open, blood pooling around her body, flashed before his mind's eye then quickly changed to *his* April, the girl with the black hair and gray eyes, lying dead at his feet after he accidentally struck her with a rolling pin.

A woman screamed.

He turned and a forty-something woman with gray-green skin, rotted in places, lunged for him. He took hold of her by the ears, her head thrashing side to side as she tried to take a bite out of his wrists. He snapped her head around. Her body dropped.

Another scream, this one clean and not garbled like those of the undead.

"Billie," he said.

Billie slammed her heel into the monster's face, breaking its nose and sending it a few inches back. Panting, heart beating so hard the pulse raced up and down her arms, she scrambled toward the side of the deck with the least amount of creatures, hoping against hope they wouldn't suddenly get down on the ground, too, and come after her.

BOOMBRACK! BOOMBRACK! BOOMBRACK!

The entire deck shook. Wood snapped above her.

She covered her face as splinters and dust rained down.

BOOMBRACK! BOOMBRACK!

Above, two burly undead men worked together and smashed a white propane tank into the deck over and over.

BOOMBRACK!

Punching through, they tossed the tank aside and reached in; four meaty hands that smelled of old fish reached for her. Two hands had her by the collar, one by her hair, another under her chin.

"Ah! Help! No!" she shrieked.

The arms yanked her up toward the hole just as the bald zombie on its belly grabbed her ankle. There was a quick tug of war then she was jerked clear of the floorboards, the sides of her body crying out when sharp points of wood ripped along her skin. She felt everything from her armpits to her waist go wet.

Two huge heads, one bearded, one not, sped toward hers.

This was it. She was going to die.

Billie closed her eyes.

BOOM! BOOM!

Gravity kicked on full swing and wind whistled past her ears as the two behemoths dragged her down. She landed atop their massive, spongy bodies, getting a full whiff of decayed flesh. She immediately threw up, sour peaches pinching her throat.

A pair of strong hands reached under her arms, pulled her up and planted her on her feet.

When she opened her eyes, she saw Joe staring back at her.

"Let's go," he said and shot two more zombies. He cocked the hammer and took down another two.

"Wh-where . . ." she said, her voice cracking.

There was no way off the deck. The undead moved toward them in an unstoppable horde. Getting through would be impossible.

A violent jerk to her arm pulled her through the patio door of the house and before it even registered she was standing in somebody's kitchen, four more creatures came walking in. Joe dropped two of them then was pushed to the side when one came at him while he was doing something with his gun.

Another was coming for her. The guy grabbed her hair, pulling on the already-sensitive strands so hard she thought he'd rip them clean off her skull. She scrambled for something to latch onto and the only thing her fingers found was a metal kitchen chair. Its legs rumbled as she pulled it across the linoleum. The undead man moved in, mouth wide, and she swung the chair to the side, slamming it into the zombie's leg. The man fell to his knees.

Suddenly filled with a renewed sense of rage, she picked up the chair and brought the bottom two legs across the dead man's face. Black-red welts immediately streaked the guy's skin.

112

More came in through the patio door. Billie hurled the chair at them then instinctively ducked when more shots rang out.

The next thing she knew, Joe was beside her, dragging her along as they darted out of the kitchen and into the living room beyond.

"Stay beside me!" he said.

She thought it was a weird thing to say but soon realized it was for her protection. If she was behind, the dead could get her. If she was in front, she'd be acting as a shield for him, which was something he obviously didn't want.

At the front door, Joe went to unlock it then paused—it was already unlocked.

"Hmph." He opened the door.

He shoved open the wind door beyond and the two took the steps in one jump.

The dead appeared in the doorway behind them.

More were coming up the driveway.

Joe led the way, zigzagging around the dead so quickly Billie felt as if she were waterskiing, the driver of the boat a maniac who was trying to dump her. Left, right, back, side, other side, forward, back, right, back, left, front—she could scarcely breathe.

BOOM! BOOM! Joe dropped another pair of creatures.

They didn't stop running till they reached the end of the street.

Joe stood with his hands on his hips, staring off down the street as Billie stood beside him, bent at the waist, wheezing.

"Breathe slow. Panting will only make it worse," he said.

"I got a stitch in my side sharper than a freakin' dagger and . . ." There was a pause.

When he looked at her, he saw she was staring at her palms, which were coated in blood.

Quickly, he grabbed her by the wrists, straightened her up, and examined her hands. "What happened?"

"You blind?" She raised her arms. The sides of her white T-shirt were wet with blood, right up the ribs like a couple of wild brushstrokes.

"Lift your shirt," he said.

"Forget it. I already took my shirt off once for you. I'm not going to do it again."

His gun came up as if his hand had a mind of its own. He pointed it at her head. "Do as I say or so help me you'll join them."

Her blue eyes went wide. When she spoke, her voice was soft, timid and afraid. "You're serious."

You bet I am. If they bit you, you're gonna die right here. "Now, Billie." He cocked the hammer. It could have been the adrenaline, could have been losing April and his failing to keep Des safe, but right now he'd love to see her die.

His head suddenly spun and the world seemed to pull itself a million miles away. He couldn't believe he just thought that. Couldn't believe he *wanted* that. He debated lowering the gun, but if he did, then he'd let the old Joseph rise again and that was something he'd never let happen.

Joseph had died with April.

Tears glazing over her eyes, Billie reached the hem of her T-shirt with shaky hands and slowly pulled it up.

Long, red lines ran up the sides of her waist and ribs, stopping on either side of her chest.

Billie looked away as he leaned in close to examine her. No teeth marks. Nothing that hinted of gummy white saliva.

He kept the gun pointed at her. "Lower your shirt then raise your arms."

She obeyed, frowning. He checked the shirt and it was torn on either side in a clean line, not chewed up or ripped in places the way nails or teeth would tear it.

After taking a deep breath and exhaling slowly, he lowered the gun.

Billie slapped him hard across the cheek, stormed off past him and gave him the finger.

"I'm sorry," he whispered. He just didn't know to whom he was apologizing: to her or to April, for what he had become.

15
EMPTY BUILDING

The world had disappeared last night. August had mustered up enough courage to head back downstairs and sleep in the vault, both hands on the rifle, the rifle on his chest. The droning bangs of the dead slamming their palms on the thick glass upstairs kept him awake at first, but soon its monotonous noise became a background beat to his thoughts and, eventually, he drifted off to sleep. Just before he closed his eyes that final time, August expected to wake every half hour or so, his racing heart forbidding him any sleep. Instead, darkness prevailed and a black sleep took him, shutting out the noise from above, the apprehension of something lurking in the shadows beyond the safe's door, the discomfort of the rifle weighing on his chest. He didn't dream; he closed his eyes one moment and opened them a few minutes later only to discover, as per his watch, a little over nine hours had gone by. The room was as dark when he awoke as it was before he fell asleep.

He stood slowly, a sharp ache filling his muscles. It'd been a long time since he'd slept on the floor, never mind without a pillow. It took several minutes for the blood to flow into the muscles to make them usable again. Still, his elbow and knee joints felt as if they were made of wood and that something would break if he tried bending them.

Head far more clear, he still couldn't get over how long he had slept. You'd think you'd be *very* awake with a throng of the dead beating at your door all night long, the thought of never seeing morning prevailing in your mind.

The drive into town then the long walk all the way from the TransCanada must have gotten to him more than he realized.

His stomach growled; the inside of his mouth was sticky.

August stood inside the vault door, listening.

The banging had stopped.

Checking the rifle, he decided his first order of business was to hit the water fountain near the escalator. After that, he'd head upstairs and see if the windows were still intact. He'd worry about breakfast—lunch—later.

His old bones creaked and ached as he opened the heavy vault door and, after poking his head out, he ventured into the bank beyond.

The flashlight was dead so he tucked it into his back pocket. Hopefully he'd find some batteries later.

The hallway beyond the bank was quiet. No dragging footsteps, no groans. No anything. The only sound was his breathing and his own footfalls.

After getting a cool drink at the water fountain—and thanking God a hundred times it was still working—he cautiously approached the escalator, ready for a walking corpse to appear at its top and charge toward him.

One step. Two. Two more. Slowly, now.

No banging.

No groaning.

No breathing save his.

At the top of the escalator, August surveyed the lobby. The blood-splattered windows were still intact.

Carefully, he turned on his heels and moved toward the back doors, something he didn't look into the night before, his brain too tired to even have thought of it. These windowed-doors were boarded up.

"Wonder why they didn't do up the glass at the front?" he said. But he already knew the answer. Either those who were here before him were overtaken by the dead that had come in through the Square, or they had fled because some form of rescue came.

August went back toward the escalator down a hallway with a row of elevators on either side.

This joint's got over thirty floors. To check every one would take all day never mind checking the Square. "Are you planning to stay here?" *Maybe. Could have everything I need till I figure out why I was supposed to come here. If I was supposed to come here.* He still wasn't one hundred percent sure that whole "exodus" thing at his cabin was Divine or not. The further that special event receded into the past, the more doubt was able to creep in. *What would You have me do?*

No reply, just a sense that he should stay put for now. Whether that was from him or Upstairs, he didn't know.

"Got a big day ahead of me," he said, and pressed the UP arrow on the elevator.

All the floors were clear, just empty offices, some with papers strewn everywhere and phones off the hooks (which didn't work when he checked).

By the time August finished scouting the top level, he was exhausted. But there was still one more place to check: the stairwell next to the elevators.

This is probably useless, he had thought more than once. *I go inside one elevator, but there are nine others that could very well be holding the dead. Or those monsters could be riding them up and down and I'd never know. Wait, that's not true. I never heard the elevators going when I wasn't in them. Maybe I am in the clear, here?* "But that stairwell . . ."

He opened the big door a crack, the barrel of the rifle poking through. After waiting a moment, he quickly shoved it open all the way in case a zombie was on the other side. If someone was there, the door would plow into them and buy him a moment to aim his shot. The door slammed open hard, banging into the wall. A bit of drywall crumbled to the floor.

August approached the railing, looked down, couldn't see anything except for the sides of some stairs, then glanced up at the steps going two flights to the roof.

"Could use a little fresh air," he said and, using the railing, helped himself up the steps, already dreading the trip all the way back down.

"Wait." He stopped two steps up.

He quickly went to the elevators, called them up to his floor and when the doors opened he pressed the emergency stop buttons in each. Smiling, he thought, *There. The only problem is I may need them later. Well, maybe I'll send one down and lock it on the second floor or something.*

Back inside the stairwell, he carefully made his way up even though he could already see these two flights leading up to the roof were clear. At the top, he thought he heard a tap coming from the other side of the roof door. Waiting, listening, wondering if it was his imagination or not, August brought up the rifle and got ready to fire.

No other sound came.

Was probably me.

He put his hand on the steel horizontal door handle and pushed. The handle went down and in, but the door didn't open. He tried again then a third time. Same thing.

"Oh," he said at the silver and black key-coded lock box beside the door.

He examined the tiny silver buttons on its face. They were numbered 0-9.

"It could be anything." *Four- or five-digit combos. Maybe more.* He punched in a couple just for the hey of it. You never knew. He glanced up. "Wanna gimme a hand?" He closed his eyes and the numbers 2, 5, 3, 7 and 9 appeared one at a time in his mind's eye. He tried them. No go. Those numbers were just him.

"Thanks anyway," he breathed. Staring at the lock box, he added, "You send me out here then hightail it when I need a hand." With a grin, "Hmph. Sounds familiar. Moses had a time of it, too. Not that I'm him or anything." After a chuckle, "Don't got a beard down to my feet."

He thought for a moment. "I could blow the lock." *Yeah, but if something's on the other side, how're you gonna lock it again?* "Okay, fine. I'll leave it for now. Bring something up to reseal it later."

August went down the stairs.

By the time August reached the bottom of the stairwell and stood before the door that opened up into the Square, he could barely stand.

Going down is worse than going up. And he had to leave the elevators on the higher floors. *If* an undead or two were in the other elevators, they were now trapped between the floors. Thank goodness for elevator control on the security level.

August leaned forward slightly and caught his breath. His rifle suddenly doubled in weight. He set it down and did a few stretches before picking it up again. It was a little lighter.

His stomach growled and the inside of his skull felt hollow. He'd have to get some food soon.

"Now You're making me fast, too, huh?" he said. A sharp ache pierced his heart. Before, he wouldn't dare take a shot at God; he knew far better than to aim an arrow at the Throne. This was the one thing that, throughout his entire Christian life, he still had a hard time dealing with: trusting Someone he didn't see. He wasn't stupid. A Christian's life was one where your faith would be constantly tested. He knew the prize. But he also knew the cost: "Take up your cross and follow Me," Jesus had said nearly two thousand years ago. He just wished Jesus would have emphasized how *heavy* that cross would be sometimes.

Checking his rifle over, ensuring a bullet was in the chamber, he opened the door.

The wide hallway beyond was empty; stepping out into it was like planting yourself into the middle of a field with nothing for miles. The walls and doors lining the hallway held no meaning.

"Let's go," he said, "one at a time."

And August began his hunt for anything or anyone alive.

Or dead.

16
ALONG THE RIVER

More than once Billie stopped and put a hand to her eyes, trying to conceal the tears.

Des was gone.

"Yo, Billie!" Joe shouted from several paces ahead.

"In a minute," she said quietly.

Brown and dry leaves crunched beneath his feet as he neared her. He pulled her hand away from her face. "Look, I know it's hard, but we can't sit and mope right now. You don't want to be caught out here with the dead walking around."

"Think I don't know that?" she snapped, sniffled, and stormed past him. A moment later: "Why are we taking this route, again?"

"The river's our best bet. So far as we know, they don't like water. The nearest zombie is probably two hundred meters that way." He nodded to their left, beyond the trees and bush, to what was left of Henderson Highway and the houses and neighborhood alongside it.

"Yeah, but we got no boat. If one of those things comes for us, there's nowhere to go. Can't just jump in the river, man. The undertow'll suck us down to the bottom."

She glanced at the river rushing by at a good clip beside them.

"At least we haven't seen any of them. That's a good thing, ain't it?"

"I suppose."

They walked in silence, stepping over and around trees that had fallen over or been bent at obscure angles thanks to the river's seasonal rise and fall from melting snow. The funk of stale water hung on the air and more than once Billie longed to go up to street level and get a lungful of fresh air. Not that that was any better, though. Having the dead walking around for a year had polluted the air so badly that it was a wonder she and the other survivors hadn't come down with any diseases. It still had yet to be discovered why they hadn't been affected the day the rain came and why, a year later, the disease—if it was a disease—still hadn't harmed them.

The duo walked on. It was slow going, the uneven debris-covered ground making the trek toward downtown difficult. When she asked Joe multiple times why they had to go into the city, his best answer out of all he offered was, "You saw them before we hit the river. They're coming down toward the Haven. Can only presume they're emptying downtown. The safe zone's being switched. Besides, we can get off the ground when we get there, clear a floor or two in either the Richardson or CanWest Global. Maybe even one of the hotels."

Joe seemed to be lost in thought because he didn't say anything for a long time. Not that he really said much at all, but despite living alone and being so secluded for so long, Billie still wasn't used to silence. At least when Des was alive, she had him to talk to once in awhile.

Oh, how she missed him. Despite how annoying he could be, he was the most down-to-earth person she'd ever met, a guy who didn't care what people thought of him. He wasn't a looker, by any means, but on the inside? Yeah, she could really go for that.

She could really go for that right now.

"You never told me where you got your gun?" she asked Joe just as they ducked under a low-hanging tree branch.

"The X-09. Didn't 'get it' anywhere. I built it."

"X-09? Mean anything?"

He pursed his lips. "'X' for 'extreme.' Wrong spelling, I know. The nine . . ."

It appeared he was going to say more, but he didn't.

She didn't want to pry any further so asked, "Where'd you learn to do that?"

Joe paused before answering. "The Net, before I got rid of my connection."

"You still never said why you did that."

"And I'm not going to."

"Oookay. So, what, you looked up a gun-building site and got lucky?"

He glanced back at her and offered a cool stare. "No." Then, "Well, kinda. You'd be surprised what you'd find on the Web. Just about anything."

"Oh, believe me, I know. Trust me. I spent most of my life on there. It's how I survived, actually. You know, getting plugged into other people and all that. You hungry?"

"Not really. Used to going without food."

"Yeah?"

"Yeah."

Something caught her foot and the ground rushed up to meet her. Palms out, she stopped her fall, but something small and pointy jammed into her palm.

"Billie?" Joe said, coming over. He knelt down beside her.

"Aaarrghhh," she growled and shoved away from the ground, accidentally pushing whatever was in her hand in further. She sat back on her knees.

"You okay?" he asked.

Her palm was smeared with blood. At its center was a shard of broken beer bottle.

"Of course," she said and not in answer to his question. Why would she expect this little jaunt downtown to go smoothly? Carefully, she pulled out the shard. Blood bubbled to the surface of the wound, leaked out, and dripped onto the ground.

"Oh man, that stings." She looked around for something to wipe her hand on. There wasn't anything out here and the river was too filthy to rinse it in. And as far as she knew, it could be loaded with dead bodies, their germs circulating through the water like salt.

"Here." Joe tore off a strip of fabric from the bottom of his shirt. He offered it to her.

"Thanks," she said and, taking a deep breath and holding it, wrapped the fabric around her hand.

She was able to wrap it around her hand three times before Joe reached over and helped her tie it.

"The second we find clean water, we'll wash it up, okay?" he said.

"Yeah . . ." she breathed and stood, cradling her hand.

They walked even slower, the vibration from each thump of her footfalls aggravating the wound.

She nearly bumped into Joe when he stopped suddenly in front of her, his hand up. "Wait," he said.

"What?"

"Something's out there."

17
EMPTY SQUARE

The bulk of Winnipeg Square had been covered and by the time August sat down on the steps leading up to the catwalk, which were near the food court, he was ready to pass out from fatigue.

The shops were empty, the only dead a few dismembered limbs. Where the rest of the people had gone, he could only guess into the creatures' stomachs.

With each pass into the shops, the side rooms, the bathrooms and beneath stairwells, he kept a sharp ear out for whatever it was that had been making noise last night.

But Winnipeg Square had proved empty.

He had made sure the doors leading outside were secure every time he encountered some and all were boarded up save for a pair that opened up onto Fort Street via the Royal Bank building. Those he secured by simply locking the door and stacking desks and paper-filled boxes from the bank offices in front of them.

The next order of business would be to block the stairway where he now sat with whatever he could find and maybe line the top of the barricade with pots and pans from the food court so that, should something try and get through, the kitchenware'd tumble to the floor and raise a sound he could hear all the way down by the vault door.

He just needed to catch his breath first.

Boy, was he starving. He had put off scouring the food court for any canned goods on purpose until he verified he was alone down here. Now that he was fairly sure there was nobody around but him, his heart leapt in delight at the prospect of finally getting some grub. Maybe, just maybe, there'd be power in one of the kitchens and some coffee and he could boil himself a cup.

August got to work. It took awhile, but eventually a makeshift barricade was set up along the bottom of the non-running escalator and the flight of stairs that ran up alongside it. He dragged heavy tables from the restaurant next to the barricade and piled chairs on top of it. Then, as planned, put the pots and pans in place, some acting as a base, others half-on-half-off, so that any jostling of the chairs and tables would force them to fall.

"Not bad," he said, hands on his hips as he surveyed his work. "Ain't Fort Knox but it ain't out in the open anymore either."

Stomach growling, he went to the food court and worked his way through the various eateries, seeing what he could find. All the perishable stuff was rotten, stinking and covered with so much thick green fuzz that he couldn't even look at it.

"How's that? Can look the dead in the eye but rotten tomatoes make you gag." *What a time to live.*

Some of the places had freezers, many of which still had a few slabs of meat, stuff which had been left behind by previous ransackers for some unexplained reason. Didn't matter though. There was no power circulating down here and the meat was all grayed-out and, even though still wrapped, stunk so incredibly bad it made the zombies smell like roses.

One of the last eateries had a series of cupboards in the back, lining the grills. A few cans of mushrooms, one of tomato paste, three tuna and four canned wieners remained.

"Mmmm, lovely," August said. "So what's it gonna be? Fungus grown in crap? Ketchup paste, dead fish or meat scraps?"

He opted for the meat scraps and dined alone in the dark at a corner table, putting away two cans of wieners. Even though he was still hungry, he put the other cans in his pockets for later, already choosing a one-meal-a-day plan unless other food options presented themselves.

There was still no telling how long he'd be here.

As he slowly chewed his food, one question hung over him: what was on the roof?

10

GOOD DOGGIES

If this were a normal day, it would already be getting dark. But these weren't normal days anymore.

The city skyline loomed not too far away.

Joe waited a moment for Billie to catch up from behind.

"Doesn't seem this long a hike by car," she said.

She came up beside him.

"We're almost there. Big thing is we gotta get over the overpass. Not sure if you've ever walked those humps, but they take awhile."

"Know where we are?"

"Sort of. Should be a street or two's worth to go. Can't really tell from down here. We have two choices: we either follow the river and head up by the bridge or we go up now and take a chance with the streets."

"Well, you said the river was safer so let's do that."

"Agreed."

They walked on for about ten more minutes. Then Joe's heart sank in his chest.

"Oh, that's nice," Billie said.

A wall of cars and trucks that had gone off the roads and barreled through the trees and bushes stood before them. There had to be at least thirty or forty cars, all stacked and smooshed together like a Hot Wheels race gone bad.

She stood with one hand on her hip, the other gesturing toward the heap of smashed windows, tires and twisted metal. "How's that even possible?"

"Panic. They probably freaked out the day of the rain and tried to outrun the dead."

"Yeah, but they would have had to blast through how many trees and yards to get down here?"

"Don't underestimate folks under pressure. I've seen too much to discount it. These trees aren't densely packed and some are small. They probably bulldozed a whole bunch before hitting one or two their car couldn't handle. Look, doesn't matter. We got a problem. One side is blocked by the river, the other might be open. If not, we go uphill. No choice."

"Fine," she said and huffed.

What's her problem?

Billie stepped around him and got closer to the cars. "Can't climb them?" She pushed against a Volkswagen sitting partly atop a Caravan (how that happened, Joe hadn't a clue). It rocked. Metal groaned. For a second Joe thought it might lose whatever slight hold it had on the van and come crashing down.

"Doesn't look like it," he said.

She threw her hands up in the air. "Okay, then. We go around."

Joe stared after her as she made her way along the wall of cars, stepping over tree stumps and large, fallen branches. He realized her problem. It was so simple: she was scared.

He pulled out the X-09. Billie must have heard him draw it from its holster inside his coat because she looked back at him.

"Just in case," he said, with a smile.

She didn't return it.

Now right behind her, Joe offered to take the lead.

"No, I'll be fine," she said as she walked with hands partly spread out to either side to maintain her balance on the uneven terrain.

A second later she slipped and fell backward into Joe's arms. He held her from behind, arms tightly around her waist. The way her small body fit into his reminded him of April.

Something didn't feel right.

Billie struggled to get back onto her feet. "Okay, you can let go now."

Joe held on. "Wait a second."

She froze. "What?"

The air was still. Leaves crunched somewhere not too far away.

Billie squirmed. "Would you let go?"

"Quiet."

"Don't you dare talk to me like that. I'm not some damsel in distress that needs your help. I'm—"

That was it. He pulled her up, set her on her feet and gave her a shove forward. "Happy now?"

Her hot glare burned right through him. No matter. She was a pain anyway.

Crnch. Crnch. Very faint, but near enough that Joe knew they had to get moving.

"Walk. Now," he said and motioned with the gun for her to get going.

She just stood there. "Jerk."

Joe shook his head and walked past her. "Something's coming."

Billie got in line.

Their own footfalls on the twigs, branches and leaves masked the crunching sounds from earlier. Joe scanned the trees for any sign of movement. Nothing but browny-gray skeletons, dead bushes and a few dry brown leaves swirling on the air from a breeze that had just picked up.

The cars hadn't smashed into each other in a perfect line, but instead weaved their way around the trees like a snake. Already the river was pretty far behind. The city was over to the right. They had to get over that way lest they take a detour that could get them ki—

Fierce growling followed by a low guttural bark shot through the air, sending a jolt through every bone in his body.

A big black wolf of a dog bounded out from behind a tree, its heavily-haired body slicked with greasy blood, its eyes dead and white, its fangs caked with rotten flesh.

Billie shrieked as five more appeared from behind the bushes, all six racing toward them.

"Billie!" he shouted.

She was already moving, dodging to the left, one of the undead dogs missing her, skidding to a halt, then twisting its body to come at her again. She was in mid sprint when Joe blasted a hole through the back of the dog's head.

It didn't even yelp.

The other five bowled over them like a tornado to a house; Joe hit the ground hard and fast, one of the beasts on top of him, its foul breath cool and smelling of rotten hamburger.

It's breathing? No sooner did the thought enter his mind than he put the barrel of the gun under the dog's snapping jaws and pulled the trigger. A spray of black blood shot up through the back of the dog's head then showered down, putrid and sticky.

Beside him, Billie had her forearm pressed against another dog's throat. It was all she could do keep the animal's snapping mouth away from her.

Joe cocked the hammer, two more shots falling into the chamber. Before he could aim, one of the beasts grabbed him by the foot, its yellow, meat-caked teeth digging into the leather and steel of his boot.

Thank goodness it didn't get me. It would have bit my head clean off.

The dog dragged him through the leaves to one of its kin that was not far off, who bowed with hindquarters straight, front legs pressed to the ground, snapping. Its bark was loud, carrying the tone of more than one voice.

It missed my toes but its teeth are lodged in my boot. It bit through steel?

Joe aimed and took the dog out. It flopped over, forcing his ankle to the side, a numbing jolt rushing up his shin.

Screaming, Billie scrambled against the ground, trying to get away. She had somehow managed to flip over onto her stomach—a stupid mistake—and now the beast was standing on her back, about to take a bite out of the back of her head.

"AAAAHHHH!" The scream came out of nowhere.

It wasn't hers.

Joe only caught it in his peripheral, the blur of an iron pipe, someone wielding it. Who it was, he couldn't see.

He shot the dog at his feet. It dropped, its face still stuck on his boot. Immediately the dog on Billie's back straightened then pounced on him, its lower teeth just missing his scalp and grazing his head. Thick gobs of funky saliva slapped onto his shaved head like a bad bath. He twisted his arms underneath it and used both forearms to push the dog off to the side. The moment the dog hit the leaves, he sat up and put a bullet in the dog's ear, straight through to its brain.

The dog stopped moving.

One left.

He tried to stand but the dog still stuck onto his boot made it impossible for him to get the heel of his left boot under him. He fell over the moment he put any weight on it.

The remaining dog growled, tore for him and its paws left the ground. Its dark, blood-soaked body sailed through the air.

"Watch out!" Billie shrieked.

Just before it landed on top of him, a blur of silver-gray struck the dog in the chest, followed by a dull *clunk*. The dog flew backward through the air like a foul ball.

Another *clunk*, and the iron pipe smashed into the dog's head.

The young man holding the pipe turned to look at him.

It was Des.

19
ON THE WAY UP

Unable to get around the cars, the three made their way uphill away from the river, the first order of business to get out of there before having a small reunion.

Billie and Des walked ahead, Joe trailing behind. They were talking about what just happened, but too softly for him to get in on the conversation. Not that he wanted to. The gloating look Des gave him as he used the iron pipe like a crowbar to pry the dog's teeth out of his boot was enough. It clearly read: how's that for a heroic entrance? See? I can be cool, too.

Or maybe he was reading too much into it. Whatever the case, Des was now the hero and Billie looked at the guy with star-filled eyes because he had saved her life.

Despite not wanting the thought to be there, it was. *I saved her life, too, and she didn't look at me that way.* As if he wanted her to. There was only one girl for him, and she was dead.

But there was a piece of April in Billie, that same carefree spirit, the kind that seemed rooted in disguised insecurity, the kind that took pleasure in the small things, the important things.

Des walked boldly, tapping the iron pipe on an open palm, as if telling any onlooking zombies to "come get some."

That guy's gonna get slaughtered if he's not careful. Joe grimaced. *I can't believe Billie is falling for it. She's smarter than that! Um, right? Relax. You don't know her. You shouldn't even care.*

But he did.

"Where were you?" Billie said loud enough so Joe actually felt part of the conversation.

"I called and called," Des said. "Didn't you guys hear me? I wasn't *that* far behind."

Joe picked up his pace so he was right behind them.

"We didn't hear anything," Billie said.

"You guys deaf?" Des asked.

"No," Joe said. "We didn't hear you because there was nothing to hear."

"I must have yelled at the top of my lungs."

"Don't forget we were also walking along a moving river, wind was blowing through the trees. Lots of ambient noise."

Des was about to reply but seemed to be considering that last part.

"Means background noise," Billie said quietly.

"I knew that. Still think you should have paid more attention."

They reached the top of the hill. A wall of trees concealed whatever was beyond, likewise what was off to either side. The three stopped; Billie and Des caught their breath. Joe was just fine, his body used to being active.

"Did you see anything in the woods?" Joe asked.

"No. Did you?" Des replied.

"Just the dogs."

"Where'd you get that?" Billie asked, gesturing toward the pipe.

"Side of the road. Looks like someone warmed it up for me. See?" He held up the pipe and showed the dried blood on its end peeking out from the fresh blood glistening on it.

"You should really clean that off," Billie said.

"Why? Kind of a badge of honor, don't you think?" he shot back.

"Do as she says. The undead can smell blood. It's what attracts them to us." *Has to be, anyway.*

"Even if that was so, this is *undead* blood on this thing, remember? Should be fine."

"Do it anyway. Don't take any chances."

"Why, Joe? You scared?"

"Whoa," Billie said, putting her palms up and taking a few steps back.

"You wanna run that by me again?" Joe said, taking a step toward him.

"Just saying that you take things a little too seriously, all grim and dark like some kind of Batman."

"Do you forget how long I've been doing this? Is it not reasonable to assume I know what I'm talking about?"

"If you did, you wouldn't have needed me to save you."

"Des," Billie said firmly.

That's it. Time to set this guy straight. "You killed some dogs. Good. Billie and I are alive. Good. But don't start going around thinking you can take on the whole world, one filled with creatures that are stronger than you, just because you killed a few pups."

Des's green eyes bore into him. "I don't know why you're being such a jerk to me."

"Yeah, Joe," Billie said. "He saved your life. And mine."

"Don't start, Billie. His head's full of hot air right now. It's gotta stop now or we'll all wind up dead."

"So you're gonna blame it on me if something happens to us?" Des asked.

"No," Joe said. "But you gotta come down off your throne and get back to the real world. I'm only going to ask you to do this once."

"Or what? Think you can take me?" Des raised the pipe.

On instinct, Joe balled up his fist and sent it into Des's nose.

"Gargh!" Des muttered, dropping the pipe and covering his face with his hands. Dark red liquid leaked out from between his fingers.

Billie was at his side in no time, one arm around his back, the other catching the blood dripping off his hands.

"Screw you!" she shouted.

Joe ground his teeth. "Fine." He stormed off up to the trees.

Behind him, Billie whispered words of comfort to Des. In front of him, he didn't like what he saw through the trees.

A cemetery.

20
AT THE TOP OF THE STAIRS

August sat on the top step with his back against the makeshift barricade next to the door at the flight of stairs leading up to the roof of the Richardson building. It should hold. Before he had opened the rooftop door, he had taken a desk from one of the offices on the top floor, emptied its contents, dragged it up to the top of the stairs then went about filling it with as much paper as possible. He did the same with a couple filing cabinets before bringing up a couple of chairs to lock things in place once he was done.

Now, the door jerked in its hinges as the undead outside banged against it.

The entire rooftop was covered with them. Who knew how long they'd been up there, but the way they charged at him the moment he peeked his head out the door, he was lucky to move fast enough to close it and shove the desk in front of the door before they could break through. The filing cabinets were the hardest to move, even just the one foot from where he placed them to right up against the desk. The chairs were easy. But those zombies . . . . Their eyes, buried in deep and decayed sockets, were white and bloodshot; bloody drool oozed from the corners of their mouths.

They were hungry.

Yet that wasn't what bothered August the most about what he saw.

There was something else.

21
THE CEMETERY

"Jerk," Des said right after Joe disappeared between the trees in front of them.

"Yeah, you said it," Billie said.

Quietly: "Did I do anything wrong?"

"Nuh-uh."

"Did I say anything?"

"Nope."

Man, did his nose hurt. Des slowly pulled his hands away. Blood was pooled in his palms. He shook them out then checked his nose. The bleeding seemed to have stopped. He pinched the bridge and tilted his head back, just in case.

"You gonna be okay?" Billie asked.

"I'll live." His voice was all nasally.

A soft ringing bounced from one side of his brain to the other, back and forth. Joe had popped him hard but, obviously, not hard enough to do some serious damage. Whether that was intentional or not, he didn't know. The guy had no right to get all upset. *He* had been the one who saved him.

Zombie wrangler? Not today. More like zombie smacker or something. It still felt good, though, to line drive those deranged dogs.

"Think we should go after him?" Billie said.

It'd be better if we didn't. But we can't leave him alone despite what just happened. Grrrgh! I hate being all moral inside! "Might as well. Dude'll get himself killed if we don't follow."

"I don't know. He's got a gun."

"Yeah? Well" —he bent down and picked up the iron pipe— "we got a bat." Didn't sound as clever as it had in his head. He pulled his fingers away from his nose and checked for blood. It seemed to have stopped for good. He wiped his nose with his shirt then gestured to Billie for them to get going.

They went up to the trees, parting the jagged branches with their hands, and pushed through. Just on the other side was a chain-linked fence. And just beyond that was a graveyard.

Cemeteries always got the best of Des. When he thought about them, he only envisioned a few tombstones, a couple shrubs and some flowers. Every time he saw one up close—and he'd only been to two real funerals in his life—he was always reminded how serious a business death was. Everybody wound up in a place like this at some point or another. Everybody had their place amongst a sea of graves, just another number in the long, long list of life gone bad.

He always pictured his grave as out in the open, the tombstone a lone marker on a hill, a few daisies in small, pottered vases on either side of the stone. But, he realized, looking out on what had to be over a thousand graves, his would more than likely be in a place like this, his tombstone just one among many, passed by without second thought by everybody not there to visit him. And even if humanity did pull through this season of death, none of his family was left or his friends. And so far, aside from Billie, he hadn't made any new friends either. Relationships had never been his strong point. He'd only had a few friends while growing up but even those relationships were distant, as if those guys never really wanted to get close to him but only wanted to use him for his Nintendo.

"Need help?" he asked her, one hand on the top bar of the fence.

"I got it," she said and climbed over.

He tossed the iron pipe to the other side, hopped over, then picked it up.

He scanned the cemetery. "See him?"

"No. Should I call?"

"And wake the dead?"

She gave him a screwed up look.

"Sorry. Couldn't help it," he said, smirking.

They walked slowly between a row of graves, their eyes going between the plots and the rest of the cemetery beyond.

"Juice box hero, na na na na na," he sang softly to calm his speeding heart. "Juice box hero, na na na na na."

Billie stopped and turned to him. "What?"

"Huh?"

"What're you singing?"

"That 'Juice Box Hero' song," he said, not believing she hadn't heard it before.

134

"What?"

"You know, 'Juice box hero, na na na na na.'"

She huffed and rolled her eyes. "It's 'Jukebox Hero,' Des." And walked past him.

He stayed there a moment. "Thought it was 'Juice Box Hero.'" He shrugged and whistled the melody as he caught up to her.

After, once they cleared the first section, Des's heart skipped a beat when they entered the next.

The dry, yellow grass on top of some of the graves was torn up, soil and a few shards of wood lay scattered atop the dead blades.

"Do you believe this?" he said. She didn't seem to hear him, her eyes transfixed further down the line. He tugged at her shirt and only now saw the thick lines of blood running from her waist to just under her arms. "What happened?"

She followed his gaze to her T-shirt. "Oh. Had a problem with a few broken boards. It's nothing." She winced as she bent from the left to the right.

"You sure?"

"Yeah."

He cleared his throat. "Do you see this?" He pointed with the pipe to one of the torn-up graves.

Billie took a step closer to examine it. "The rain must have gotten to them, too."

"How?"

"I'm only guessing, but it probably soaked into the earth and got in between the cracks in the cement casings that hold the casket. I'm also betting some of these graves are just a wooden box buried in the earth, too. The really old ones, anyway." She checked the tombstone. "Yeah, see? Elizabeth Martin, born eighteen-oh-four, died eighteen-sixty-eight. This one's a hundred-and-forty years old."

"That's heavy duty, man."

"You're telling me."

"Think any of them are walking about? I mean, around here?"

She looked around. "Don't see any, but you never know. If there were any, they're probably en route to the Haven like the rest of them. Which is why we better get moving. The highway's just over there, right?" She nodded straight ahead of them.

"Yeah. Leads up to the Disraeli then it should be just up and over, twice, and we're done."

"It's a long bridge to walk, Joe said."

"Speaking of which, where is he?"

"Those idiots better follow me. I'm not going back for them," Joe muttered as he made his way between a row of graves. Already having taken note of the several he saw with stirred-up tops, he had the X-09 drawn and at the ready.

He shouldn't have hit Des despite how much the guy deserved it. And it wasn't even that. A shot to the face for acting like a jerk? That kind of thing didn't merit a bleeding nose.

But jerks did.

He'd encountered too many in his life, the last real one being Dan, April's boyfriend or ex-boyfriend or whatever he had become to her after that glorious weekend together. Dan had been your typical tough guy, the kind that bullied up on the girl. He had even hit her once, April told him. What drove Joe nuts about the whole thing was that April had taken him back on the promise it would never happen again. And Joe had no way to verify it didn't happen again either.

Smacking Des was just a knee-jerk reaction, nothing more.

Yet Joe didn't feel the need to apologize. If the guy thought he could handle himself and Billie out here alone, fine. Let them see that fighting the undead wasn't a joke and unless you knew what you were doing, they'd take you in a second. Wait, they already knew that. He had saved them *twice*!

Joe passed by a mausoleum, where banging and muted groans came from behind its stone door.

At least those ones are trapped, he thought.

He turned around and surveyed the cemetery for Des and Billie. There they were, four rows over and two sections behind, just two dots amongst a plethora of tombstones.

Another dot was moving slowly toward them.

Then another.

Then another.

"I'm not going to wander around this cemetery till tomorrow, looking for him," Des said.

Billie didn't have to look at his eyes to know he was dead serious.

Des spun the iron pipe with his wrist then planted one end of it on the ground.

"No, you won't have to. We'll just keep going toward the highway. He's probably standing there, waiting for us."

"You think?"

"Probably. Seems a decent enough guy to not leave us hanging despite how cold he sometimes seems."

"Wonder why he's like that?"

Billie thought back to her chat with Joe in his kitchen and the way his eyes went vacant when he talked a bit about his old life.

"Just don't think we need people like that right now. You know as well as I do that people need to get together when crazy stuff like this goes down," Des said.

Out of the corner of her eye, she saw someone approaching them. Still mad at Joe, she didn't feel like looking up at him right now. "Shh. He's coming."

Des must have felt the same because he didn't look up either, not until the humanoid shadow came up behind him and wrapped both hands around his neck. "Hey! Quit it! Where do you" —he twisted himself around, trying to wriggle out of the hold; instead the hands held on— "get off?"

"Des!"

He shrieked, dropped the pipe and grabbed the pair of wrists attached to the hands with gray and dead fingers around his neck. The zombie must have been a local because it wore a dark, navy suit appearing to be from the '40s, its owner's head a shrunken skull with a couple tufts of black and dried, curly hair. Its face was all sunken in, its eyes deteriorated to nothing, just black vacuous holes in a crusty gray, patchy-skinned skull.

Billie shot out both arms and drove them in between Des and the zombie, attempting to use them as a crowbar to pry the two apart.

More shadows.

Three more undead, all in outdated clothes, were drawing near to them.

With a grunt, she shoved her elbow into the zombie's chest with one arm and the palm of her other hand into Des's, shoving him away.

"Run!" she shouted, and she and Des turned tail and darted away from the walking dead.

Des doubled back.

"What are you doing!" she screamed.

He grabbed the iron pipe off the ground then zipped back toward her.

They poured on the speed and leaped over a pair of tombstones and kept cutting across the rows, running, leaping, running, leaping, until it felt like she was flying. Another leap at the next set and—*floonk!* Her toe caught in between a pair of headstones and her body went horizontal. The next moment, she slammed chest first into the ground, the bottom of her chin smacking into the packed earth beneath the dead grass, sending her bottom teeth across the tip of her tongue. Her mouth immediately filled with blood.

Tears springing to life, her vision went and all she could see was the blurry yellowy-brown of the dry grass and the dark lines of shadow running in between the blades. When she looked up, a murky figure was running on ahead. Des didn't seem to have noticed she fell. She seemed to be tripping a lot lately. Maybe she had been pushed so past her limit that even her coordination was giving out on her?

She tried to cry out but instead only produced a semblance of his name followed by a gush of blood from her mouth. Fire lit the tip of her tongue and she wondered how bad the damage was. Hand to her mouth, she flinched when her fingers touched the sensitive flesh.

Unable to help herself, she dragged her caught foot off the tombstone, let it thunk against the grass, then, sobbing, got on all fours.

Crunch. Crunch. Crunch.

Footsteps on the grass.

Des?

She glanced up. An undead hand with bruised fingernails reached down toward her and grabbed her by the back of the neck and jerked her to her feet with remarkable strength.

Shrieking, she plowed her fist into the side of the dead man's jaw, the bone so brittle that the jaw broke and just dangled there to the right side, hanging on by a few, purply-gray ligaments. She shoved the zombie away and ran like a mad woman, screaming, arms flailing, not caring if she looked like an idiot.

Wiping her eyes with the bottom of her shirt helped clear her vision a little, but it still didn't help the inferno inside her mouth.

Blood filled her mouth so badly she had to spit every few seconds as she ran, each spurt of crimson mucus either landing on her shoes or, because of the wind caused by her sprint, splashing back onto her in sticky strands.

Des was nowhere to be seen. She cried out his name, thought she heard cursing somewhere to the left, but was quickly distracted when two rows over a throng of twenty or so undead moved between the headstones, a few of them stumbling over the markers.

The highway! Where was the highway?

Spitting then gathering her focus, Billie forced herself to slow down enough to get a clearer look around. There! The road was just ahead and over to the left.

Where was Des?

Giving it all he had, Des swung the iron pipe into an old fat woman's head, the heavy end lodging itself into the skull bone and sending up a sploosh of blood like a basket of eggs getting smacked off a T-ball stand.

Another heavyset woman came in from behind, this one much younger, maybe even this old one's daughter.

Des whirled around and brought the pipe down like an axe onto the woman's head, passing through her curly blonde hair and delivering fifteen pounds of iron into her brain. She dropped to her knees, fell forward and, pipe still lodged in her head, clawed toward him on all fours, trying to get a piece of his ankles. Des yanked back hard on the pipe, the motion strong enough to dislodge it but also enough to throw him off balance. He landed hard and fast on his keester. The blonde took hold of his foot and pulled it toward her mouth. About to sink her teeth into him, her head suddenly spun on its neck as he brought the pipe swiftly across her face, the edge of the pipe cleaving off a chunk of cheekbone. Black blood gushed out. It got on him, got on her, got on the grass.

Getting to his feet, Des was about to sprint off toward the highway when he came to a halt just as a teenage boy in a nice black suit raised his arms at him. This one's clothes weren't dated like the others. He wasn't even that gray. The young man must have died just before the rain came.

"Sorry, man," Des said and brought the pipe to the ground, holding it like a hockey stick.

He allowed the dead teen to get a little closer then, bringing the pipe back, delivered a slap shot to the kid's knackers, the blow so hard it lifted the young man off his feet and sent him onto his back. Des then rounded to the boy's head and brought the pipe down, mashing iron into bone like one driving a tent stake into the ground.

"I'm gettin' the hang of this," he said.

Billie . . .

He couldn't see her, just a pack of the undead off in the distance, with a few more ambling through the rows on either side toward him.

Barely able to breathe, Billie ran in between a couple of trees then stopped to catch her breath. She spat another wad of blood to the ground, wiped her mouth with her wrist, then walked quickly around another tree and came to rest against the doors to a mausoleum.

Panting, she closed her eyes. *Just one second. Maybe two. Just one second.* Her chest heaved up and down, each breath feeling as if her lungs had to rise up against a hundred pounds.

I'm not that out of shape, am I? she wondered.

The tip of her tongue was more numb than painful and the blood flow seemed to have slowed. She touched it and pulled her finger back when the salt of her skin stung the open wound.

Someone wheezed behind her. But there was no one there. Just a couple of large, stone doors.

Hheeehnsh . . . hheeehnsh . . . hheeehnsh . . .

DROOM!

Billie yelped as several pairs of dead hands popped out of in between the pair of mausoleum doors. She bounced off the wall and backed up a few steps. Gray-green hands blotched with purple flesh clawed and grabbed from the crack. She scanned the door and saw the hinge-and-lock was nearly broken off, the hinge bent so much it allowed a bit of space for these creatures to get their fingers through.

Must be cracks in the roof or something, for the rain to have gotten through.

It took a few moments, but she realized the mausoleum was getting further and further away. An unsettling feeling rose in her stomach a moment later: she had decided to stop her instinctive backward steps at the same time she bumped into something.

Something soft yet with an underlay of bone and—

Billie screamed.

A shot rang out.

Billie ducked and covered her head.

The body dropped behind her.

Des turned his head in the direction of the gunshot.

Joe, he thought with a grimace. *I don't need to be there to know you saved her.*

"Fine," he grumbled and smacked the pipe into another of the undead. "See you at the bridge."

Billie looked up at him, blue eyes wide, pink hair a mess, blood covering her chin.

Joe held his hand out to her. "You all right?"

Her hand shook as she extended it to him. When he took her fingers in his, there was a moment there when he realized how small they were, how smooth.

How perfect.

"No," she said softly. When she straightened, she had her hand over her mouth.

"I already saw it," he said. "Let me take a look."

She shook her head and pulled away her hand. "Mm-uh. I don't like it when you look me over, and I'm not taking my clothes off for you again."

Was she flirting with him? *No, you idiot. She's mad at you. Besides, even if she was, you don't have room for her in your life. Too much at stake as it is. Anyway, what would April think?*

"I just want to see if—Get down!" He pointed the X-09 just past her and took out a zombie coming in from behind.

With a wave of his hand, he said, "Come on!"

Billie didn't move.

"What's the matter with you? Let's go!"

She just stood there.

She's in shock, he thought. *Great.* It didn't quite make sense. She'd been in worse. Perhaps it was finally all piling up.

He ran over and gave her a shove from behind.

Finally her feet started to move.

Des tried the cemetery's front gate. It was chained shut and bound with a padlock.

"Grrgh!" He gave it a shake then climbed over the black metal fence.

The Disraeli was a long sidewalk length to the right. He started walking down it.

Three more shots rang out.

Joe and Billie ran toward the fence, Billie with a dazed look on her face, Joe pointing the gun every which way and dropping zombies as fast as he could.

When they got to the fence, Des debated going over there to help Billie over.

Let the hero handle it. He kept walking.

"Des! Hey, Des!" Joe shouted from behind.

He just kept going, and didn't look back.

22
THE BRIDGE

"Hey, Des, wait up!" Billie called after him. She didn't like the way her words came out all muddled and fat thanks to her sore tongue.

He kept on walking and only stopped when she caught up to him.

"Hey, didn't you hear us?" she said.

"What? You guys called me?" he said.

"Ah, yeah, like a hundred times. You deaf?"

"No. I hear just fine, thanks."

"As if you couldn't hear us."

"Well, sometimes people don't hear each other, all right?"

She rolled her eyes. She knew what he was driving at: her and Joe not hearing him when he called after them while they walked along the river. And to think she was going to give him a hug, glad that he was okay. Not anymore. And he didn't even ask about the blood on her mouth or why she sounded so funny.

Joe came up to them, gun still drawn. He cocked the hammer. Des's eyes landed straight on the large pistol. For a second there, Billie thought Joe was going to shoot him.

"Uh, I found the bridge," Des said, thumbing to it over his shoulder.

"Then let's get over it," Joe said, unmoving. He remained planted there until Des finally turned around and took the lead.

Billie wasn't sure if she should walk beside Des or hang back with Joe or just stroll somewhere in the middle between them. She opted for the latter.

The three began their ascent up the first large hump of the two-humped bridge, staying on the walkway, each with a hand on the railing. The metal was cold and covered with flakes of dried, gray rain.

From behind, the undead droned in the distance. Billie kept glancing over her shoulder and peering past Joe to see if any were following them. The undead just stood there, calling out with hoarse voices behind the cemetery fence, either too stupid to figure out how to climb over or simply unable to.

Soon they were crossing over the river. The skeletal forest lining it seemed much more peaceful from up here. If this had been before the rain, you could have mistaken it for just another fall day, if not for the boatload of abandoned cars on the bridge, some smashed into each other, others piled onto the cement divider separating the north and south lanes, a few others smashed into the railings on either side. At one point they came up to a car that sat with its hood smashed against the bent railing at a forty-five-degree angle, its front end jammed into where the railing met the walkway, the railing having stopped it from flipping over the edge. They walked around it. Billie could only wonder how many cars had actually gone over and plummeted to the river below.

On the descent of the first hump, Des finally spoke, cracking seven minutes of silence. "What're we gonna do when we get downtown?"

Billie didn't know and she wasn't sure Joe did either. Not *specifically* anyway. He also didn't reply.

"I said, what're we—" Des began.

Joe cut him off. "Not sure."

They crossed the little valley in between the two humps of the bridge and rounded a transit that had tipped over onto its side. Billie doubted anybody was left within and when she saw the ring of glass bordering the vehicle, she knew that it was empty and whoever was within had smashed their way out. The bloodstains on the pavement suggested either these folks had been killed or had been caught in the rain and were transformed.

They began ascending the next hump.

"How can you not know?" Des said.

Joe didn't reply.

"Aren't you supposed to be the guy with the plan?"

Does he have to keep it up? What's with the jerk-change all of the sudden? Billie wondered. "Joe will probably tell us when we get there," she said, trying to reassure him. "Isn't that right, Joe?"

"More or less," he said from behind.

"What does that mean?" Des asked.

"It means just what Billie said: I'll tell you once we get there."

"Why not now? Or do you not know?"

"What's your problem, Des? You've been nothing but a—"

"Oh, like you're one to talk."

"I didn't even finish."

"Like you needed to. What were you gonna say? I've been nothing but a jerk?"

"Yeah, since we hooked up by the river."

"See, called you on it, didn't I?"

They were hitting the apex of the hump. Joe stormed passed Billie, and grabbed Des by the collar of his shirt and shoved him against the railing.

"Joe, don't!" she said. *Oh no.*

The guy had Des bent backward over the railing so far that she thought his body would snap. Des's eyes darted between Joe's and the ground several stories below.

Joe still had his gun in his hand and Billie wasn't sure if he realized it or not. If that thing accidentally went off . . .

"You wanna settle this now?" Joe said.

Des spat in his face.

With a violent jerk, Joe yanked up on Des's collar, then with a mighty heave slammed his shoulder blades against the metal railing. Des howled then took a swing at him.

With the iron pipe.

Joe's shoulder rocked in its socket as the metal crashed into the bone. His left arm immediately went numb, leaving only his gun-filled right hand available.

He aimed it at Des's head.

"Go on, coward!" Des screamed. "Wanna cap me? Go right ahead. Got nothing to live for anyway."

What? He kept the shot squarely lined up. All it would take would be a simple squeeze of the trigger and a one-inch-round hole would materialize between Des's eyes.

"Joe, stop it! Put the gun down!" Billie screamed.

"Why should I? He'll only get us killed! Look what he's done so far!"

The iron pipe was suddenly in the air then Joe felt as if his fingers had been torn off right along with the gun from his hand. He had to double check just to make sure. They were still attached but there was no feeling in them.

"GRRAAH!" Des screamed as he came in with another swipe of the pipe.

Joe ducked and the pipe smacked into the concrete next to his leg with a dull, metallic *clunk*.

His boot was in the air and he kicked Des in the gut. The guy doubled over, wheezing and pawing at the air in front of his mouth, as if trying to scoop in handful after handful of sweet, sweet air.

He could barely be heard between panicky moans. "I . . . ca . . . bre . . ."

Fingers tingling, Joe forced them to curl into his palm. His fist was weak, but he didn't care. He sent an uppercut flying into Des's chin. The young man jerked backward and flipped over, landing backward on the pavement, the rear of his head smacking the ground.

He didn't move.

Joe searched for his gun. It wasn't on the ground.

"Good-bye, Joe," Billie said. She cocked the hammer.

23
JUST LEAVE ME ALONE

August sat up, waking to the dark. He was back in the vault and had gone down for a nap after scouting the Square some more.

A chill swept through him, his sweat-soaked clothes clinging to his body. He remembered what he dreamed about: his family.

It had been Christmas and all of them were there: Eleanor, Jonathan, Lydia, David and Jan; the kids: Jon junior, Bella, Finch, Katie and Stewart. His wife had served the turkey. He stood from the table, all set to carve, about to deliver the story of Christ's birth as he did so when, after he pulled off the lid of the turkey roaster, instead of a big and juicy, fat, old bird, there was his own zombified head, bloated, with oily gray skin, staring up at him with those awful white eyes. His family was gone from the table when he went to tell them what was in the roaster, each suddenly at his side as if materializing out of thin air, all dead—all *undead*—with clawing hands. August tried to ward them off with the electronic cutter, but Eleanor got to him first, grabbed the hand with the cutter and bit into it, tearing off first one finger then another, picking it clean like a turkey bone.

Screaming, August shouted at his own head in the roaster to help him. The dead head's jaw popped open; pointy teeth sharper than razor blades shot out from its face and latched onto his throat. They tore out his jugular in a blaze of pain and instead of dropping dead like he expected, August was suddenly on his back on the floor beside the table, his family tearing the limbs from his body, chowing down, blood and ligaments dripping off their chins.

He couldn't move and only awoke just as his wife bent at the waist and gave him a kiss, her breath hot and foul and filled with maggots.

Alone in the dark, August hugged his rifle to himself then, as if discovering the instrument of death anew, tossed it to the side.

He had killed his family. He had to. But he still killed them.

"How much longer?" he whispered.

Head throbbing, a thousand voices filling his brain and calling him a murderer, he lay back down, hugging himself.

"Just leave me alone."

24

IT AIN'T WHAT IT USED TO BE

The look of concentration behind Billie's icy blue eyes made Joe shudder. She wasn't kidding. He had just dropped her best friend. No one in their right mind would stand for that.

He could only hope that after today's ordeals, she wasn't in her right mind. Yet at the same time, maybe this was a good thing. It'd been a long year, one that felt like a lifetime of dragging around the pain and memory of the girl that got away. The haunting and soul-wrenching conviction that he'd murdered somebody. Murdered so many. You could call it what you wanted: self-defense, self-preservation, righteous judgment, whatever. Still, death was death and who was he to administer it?

Maybe a bullet to the brain or heart would finally cure him of the pain he was so sick and tired of carrying around. Maybe finally—finally—he could let April go because death was the only way he would be *able* to let her go.

But you don't live in a world where the dead stay dead. You could come back, if it rains again or if one of the creatures start gnawing on you. He eyed Billie squarely. She didn't flinch. Des was trying to say something but he was too low to the ground and too messed up to be coherent. *You could even still carry memory. April could still be with you.*

"Do you really want to kill me, Billie?" he asked her.

The statement must have hit her like an arrow laced with realization because her eyes glazed over.

"If you want to, you can," he said.

"You deserve it," she said, her voice curt yet at the same time uncertain.

"For?"

"You're a murderer. You were going to kill Des."

"Des was going to kill me," he said.

She didn't reply to that. He took a step toward her.

"Don't move," she said and aimed the barrel of the X-09 squarely at his head.

149

He raised his hands. "Okay."

Des muttered something else, coughed, then said, "Bill . . . don't . . ."

She flinched at hearing her name. A single tear leaked out of the corner of one eye. Even now, ready to kill him, Joe couldn't believe he thought she looked beautiful.

Stop it, he told himself. *Don't let her take you.*

"You're going to have to make a decision, Billie. I can't make it for you," he said.

She sniffled . . .

. . . and pulled the trigger.

BOOM!

Air wisped passed his face and then instantly after a jolt shot him when the car some twenty feet away blasted into the air aflame then came crashing down in a shrill metallic *BANG!*

Billie stood there, mouth hanging open.

Joe took two quick steps up to her, wrapped his hands around hers, grabbing the gun by the handle, pointing it upward. "Give me that." He yanked it away and clicked the hammer back up so another shot wouldn't go off.

Billie turned and put her face in her hands, sobbing.

Des exhaled what sounded like a breath of relief.

Joe went over and stood over him. "Are we done?"

Des nodded.

"Then let's get moving. They'll probably be here any moment."

When Joe and the others made their descent down the second hump of the Disraeli Overpass, he opted to take the lead, X-09 ready, the other two single file behind him. He toyed with the idea of Des leading the way and acting as a body shield should any more zombies show up, but he knew these streets and preferred to take the responsibility upon himself.

Downtown was his home. Its streets were where he used to spend hours just walking and thinking and dreaming up comic tales in his old life. He used to live out here. He could probably walk the majority of them blindfolded and know where he was. They were also his patrol ground, a concrete grid to hunt down the undead and wipe them off the face of the city.

The place of his redemption for killing April.

"So where were you when the rain fell, Joe?" Des asked from last in line.

"Home."

"How exciting."

Billie shooshed him.

"Why, where were you?" Joe asked.

"I'll save it for when we settle down wherever we wind up and we'll have a 'Kumbaya' moment."

Look forward to it, he thought facetiously.

As they approached the intersection of Logan, Lily and the Disraeli Freeway, Joe wondered what would be the best route to take. Go left, and they'd wind up behind the museum, concert hall and the old buildings that made up one side of the Exchange District. Go straight, and they'd land on Main. There would be buildings either way, but going straight would be more out in the open and not as confined as the zigzag route they'd have to take through the Exchange to get to Portage Avenue. He decided to head up to Main then turn left.

He informed the others.

"Works for me," Billie said.

"Ditto," Des said.

Weaving their way through and around the cars clogging up the road, they went up to Main Street and turned left, sticking to the sidewalk, it being the clearest path with only a handful of cars having driven up onto it on that terrible day long ago.

They walked in silence, which Joe found peaceful. After his and Des's exchange on the bridge, he needed the break. First *real* human contact in months and it had to be with a loud-mouthed nerd who had a bad temper. Billie, though . . . . He hated the way his neck ached to glance back and steal a look at her. He had to keep reminding himself that the only reason he wanted to was because she reminded him of April. Put a long, black wig on her and, from the back, they'd probably look the same. Even in the face Billie bore a resemblance to her, the biggest difference only being the thick-framed glasses she wore.

Snap out of it, man. She's no good for you. It's misplaced affection, if "affection" is even what it is. You're so messed up right now that you wouldn't know affection even if it was dumped on you, so who do you think you are feeling this way? And "feeling" wasn't even the right way to describe it to himself either. It was more of a haunting notion, the *idea* of April that somehow Billie possessed, that got to him.

"Hmph," he said. *That thing underneath.*

"What?" Billie said.

"Nothing." But it was *something.* "That thing underneath," was what he called it back when he met April, that invisible quality that attracted one person to another, the one thing in all of human thought and feeling that was utterly intangible and completely indescribable yet was known all the same. It was like everyone was built with an invisible sensor, one designed for a single purpose: to detect that secret, hidden, amazing attractable quality in another person. Some would probably call it "chemistry" or some other dumb name, just a feeble attempt to rationalize what they didn't understand. Joe didn't understand it. He just knew it was there.

April had it.

He had thought that, maybe, he had had it, too, and that April had found it in him. But he had been proven wrong the morning after they spent the night lying side by side in his bed and April was gone. He hadn't even had to roll over to confirm it. He just knew. She had left a note, one explaining she had some things to work out but that she'd never forget him.

So lost in his reverie, it took several pokes from Billie from behind to catch his attention.

"What?" he said.

"Over there."

Her finger pointed over his shoulder to the staggering corpses walking down the front steps of the Centennial Concert Hall.

The three stopped.

Des drew out the iron pipe.

The four undead moved down the steps with much more control than Joe thought them capable of. There was purpose in their stride. Even from across the street, the hatred in their dull, white eyes was apparent. Four men. Two middle-aged, two younger, all dead for so long that their skin was completely gray, blotched with brown spots, eyes fully sunken into their sockets save for those awful whites. Only one of them had hair, just a touch of black and unruly strands on top of its head.

Once at the bottom of the steps, the undead locked them in their sights and picked up their speed.

"Joe . . . ?" Billie said. She was right beside him. He hadn't even noticed her get so close.

152

One look told her to take a step back, which she did.

X-09 raised, Joe cocked the hammer and lined up his shot, picking off one of the zombies just as it crossed the median. Another loud crack of the gun and he took a second. Their bodies dropped to the pavement in dull, fleshy *thunks*, black blood oozing from their skulls.

Des had the iron pipe raised like a baseball bat.

Billie took a few quick steps backward.

The remaining two zombies ran for them, one for Billie, one for Des.

Pulling down the hammer, he took aim and blasted the forehead out of the skull of the one coming for Billie.

Des wound up like a star hitter, ready to sink the pipe deep into the last zombie's brain.

BANG!

The corpse dropped before Des could take a swing.

"Hey!" Des said, whining.

Joe just winked at him, turned, and continued down the street.

"You know, you should really get a silencer or something for that thing," Billie said to Joe. He didn't reply. "Don't you think its noise will attract them?"

"It does," he said, though reluctantly. "I tried building one but every prototype failed. They only muffled the sound a little."

"So you can build a gun but something like a muffler is difficult?"

She was obviously busting his chops but Joe didn't care for it. Not now. Not after a kill.

"You should look into that online if we ever find a working computer that's hooked up to the Net," she said.

"Yeah," he said flatly.

Des hadn't said a word since that last kill. He was obviously pouting but Joe wouldn't give him the satisfaction of it actually working by saying anything.

The three reached Portage and Main. They stopped, scanned the streets for the undead and, with the coast clear, took a breather.

"So here we are," Billie said after a few moments.

Joe nodded, not feeling like speaking.

The buildings were empty, with no sign of life in their windows. Empty cars littered the street like trash from an enormous garbage can. Many of the buildings had their windows smashed, especially on the lower levels except for the Richardson building, which had its lower windows covered in blood, a few corpses lining the lower windows like a cheap ledge.

Across the way, through the dark lower windows of the Scotiabank building, the silhouettes of the dead were like paper cut-outs, piled four or five high.

The ever-present gray clouds hung thick overhead, their very presence seeming to muffle any and all sound. The brown blotches that weaved their way in and around the clouds looked extra ominous today.

This wasn't the Winnipeg Joe knew. Though he'd seen it torn apart like this before, it was still new every time he laid eyes on it.

This place—this *center* of downtown—was meant to be a hub for life. It was one of the most famous landmarks in Canada. It was the very symbol of downtown Winnipeg and the one place people usually offered as a starting point when giving directions on how to get from Point A to Point B.

Now it was dead, the buildings stained with that pukey gray crud that came with the rain, each one appearing a hundred years older than what it actually was. Traffic lights hung limp off their metal poles, like dead fish off a fishing rod. The streetlamps, some with broken bulbs, hadn't been on since shortly after the rain fell.

"So sad, isn't it?" Billie said softly.

"Yeah. It ain't what it used to be, that's for sure," Joe said.

"To be honest," Des began, "I didn't expect it to last this long."

"What do you mean?" Billie asked.

He drew near to her. "After the rain, I thought for sure the boys in green—the military, I mean—would have come and just bombed it or something, you know, to get rid of as many of the undead in one go as they could. The zombies used to be like a swarm down here."

"I doubt they could have bombed downtown even if they wanted to," Billie said. "Canada's army's more like a few pissed off guys wielding hockey sticks than actual soldiers."

Des chuckled, seemingly because he couldn't help himself. "Yeah, a stick in one hand, a bottle of beer in the other."

Joe turned away to conceal his smile. It was true. Compared to most other countries, Canada really fell short in the warfare department. It was probably why it had been overrun by the undead as quickly as it had.

Elsewhere in the world, from what he had been able to piece together from the Internet and the bits of radio before the signals went out, their military efforts had lasted much longer. Months longer.

There was movement up the street and decayed heads peeked out from behind the roofs of cars and the sides of buildings. At first only a few, but with each second that passed, the number seemed to double.

"They're here," Joe said.

"I thought they were supposed to be gone?" Billie said.

"Me, too," Des said, pipe already held tight with both hands, ready to roll.

Joe reloaded the X-09, pulled the hammer down and kissed the barrel. "Follow me."

He meant to take them to the left, further down Main, but had to stop when more of the undead came out from behind the cars. Was it an ambush? Seemed like it, some kind of surprise attack. But there was no way the undead would have known they were coming.

"This way!" Billie said, pointing back the way they came.

All three stopped running after a few steps when more ambling corpses came out of the side streets and from behind crashed cars.

They snuck up on us, Joe thought. *That would mean that they* can *think.* As an afterthought: *Or maybe just some of them?*

They backed up to the front doors of the Richardson building.

The undead drew closer.

25

SNIPER

No matter how many times Joe had laid bullet to marrow on one of these things, he still wasn't used to them. He could see them from afar, they could be rushing in up close, and each time a flash of panic still burst through him, throwing off his insides and momentarily detaching his mind from his body in a fit of surrealism.

The walking dead weren't natural. None of this was. The human race wasn't meant to end in a splash of blood at the jaws of the unworldly dead. He didn't know *how* it was supposed to end—if it ever would—but a storm of gray clouds that brought death-giving rain not once crossed the minds of those who planned for chaos.

"Got any ideas?" Billie said beside him.

"Just one: try and survive," Joe said.

"I could have told you that."

"Me, too," Des added.

Joe didn't have to look at Billie to know she was panicking; her frantic breathing gave her away. He couldn't blame her. She was unarmed, for one thing, and, as much as he believed in equals, she was a girl, the lesser in regards to strength and old fashioned wear-and-tear.

White, haunting eyes locked onto them anew. Hundreds of them, a stampede of wild animals with no thought except for the satisfaction of blood and flesh.

Surrounded, Joe did his best to remain calm though he was certain he was either going to die or soon become one of them.

The undead stopped their advance, as if all were waiting for a signal to go ahead and feast.

"What are they waiting for?" Billie whispered.

"I don't know and I don't care to find out," Joe said. "Des?"

"Yeah?"

"Get ready."

"O-okay."

He raised the gun and blasted holes into the heads of two of them. The sweet dual crack of the gun made his heart sing.

Just pretend there's only a handful, nothing more.

Bellowing, voices hoarse and ethereal, the undead charged.

Joe pulled the hammer back and took out two more before grabbing Billie by the hand and leading her to the left, just missing the scaly gray hands from four zombies.

Bang! Bang!

Two more down.

Bang! Bang!

Another couple and he made headway into the patch of zombies to the side. Behind him Des screamed in between dull *thonks* as he drove the end of the iron pipe into the skulls of the deceased.

Billie yelped, swore, and kicked and punched at those who came near her. Joe helped her by quickly firing as many shots as he could into those who got too close.

Soon, they and Des were separated.

"We can't leave him!" Billie shouted amidst the wails of the dead.

"Can't help it. We need some room."

He jerked on her hand and, taking out a few more zombies, carved a clear path to the side of the building, reloading the X-09 with a packet of bullets from the straps crisscrossing his torso inside his coat.

Sprinting, they rounded the corner.

Only a half dozen undead here, all coming toward them, some walking almost normally, others dragging their feet.

Gray-green decrepit faces snarled at them; others held vacant expressions, drones in their lust for flesh.

Bang! Bang!

Two more fell. The others coming up behind them tripped over the bodies.

Joe pulled Billie by the hand and they ran past them, not bothering to finish them off. Every bullet spared meant more chance for survival later.

The anguished groans of the dead filled the streets like a stadium of hissing fans.

At the rear of the building, Joe saw them first. Billie ran past him and he had to grab her from behind by the waist, pick her up off her feet and pull her back.

The corpses were everywhere.

The doors at the back of the building were boarded up.

There was no way in.

"Aaaaaaagggggghhhhhhh!" Des screamed as he came running from the side of the building, pipe in one hand, the arm of an undead torn at the elbow in the other.

When he reached them he spun around and hurled the arm at the horde of zombies moving toward them.

There was a parkade to their left, the wall high, impossible to climb over, its entrance way blocked with empty cars. Zombies closed in from front and back. The Richardson building stood over them like a giant silent observer of a murderer's dream.

"Got any other bright ideas?" Des asked. "No? That's what I thought."

"Shut up, Des. Let me think," Joe said.

There was no place to go but up and unless each were suddenly bestowed superpowers, that wasn't going to happen.

It was over.

The undead were no more than fifteen feet away.

Billie was crying.

"Hey," Des said softly and for the first time since Joe knew him, genuine affection crossed his face.

Billie reached for him and put her arms around his neck.

"There's something I have to tell you, Billie," Des said.

"I . . . just . . . just hold me," she replied.

Des appeared disappointed, but Joe had a pretty good idea what the guy was going to say.

"We have about ten seconds, folks," Joe said. "I don't know about you, but these guys aren't going to take me. They've stolen enough already." He raised his gun eye level, grinned, and said, "See you on the other side."

He stretched out his arm and aimed the barrel at the nearest zombie.

Billie let go of Des and the three stood side by side.

One last stand.

Joe only managed to squeeze off one shot when the zombies rushed them and took them to the ground.

Screaming inside and out, Des kept the pipe across his chest, using it as a barrier between him and the chubby woman with yellow teeth and purple lips pressing down from on top of him. Another zombie wrapped its sticky fingers around the bottom of his chin from behind, pulling so hard against his jaw and putting such pressure on his throat that it silenced his cries.

Still screaming inside, Des tried to ignore the pain building in his neck as this thing tried to separate his head from his body.

Pressing forward with everything he had, he tried to get the heavy dead woman off him. He only gained a few inches of space before she shoved the pipe into him, the iron plowing into his ribs. Something cracked inside.

Grunting, Des squeezed his eyes shut and braced for the end.

A crash of glass. A shot rang out.

The fat woman fell on top of him.

Joe?

Billie frantically slapped and hit and pushed and punched the two corpses trying to take a bite out of her jugular.

"No! No! No!" she screeched.

Each time her hands struck dead flesh, they slipped right off as if these two zombies were covered in a slick goo she couldn't see.

Their stench invaded her system and she shut her eyes, trying to block out the horrible, deathly whites of theirs.

A large hand clamped down on her waist; dull pokes dug into her skin and she knew that in a moment her intestines would be ripped out.

The sound of the gunshot jolted her out of her imagination, but she dare not open her eyes lest she be forced to see the undead eat her alive.

The finger-like vice around her midsection loosened its grip.

The zombie's head exploded after Joe managed to put the barrel of the X-09 under its chin and pull the trigger. Blood and brain splashed onto his face. The familiar sensation of teeth biting into his shoe distracted him, as did the fingers gripping him about the ankle.

A hard hand crashed down onto his face, sending a spike of pain from his nose up into his forehead.

"April," he said but barely formed the words and another of the creatures shoved a finger that tasted like rotten milk into his mouth.

Gagging, Joe bit down anyway. The finger jerked and tugged between his lips.

Stop! You bite it off and the blood will get into you. Then, like another voice: *What does it matter? You're going to die, anyway.* Then another: *Go down fighting!*

His right hand holding the X-09 was yanked to the side. He fired off a shot and thought he heard a zombie screech.

Anger boiled within, filled his stomach, bubbled up his chest and exploded into his head and heart.

He cocked the hammer and fired.

And fired.

And couldn't stop squeezing the trigger even though he hadn't pulled down on the hammer.

A shock of weight suddenly pressed down on him. He didn't know what it was; the hand over his face made it impossible to see anything.

Something bit into his coat, putting pressure on his left biceps.

His thumb searched for the hammer but it was quickly grabbed by another set of fingers.

Bang!

Did his gun go off? No. Something still had his thumb. Des? Did the guy have a gun but decided to keep it secret and only bring it out now just as they were about to die? That didn't make sense either.

Bang! Bang! Bang!

He didn't care where the shots were coming from. The onslaught of hands trying to get hold of him was lessening.

Bang!

The dead hand over his face went limp. Joe shoved it away.

Straight above him hanging half out the window overlooking the back of the Richardson building was an old man with a rifle pointed at the dead.

"I can do this all day, you lousy schmucks," August muttered. *I got plenty of bullets.*

It had started as sport about a half hour ago, looking out the window and picking off the dead. Something to pass the time and, he admitted, a deep exercise in catharsis. Anything to work out that terrible dream. But when the three strangers suddenly appeared at the front of the building, it took a good several moments of looking for him to actually believe what he was seeing: people, *real* people. People who were *alive*. That's when the undead moved in and tried to kill the trio below. The three had begun their fight so fast that August hadn't been sure if he should run downstairs, get outside and help them, or just stay put and see what he could do from there.

When the young man in the trench coat and the girl rushed to the side of the building, he followed them along the windows bordering the bank of office suites on the fifth floor, running from the hallway to the windows, trying to keep up with them. When he remembered the guy in the front, he ran back to his original station to see what happened to him. The guy in the green T-shirt was gone, so August ran back into the hallway, searched the side windows and eventually found the three of them at the back of the building, surrounded.

He smashed the window with the butt of the rifle right after the three were mauled by the massive horde, figuring that even if he was too late, at least he had made an effort to save them. What he would do when the zombies looked up and saw him, he wasn't sure.

Another zombie dropped below and August quickly kept aligning his shots, taking out the undead surrounding the three people, giving them room and a moment to get to their feet.

The guy with the trench coat did something with his gun and then began firing into the throng of living corpses.

August did the same, reveling in each shot, paying them back for forcing him to murder his family.

26

THEY NEVER STOP

This is what you get, August thought, his teeth clenched, lips pressed tightly together. *You took everything from me.*

He fired as many rounds as fast as his finger could pull the trigger. Below, the heads of the undead popped one by one, each dropping to their knees then falling flat on their faces a second after skull and tissue sprayed outward.

It wasn't long before August had to reload the rifle. Even the few seconds it took for him to do so seemed an hour, he longed to squeeze the trigger so much. And when he finally was able to do so again, it was like coming home. Darkness curled its shadowy fingers around his heart and clenched the pounding muscle; blackness of soul consumed him. Despite knowing better, despite knowing he should let up, he couldn't help but fire shot after shot into the horde below. Even if he could save just one of these new folks down there, he could somehow find a way to redemption through their rescue.

This isn't you, August. The voice in his head was not his own. Though it carried the *sound* of his voice, it clearly belonged to another. *Leave them to Me*, it said.

"I c-can't," August squeezed through gritted teeth.

If you don't trust Me, if you don't let go of what happened, you will fall away. Choose.

Time seemed to slow and though the zombies five stories down still quickly fell with every crack of the rifle, August felt removed from himself. He could see the dark gray, scaly hand around his heart, its long black nails beginning to puncture the flesh, drawing blood.

"What are you?" he whispered, not expecting a reply.

Very clearly, the hand said, "You."

Tears pricked the corners of his eyes and a sharp pain pierced his chest, as if he was experiencing the loss of his family all over again. And if he wasn't careful, he'd lose something even worse: himself.

Bang! Bang! Bang! Bang!

The dead fell.

August kept squeezing the trigger, reloading when necessary.

Bang! Bang! Bang!

The live souls below shouted at each other, but August couldn't make out what they were saying.

Then one of them, the man in the trench coat, waved at him and pointed away from the building.

More dead were coming.

Now on his feet, Joe delivered a hard hook to the jaw of a dead man with one eye missing then an elbow to the face of a woman with short brown hair and several missing teeth.

He cocked the hammer of the X-09 and blasted the heads off two zombies rushing toward him.

His friends were missing.

"Billie! Des!" he shouted.

Whirling around, he caught sight of them—Billie to the left, Des to the right—struggling against the mass of walking dead.

Des slammed the pipe into the head of one then jerked its opposite end back into the face of another, plowing right through the creature's nose.

A gush of blood spurted high in a wild arc as Billie pulled a long knife from one zombie's face.

Where did she get that? he wondered.

Another came at her, this one from behind. Just as she turned to meet it, Joe cocked the hammer and fired off a bullet into the creature's brain, sending it to the ground.

"There's too many!" Billie screamed at him.

"I know!" he growled. He took the face off one, pulled down on the hammer, and took out two more, the bullet going through both at once.

To the side, Des screeched as he swung the iron pipe around like a wild man, unloading all his hatred into the skulls and faces of decaying men and women.

The old man! Joe thought.

He looked up and saw the old guy hanging partway out of the window, rifle poised on the dead below but no movement or sign he was going to pull the trigger again.

"What's he waiting for?" Joe said. "Hey! Hey, you! Yeah, I'm talking to you, old man! See what's going on down here? Let 'er rip or we're all dead!"

Still the old guy remained in the window, frozen. Was he dead? Had the excitement been too much for him and the old coot just had a heart attack and died? If so, the guy was going to be one of the walking dead very soon.

Joe debated firing a shot at the guy to put him out of his misery. His thumb pulled down on the hammer. About to the pull the trigger, a gray hand slammed down on his arm and a set of teeth rushed for his neck. Joe wrestled the zombie away, kicked it once in the gut, then put a bullet between its eyes.

Another shoved him from behind, then another and another.

Billie was screaming. So was Des, as each was shoved toward the building by a mass of the undead.

Joe looked up.

The old man was gone.

This is it, Billie thought for the millionth time that day. Even though this wasn't the time to be thinking it, she thought it strange that each time it seemed death was coming for her it scared her anew. She thought she'd be used to it by now.

"Joe, help!" she cried.

"Billie, I can't, I—" came his voice from somewhere far away. It was quickly shut out by the raspy groans of the undead as they pushed against them.

So many hands, so many teeth. Billie pushed and pulled and twisted her body every which way, trying to worm her way out from under and in between them. Head spinning, she lost all sense of direction and quickly found herself hoisted up above the creatures' heads, her body tossed around on top of them as if it were some kind of crazy mosh pit.

Over on the right, Des drove his pipe into the ear of one of the corpses, lodging it in. Before he could withdraw it, another creature grabbed him and pulled him away.

"No!" Des screamed, still reaching for the pipe. "It'sgoneit'sgoneit'sgoneit'sgone," he said, nearly breathless.

Strong fingers gripped his leg and pulled him down to the ground. He hit the gray-stained concrete with a *thunk*. Pain lit up inside his hip.

A mass of gray and decaying heads loomed over him.

Then a hundred fingers reached for him.

Des had disappeared beneath the crowd of the undead just as Joe had been thrown up against the building wall. The back of his head hit the wall with a sickening smack and green stars burst before his vision and a light droning filled his ears.

Moaning, he drew up the X-09, about to shoot as many of the zombies crowding in upon him as he could. He couldn't even get the gun shoulder height before the undead pounded into him like a tide into a surf. One fat one slammed into his chest, winding him, forcing him to the ground.

Heart racing, he gripped the X-09 hard and tight. If these suckers were gonna tear him apart, it was going to be *after* he was dead, not before. He bent forward, pushing his head toward the gun while pulling his arm toward himself despite the tugs of the dead wrestling it away.

Just one will do it, he thought.

He put the barrel against his forehead. *I'm sorry, April. Didn't mean to go out like this. Some hero I turned out to be. In a few moments I'll be seeing you though. Hang on. I'm almost there.*

He squeezed his eyes shut.

BOOMBANG!

27

SOME KIND OF RESCUE

Brain matter and globs of blood splashed against Joe's face.

His finger froze on the trigger.

Am I . . . had I . . . No, he wasn't dead. He was still *aware.* Then what . . .

A zombie groaned somewhere above him and a dull thunk shook the pavement as the body dropped to the ground. The pasty corpse laid prone, eyes wide and spacey, staring at him, blood oozing from its skull.

BOOM! CRASH!

A couple more of the undead surrounding him dropped to the ground, and not from gunshots.

Joe placed his palms on either side of him, pushed against the cement, and quickly got to his feet and stepped away from the building.

A thick whistle filled the air and—*BOMF!* A large gray box crashed onto the zombies, at first bouncing off the head of one, puncturing its skull, then rebounding off the creature's head and hitting the pavement, causing the others around it to take a step back.

Joe looked up and two more gray boxes flew from a window above, one near Des, the other near Billie, each box knocking the undead away from his friends.

Those look like . . . ". . . computers?" Joe said.

"Get off me!" Billie shrieked as she shoved one of the zombies to the side just as what looked like a black fax machine sped down toward the zombie behind her, nailing it in the face. The zombie stood there, muttered something, then teetered on its heels before falling over.

"FIRE IN THE HOLE!" came a loud and raspy voice from above. Just then a photocopier toppled out of the window and sped toward the earth below, landing with a resounding *BANG* as it smashed through a handful of the undead and hit the ground. Bits of plastic, metal and glass sprayed outward. The creatures surrounding it took a step back.

"Thanks!" Joe shouted to the empty window above. He hoped the old guy heard him.

166

X-09 raised, he pegged off another zombie then sent yet another bullet into the head of one stumbling toward Billie as she ran toward him.

Off to the side, the dull thwacks of metal beating against bone forced Joe to aim his gun in that direction. Des stood there amidst five undead, slamming his pipe into their faces, the look of sheer rage upon Des's face enough to make even Joe feel a tad uncomfortable.

Whoa, easy there, cowboy, he thought. Yet at the same time he was proud of the timid lad for finally standing on his own.

Another computer monitor quickly followed by its processor flew out of the window above, whistling through the air. The monitor clunked one zombie in the shoulder. The processor missed its target and landed in between two others. When it broke against the ground, the sudden bang was enough to the get the zombies to stop, look down, and slow their advance.

From above: "Get close to the building! Hurry!"

Joe fired the X-09, dropping another creature. He took Billie by the hand once she was in reach.

"This sucks!" she screamed.

"Tell me about it," he said. "Come on."

"What? Are you crazy?" she yelped as he tugged her closer to the building wall. "You wanna box ourselves in or something and die?"

"Des!" Joe shouted over the murmurs and groans of the dead.

Des turned and withdrew his pipe from a zombie's eye socket. Blood coated the young man's face. He didn't seem to care. Grimacing, Des gave Joe a nod then whirled around and slammed his pipe into the temple of an old dead lady before stepping over the bodies to get to them. One large dead black dude stumbled toward him. Des didn't seem to know the guy was there. Joe fired off another shot. The creature fell.

Des's eyes darted toward the deceased then back at Joe, shooting him a cool glare. "I saw him."

"Yeah, right," Joe said. "Let's go."

The three made it to the building.

The undead closed in. Fortunately many were slowed by having to step around or over their fallen kin. Still, there had to be at least thirty coming their way.

Glass shattered above and rained down just to the left.

"Look out!" Billie said as a mammoth wooden desk tumbled over the window frame five stories up and crashed upon a few zombies; its now-broken-in-half-top squashed what was left of those who had already fallen.

"Is this guy nuts?" Billie said, eyes wide.

"Probably," Des said. To Joe: "So, now what?"

"He said to get to the building. That's all I—"

Cloonk! Something nearly nicked Joe in the shoulder. The thing dangled beside him for a moment before he realized what it was: a fire hose.

The old coot leaned on his palms against the window frame above. "Grab on and climb up!"

The three just stood there. Was he serious?

"You wanna die!" the old guy shouted. He reached down to somewhere behind the window and pulled out his rifle. He took aim and fired.

Joe jumped just as something heavy landed on his toes. He looked down to see a teenage zombie draped over his feet.

"No," he said to himself. Then as if in afterthought: *Not now, anyway.* "Okay, Billie, you go first."

He grabbed the end of the fire hose and gave it to her.

"I can't lift myself," she said, eyes wet with tears.

"You're gonna have to."

"But . . ."

"Or you stay down here and get eaten."

A creature appeared in his peripheral. He took it down.

Billie grabbed hold of the hose and began to climb.

"Use your legs," Joe told her.

She intertwined her feet around the hose and began to ascend.

"Des, give her some space then it's your turn. Push her up if you have to."

"How?"

"Just push on her b—" *BOOMCRACK!* A chair crashed in front of them, scattering three more of the undead that had stepped hungrily toward them.

Billie was already half way up to the window. Probably all the adrenaline coursing through her gave her a boost.

Des stuffed his pipe into his belt loop then took hold of the hose. He jumped . . . and his fingers slipped and he fell to the ground.

Joe offered his hand to help him up but Des slapped it away.

"Excuse you," Joe said.

"Palms are sweaty," Des said.

"Yeah, sure."

"Shut up." And he tried again, this time grabbing on and working his way up.

A telephone spun through the air like a disc and knocked another zombie away. A gunshot took down another.

"Can't hold them off forever, sonny!" came the old guy from above.

"Just do what you can!" Joe shouted. Then, pointing to Billie, "And help her, if you can."

Billie stopped climbing and leaned her head against her palms.

"Keep going!" Des hollered at her from a few feet below.

She just hung there. A moment later, she began climbing again albeit this time much slower.

Joe cocked the hammer of the X-09 and took out another zombie before stuffing the gun away and wiping his palms on his pants. He took hold of the hose and pulled himself up.

Two undead ambled toward the bottom of the hose.

"No, not now," he muttered and tried to reach his gun. His arms were already too rubbery from all the excitement. Holding himself up with one hand while trying to reach his gun with the other would be impossible, and he was already a good ten feet up so dropping wouldn't work lest he wanted to risk twisting his ankle from landing on top of the corpses.

"Hurry! Hurry!" he shouted.

Billie had stopped again.

"I'm outta stuff up here!" the old man shouted.

"Des, give her a push," Joe said.

Des reached up, arm slightly shaking, and tried to give Billie a nudge on her bottom. She was a half foot too high; he couldn't reach her. He climbed up further and just as his fingers touched her sweat pants, the two undead below swung the hose and Des quickly snapped his fingers back and clung to it for dear life.

Billie let go.

She skimmed past Des, her hip bumping into his shoulder, sending her spinning to the left as she fell.

Joe shot out his arm and caught her around her small waist. She let out a choked gulp the second his arm wrapped around her middle. His fingers slipped on the hose and he skidded down a good couple of feet before the friction brought them to a stop.

"I got you," he said, wincing at the searing heat blazing across his palm.

All she could do was nod.

Des peered down over his shoulder at them.

"Keep going," Joe told him.

He grimaced, looked skyward, then continued his ascent.

Already Joe's hand was shaking from having to support not just his but her weight as well. Billie just hung there off his arm like a rag doll. Below, a few of the dead grabbed hold of the hose and swung it side to side. One of them seemed amazed at the hose's movement.

"I'm gonna need your help, Billie," Joe said. He jerked her right up against his body and told her to take hold of the hose. His hand slid down another few inches.

The zombies swung the hose, sending all three to the right. Joe spun and his back and base of his neck slammed into the building. A dull *thwunk* echoed inside his head and the back of his neck throbbed.

"GRAB ON!" he shouted without meaning to.

Billie adjusted herself in his grip then reached up and took hold of the hose.

"I can't . . ." she said.

"Yes, you can. You have to or we're both done for."

A couple stories above them, Des was now halfway over the window, the old timer above reeling him in by the back of his shirt.

"It's okay, Joe." She sniffled back tears. "Really. I'm finished. I can't climb on my own. I'm—"

"Shut up and climb up!"

She shook her head.

"If you let go, I'm letting go, too, but so help me I'll kill you before they do."

Her blue eyes went wide.

"Yeah, not joking," he said, locking eyes with hers. Then, pacing his words very carefully, "Start going up. I'll be right behind you. I'll give you a shove when you need it."

The hose took a swing to the left then snapped taught as one of the zombies below grabbed on and tried climbing up. It took a few tries but the thing quickly caught on and slowly ascended.

"It's either me or that dead guy down there. Your call," Joe said.

Billie looked at the creature below; tears leaked out the corners of her eyes. She took a deep breath then started to move upward.

Good girl, he thought. *Finally.*

He slipped a notch and thought he felt the bottom of his boot skim the top of the zombie's head beneath him. He kicked downward once and hit nothing but air. With his left hand he gave Billie a shove and ignored the pain in his shoulder as he helped push her up.

When he was finally able to grab hold of the hose with both hands, blessed relief washed through his aching muscles. Much easier.

The two climbed.

"Hurry! They're right behind you!" Des shouted.

Before Joe could look, the hose went to the left again but this time not as much thanks to all the weight upon it. Billie shrieked.

"Keep climbing!" Joe told her.

If I could just reach my gun I could—Billie slipped and landed rear first on the top of his head. She must have caught herself because he only slid down another inch or two.

He gave her a hard push where her tailbone met her bottom, renewed his grip on the hose, pulled himself up a little, then gave her a shove again. He kept repeating this till Billie was finally at the top.

"Grab her!" he shouted at Des. The old guy wasn't with him anymore.

Des latched both hands onto her shoulders and heaved her in like a fisherman loading in a day's catch.

Something grabbed Joe's ankle and tugged him down. Both hands slid on the hose. His palms ignited and it wouldn't have surprised him if he saw smoke waft out from under his hands. He kicked wildly at the creature below, slamming his boot into its face, all the while scrambling up the hose as fast as he could.

"Pull me up!" he shouted.

Des just stared at him, Billie at his side, tugging on the sleeve of his shirt, screaming at him to listen.

"What's your problem!" he shouted, not knowing why Des wasn't doing anything.

Again dead fingers curled around his ankle and yanked him down. He let go of the rope and plowed into a dead Asian dude who was on the hose a few stories above street level. The creature's eyebrows drew into a point above its white eyes as it growled at him. Immediately the thing went to bite his neck. Joe jerked to the side and the thing's teeth just missed him. Suddenly he had his back to the wall; the undead freak wasn't letting up and clawed at him.

Joe shot out his fist and caught the creature in the jaw then snapped out another punch to the thing's neck. That only dazed it for a second before it grabbed hold of him. His hand held the hose tight while the other was intertwined with the zombie's. There'd be no way to reach his gun now.

BANG!

Blood and tissue splashed his face as a black hole suddenly appeared in the Asian's forehead. The thing let go and fell on top of its comrades below.

Joe felt a tug on the hose and was jerked upward one foot at a time. Strength sapped from his arms, he maybe managed a few feet on his own till he felt several pairs of hands grabbing him on the shoulders and around the chest. The posh carpeted floor of an office came into view as he tumbled over the window's edge, landing against someone's shoe.

An old man with a scraggly head of gray hair and a gray beard loomed over him, a rifle in his hand. "You owe me one."

20
INTRODUCTIONS

To see people again—real, *living,* breathing people—set August's heart into a gallop, and it wasn't from excitement. Reconnecting with the "real world" after being away from it for so long . . . well, he just didn't know what to expect. The world he left was one where everyone fought for their own place, looked out for themselves and, as he learned over the course of a lifetime, didn't care who or what they had to hurt to get themselves to where they wanted to be. Eleanor often told him he was being too cynical and that if he gave folks a chance, he'd see that despite their flaws most were, deep down, decent people.

"But you forget the human heart," he told her. "Who can know it, right? The things we're capable of . . . . How many times have you thought the path seemed right but then, a short time later, you found out you led yourself astray?"

She was usually silent after that. Deep down, he knew she agreed with him. It was one of the many things they both firmly believed. It was also one of the things that made them appreciate God's Gift all the more.

But that was before all this madness. Before the dead roamed the earth.

August looked around at the faces of the three young people who had come in through the window. The four of them were now crowded into a small maintenance room off one of the hallways in Winnipeg Square. A small candle taken from one of the shops provided the illumination, the room cast in a warm glow that, at any other time in history, would be quite comforting. Now, it reminded August of the possibility of hell to follow should any of these three try anything.

The power had officially gone out not long after he awoke. That meant no running water either.

The guy in the trench coat broke the silence. "How long have you been here?"

August studied the young man's face, more specifically, his eyes. It could have been his imagination but he thought he saw a distant pain somewhere behind the man's green-eyed gaze. "Not long. Since yesterday."

The man nodded.

The young girl with the pink hair folded her arms. Though her eyes were cast to the floor, August knew she was addressing him when she spoke. "Are we safe in here?"

"As safe as can be, my dear, though I don't know for how long."

She glanced up at him quizzically. Should he tell them about the possibility they weren't alone in the Square? That a creature yet unfound lurked about? No, not yet.

"What's your name?" the other young man asked him.

"Yours first," August said.

"Why?"

He flinched inside. He thought it was expected that you answered an elder regardless of the question posed. "You tell me yours and I'll tell you mine. And be truthful. I know kids like to make up names, if it suits them."

The guy smirked and shook his head. "Okay, fine. My name is Des."

"Does Des have a last name?"

Des shook his head again. There was a pause before he spoke. "Nottingham." Des looked as if he were waiting for August to say something.

"Thank you. My name is August. August Norton."

"Joe Bailey," the other young man said.

August nodded in his direction. The three turned their attention to the girl. She unfolded her arms.

"My name's Billie. Billie Friday."

Des, Joe and Billie, August thought. *You sure know how to pick 'em, Lord.* He wasn't quite sure what he meant by that.

Silence reigned in the little room again.

"So what now?" Des asked after a time.

"We can't stay here," August said. "They know we're in here. If they're able to communicate with one another, they'll surely tell their friends that a meal is waiting for them if they're willing to dig a little."

"That's reassuring," Billie said.

"What did you expect, my dear? The promise of absolute safety?"

"What's eating you?" she snapped back.

August sighed. "Nothing. Apologies. It's been awhile since I've spoken to anyone."

"I'm sorry."

You don't have a clue. "Listen, right now we need to come up with an exit strategy, and more specifically, where we're going to go once we're out of here."

"Couldn't we just walk out?" Des asked. "When the coast is clear, I mean."

"If that moment comes, that's a possibility. But first things first. I need you boys to help me board up the windows upstairs. The dead saw us climb in. They could be trying to climb in as well. They could already be inside, for all we know."

"Agreed," Joe said. "When?"

"The sooner the better."

"And we'll use *what* to board them up?"

"There's a lot of office furniture up there. I'm sure we'll find something," August said.

"All right. I also propose we use the buddy system. No one goes anywhere without someone else. Not even to the bathroom."

Billie shifted uncomfortably. "If that's the case, I choose Des as my partner for that."

"Gee, thanks," he said.

"Arms are important," Joe said. To August: "Have anything?"

"Just what you see here." He hefted his rifle. "That and a lot of prayer."

The other three made a face.

"Think what you want," he added. He surveyed the room. "I haven't had a chance to go through everything in here so look around. Find any tools, bring them out. We'll take them upstairs and do what we can. I also want all of us going up there together in case we run into trouble."

29

UPSTAIRS

The four returned to the office upstairs, Joe and August taking the lead because they were the ones with the weapons. Billie followed closely behind them with Des trailing at the end. He clenched the iron pipe between his fingers as they trudged up the multiple flights of stairs to get up to the fifth floor.

I'm getting tired of this, Des thought as he adjusted the small pouch of tools over his shoulder. He'd taken them from the maintenance room. His eyes and head ached from exhaustion. It was well past time to go to bed. Couple that with all that happened . . .

His stomach rumbled and every muscle in his scrawny body seemed to protest this further strain he was putting on them as they climbed. He knew full well he was grouchy, but he still couldn't shake the swell of anger and frustration bubbling within his chest.

Up until now—namely up until Joe showed up—everything had been fine. He was finally getting used to living in an undead world and having to be "always on the run." What's more, he was also getting himself ready to talk to Billie, to *really* talk to her, and tell her how he felt. Des figured the odds of her accepting him were in his favor. There weren't too many other "live folk" around for her to choose from. They were close. Best friends, even. But Joe changed everything. The guy, as much as Des hated to admit it, was a hero. He came out of the dark and saved their lives. He had appointed himself leader of their little band and now that they met August, he seemed to take to that role even more, though Des sensed a bit of unease on August's part. The old guy probably figured that since he had lived nearly three times as long as each of them, he should be the one in charge. The guy had to at least be in his sixties. That and a respect-for-your-elders tradition probably played a strong part in it. With each passing moment, Des felt as if Billie was slipping away, especially because of his behavior as of late.

Keeping cool had never been his strong point. When things got intense, it was fly by the seat of your pants for him. He'd always been one to listen to his heart even when it sometimes landed him in trouble.

August opened the door leading onto the fifth floor and the three others walked past him as he held it open. The old man quickly moved past Des and Billie and rejoined Joe at the front.

"This one here," August said and led them into the office where not long before he had hurled computers and office equipment onto the street.

August drew up his rifle and pointed it into the room before entering, just in case. Des braced himself for a rush of the undead to come pouring out.

"Clear," the old man rasped.

They all went into the room. Des, Joe and Billie stopped in their tracks when August raised a finger, motioning for them to be silent.

The entire floor was quiet, and no sound indicating movement came from the street below.

Des and Joe went to the window and peered out. Below, dead bodies rimmed the lower edge of the building. A few straggling zombies milled about, some stopping to inspect their fallen kin, others just walking aimlessly here and there.

"Not very intelligent, are they?" August said as he came up beside Joe.

"I don't know about that," Joe said. "We've encountered a few who seemed to know what they're doing. And there're some out there who are fast, too."

"Different breeds?" Des asked.

"Maybe," Joe said. "Or maybe it just takes time for them to learn from one another or, even, for them to come to conclusions on their own in regards to what they're capable of. Let's face it: those are shells of human beings down there. Brain dead, for the most part. That is, smart enough to know what they have to do to survive but not so smart as to go about it in the best way. Thankfully, that works to our advantage. They have the IQ of *maybe* a one-year-old, if that."

"I think it's instinct," August said. "Think about it: what's their goal? To eat. Why does anyone eat? To survive. Why does anyone fight? To defend themselves or to survive, right?"

"But why us?" Billie asked. "Why eat us? Makes no sense."

"I'm sure there's an explanation for it," August said.

"Do you know what it is?"

"No."

"There's probably no way to find out either." She slouched her shoulders and walked to the wall on the other side of the room.

"What if there's more to it than that?" Des said. "I mean, think about it. Look back to a year ago when this all began. The rain came. People turned into, well, zombies. But some people didn't. *We* didn't. If this was just some freak thing, wouldn't all of us be like them?"

August glanced at Joe. "The boy raises a good point."

Des smiled. "The question, of course, is how do we know?"

August let go a deep breath. "Like all things, answers reveal themselves in time. If we're looking for them, of course."

Billie turned away from the wall. "How did you get here?"

"Me?" August said.

"You're the only one we don't know."

Des thought he saw hesitancy in the old man's eyes, as if he didn't want to give an answer.

"I, uh—I walked. Drove. I'm from here but had gone out of town with . . . with my family."

"Where are they?" Des asked then Joe shot him a look that said he shouldn't have asked that question.

August cast his gaze to the ground. When he spoke, his voice was just above a whisper. "Not here."

The hurt in the old man's voice was real and Des suddenly felt ashamed about his own selfishness and the sense that Billie was being taken from him. "I'm sorry," he said.

"Me, too," August replied.

"Will you be all right?" Joe asked the old man.

August put a hand on Joe's shoulder and gave it a squeeze. "I'll be fine. Got some things to work through, but don't we all, right? There's more, but I'll talk about it if and when the conversation allows."

"I say we make a pledge," Billie said.

"Pledge?" Des asked.

"Yeah. We need to stick together. Us four. Maybe more, should we come across anybody." She looked at Des intently. "I know we don't know each other all too well, but that's fine. This isn't about that. Not right now. Look at . . . look at what we've been able to manage when we worked together, when we backed each other up. We'd be dead otherwise. Maybe even like *them*."

August nodded. Joe did the same.

So I guess there's no going back to the way things were, Des thought. He supposed it was for the best. Wait, what was he talking about? Of course it was for the best. He just had a hard time accepting it, was all. But this wasn't about him. Wasn't about Joe or August or even Billie. It was about trying to get things back on track, about, possibly, even reclaiming a dead world from those who owned the keys of death.

A low groan came from the street below and all four turned their attention toward the window. About seven or eight blocks from the building, a long procession of the undead were making their way toward it.

"They know we're here," August said. "Quick, let's close this window up. They can't come in."

Billie felt out of place as the men worked. Her main job was to simply hand them tools when they called for them. It was all she could do. She wasn't that strong so she couldn't lift and turn table tops once they had been detached from their legs. She couldn't hold the heavy tops up against the wall as August worked to fasten them into place. Her arms were still fatigued from having to climb the fire hose. But it made her smile inside when August looked her way now and then and gave her a warm grin, when those old eyes bore a little twinkle as he tried to make her feel included. And for a moment, she was able to forget about the blood, the undead, the nearly dying.

Able to forget about her family.

She had a new family now, one that had shown it was willing to give anything and everything to ensure she was taken care of and that she was safe.

It took over an hour before the table tops were secured across the window frames, the men working as fast as they could. The undead they had seen advancing toward the building were down there somewhere, probably right up against the outside wall, searching for a way in. Every so often she could hear their mutterings and groaning below, their hollow banging on the glass lining the lower level.

"We're okay, right?" she asked August.

"Hm? Yes. For now. But there's strength in numbers and those things are multiplying. We can't stay here. We need to get out. There's also—" The old man cut himself off.

"There's also?" Des prompted.

"Let's finish this up then go back downstairs."

The men quickly finished blocking the large window and examined their work as Billie put the tools away. She slung the pouch over her shoulder and waited for them by the door.

Her heart jumped when a low *badoom* banged somewhere at the end of the hallway.

"Guys?" she said.

Joe looked back at her from the window. "Yeah?"

Badoom.

Joe's face hardened. He had heard the sound, too. He quickly snapped out his gun and walked briskly to the door.

"Out there," Billie said, pointing down the hallway.

Badoom.

"August, rifle. Let's go," Joe said.

August brought the rifle forward and marched toward him, grimacing.

"What about me?" Des asked.

"Stay here with Billie. Holler if you see anything."

Badoom.

"Ready?" Joe asked the old man.

August nodded.

The two went off toward the stairwell at the end of the hallway.

"There's something I have to tell you . . ." August said to Joe as they walked away. Whatever else he said Billie couldn't make out, but she didn't need August to finish his sentence to know what was up. Joe's momentary stopping in his tracks told her everything.

There was a zombie in the building.

Badoom.

30
WHEN BAD THINGS HAPPEN TO GOOD PEOPLE

The front two legs of the wooden chair slammed back down, jolting August out of sleep. After getting his bearings and making sure the chair he sat upon was firm on the floor, he frowned for having dozed off.

The maintenance room was quiet, Joe curled up against the far wall, trench coat still on, its collar bunched up around his neck as a makeshift pillow. Des lay sprawled out on the floor to the side of him, snoring.

The small candle on the workbench was burned down near to nothing and would soon need replacing.

Billie wasn't there.

You should have been watching, August thought. The plan was to take turns keeping an eye out. He had volunteered to go first in spite of how tired he was. That, and he still didn't completely trust his new comrades. To just hand over his rifle and say, "Shoot anything that moves and is not alive," well, might as well just give your life over to a stranger and hope for the best.

Should he go look for her? Earlier, when he and Joe had gone after the zombie that was lurking in the building, they came up empty handed, even after an hour of searching. Wherever the thing was, it was still out there. How it evaded them so easily, especially given how slow the dead were, he didn't know.

Billie couldn't have been gone that long. She was still there, lying near the door, when August last surveyed the room before falling asleep. It certainly didn't feel like he had passed out for long, maybe five or ten minutes. Twenty tops.

She probably just went to the bathroom. He stood. *But we're on the buddy system. She should know better. Besides, she and the others had already gone to clean up. I kept watch for them.*

It had, however, been difficult for the others to clean up and use the facilities now that the plumbing no longer worked.

He double checked the room just in case she had decided to switch corners or sleep under the workbench.

Nothing. She was gone. The door to the room was unlocked.

No sound came from the hallway beyond.

"Going to go check," he told himself and moved toward Joe so he could wake him and tell him what was up.

Just as he was about to give Joe a shake on the shoulder, the maintenance door screeched open. August spun around, rifle aimed at the human-shaped shadow at the door.

"It's me," Billie said, her voice quiet.

He lowered the weapon.

She came in, turned to close the door behind her and locked it, then, hands dropped down at her sides, slowly slumped down against the wall adjacent to the door. She didn't look at him, but instead kept her gaze toward the door. In the faint light, her eyes glistened amidst red cheeks and puffy skin.

She had been crying.

August returned to his chair and eased himself down. Planting the butt of the rifle against the floor, he leaned against it like a walking stick.

He didn't say anything. Neither did she.

The minutes ticked by.

"I didn't want to wake anybody," she said softly.

"It's okay. I'm sorry for falling asleep," he said as gently as he could. It'd been a long time since he had to comfort someone so young. The last had been his son over some trouble he'd been having early on in his marriage. "But next time wake me up, okay? Or Des or Joe."

She nodded and turned further away so she could wipe her eyes.

"Want to tell me what's wrong?" he asked.

Billie sniffled and wiped a lock of pink hair away from her eyes. When she spoke, her voice cracked. "I just . . . I just miss my family. That's all. I spent a lot of time trying not to think about it, but it comes back, y'know? I wanted to . . . . I thought I could be strong, but after today . . ."

He waited for her to finish but the words never came.

An aching warmth filled August's heart, catching him off guard. For so long now he had tried to suppress what had happened with his own family, tried to hide the pain, but now . . . now he had found someone else who understood what he was going through and someone whom he could understand in return.

"Do you want to share what happened to them?" August asked, hoping he wasn't pushing to hard.

At first it didn't look as if Billie was going to reply, but after wiping her eyes again, she told him what happened the day the rain came. Told him how she killed her sister Audrey. Told him that even though she and her folks never got along, she'd give anything to see them again.

To have a normal life again.

"I'm sorry to hear that," August said. "My family was taken, too."

"Really?"

He nodded. "The rain came and so my family and I went out of town once we saw what it did to everyone. We thought we escaped it but one night my son went outside and never returned. It wasn't long before someone went looking for him, then another, then another. When they came back, they were changed. Transformed. In the end I had no choice but to . . ."

Billie's eyes grew wide.

Tears stole August's breath and getting the next words out took all he had. "I couldn't . . . couldn't let them go on like that."

"You killed them," Billie said then shot her palm over her mouth in a futile effort to catch the words before they had escaped.

August sighed, picked up the rifle, laid it over his lap and sat back in the chair. He couldn't even bring himself to nod let alone answer her directly. "I just thought that, when all was said and done, God'd save us. But instead He didn't. Or at least didn't save them."

She furrowed her brow. "You know . . . I'd never been one for believing in God. I was raised with it but that's as far as it went." She wiped her eyes again. "I just don't see how a loving God could allow this to happen. If He exists, I mean."

"Well, I know He exists," August said. "I'm sure of that. But as to what's going on, I just don't know. The world wasn't supposed to end this way."

"No?"

"No. Other things were supposed to happen. Maybe they still will and this is just a bump in the road?"

"So the, what, Bible doesn't talk about this? About zombies?"

August couldn't help himself but smile. "No. Not about zombies and you'd think something as important as this would show up in its pages. This is a pretty big deal."

"Pretty big?"

"Okay. A very big deal. You know what I mean." He felt the fatigue setting on again so he shook his head to wake himself up. "I spent some time thinking as I drove here then walked to Portage and Main. I tried to figure this all out. I thought that maybe I'd remember some verse or scripture that would give a clue as to what was going on and how I could survive it."

She grinned. "I'll play along. Think of anything?"

"Just one thing, well, two, actually: trusting God and just accepting that I'm not going to figure this out."

"See, that's no good. That's a big problem with you people." She snapped her mouth shut. "Sorry. I meant you Bible guys. If you don't mind me saying so, all you guys talk about is faith and trust and whatever, and expect the rest of us thinking people to just accept that."

"Billie . . ."

"Not good enough, August." She stood. "People are dying. You three guys are the only living people I've seen in ages. There are others out there, but how many, I don't know. You can't tell me that some loving God is in control of all this. It makes no sense that He'd allow this to happen. Let so many people die."

"So you're going to play that card, eh? Fine. I'll play one of my own. One time Jesus saw a man who had been blind from birth. His disciples asked Him who sinned to make the guy born blind, the blind man or the blind man's parents? Jesus said neither the man nor his parents did, but that God allowed it so that, later on in the man's life, the work of God might be revealed. Same deal, Billie, for you and me. For Joe, for Des. What has happened is being allowed so that, later, God can show Himself. Bad things happen to good people, Billie. That's just how it is. Tragedy can be turned to God's glory, if we let it." August perked up at that old fire rekindling within. It'd been a long time since that flame brewed. "It can turn around, if we're willing to seek God on the matter. I'm just as upset as you. All I know is that we're gonna have to ride this out. Your call."

"Sorry, August, but that's not good enough."

"Are you sure?"

31
OUT OF OPTIONS

The incessant banging coming from upstairs forbade anyone from further sleep. Des had jumped from the floor with a shout, only to be met with an "It's okay, it's okay," from August.

Joe sat up, blinked some of the drowsiness from his eyes, then looked to Billie in the corner of the small room. Her eyes met his, concern written all over them. For a moment, the low, distant drumming of activity faded and Joe wished he could offer her some words of comfort.

He had heard her and August's entire conversation, but hadn't let on he was awake for fear of launching into his own story about April, Dan and losing everything he loved. He'd been making an effort to just set it aside, put it away for the time being so he could be of better service to his new friends.

Boomboomboomboomboomboom. The bangs were muffled yet loud enough and firm enough to assure that the creatures making them meant business.

August stood and cocked his ear toward the ceiling. "Probably coming from the Richardson building. The windows that line the back are boarded up; the glass in front is coated in blood. You can't see a thing to the outside." He put his hands on his hips and clucked his tongue a few times. "They want to come in. They've been throwing bodies against the building."

"How much time do we have?" Des asked.

"I don't know," August said. "They haven't gotten in yet. Either they're too stupid to figure it out or someone who knows what they're doing hasn't yet come along. Either way, I don't want to be around when they do."

Joe drew closer to the old man. Des did the same.

August carefully eyed each of them. "If they come in and we're still here, we'll be trapped. They'll siphon in through the Richardson and fill the Square in no time. All other exits are either boarded up or blocked. I checked the Fort Street exit earlier. That I blocked with desks. They're standing there outside it, as if waiting for us to come out. Unless that's changed, there's no way out. There's probably hundreds outside. Maybe more."

"Thousands," Billie said softly.

"And then there's still that window we closed up upstairs," Joe said. "It wouldn't surprise me if they figure out how to get in. They don't even need to climb to the fifth floor. They just need to know about it and resolve to get inside."

"We have to leave," August said. "Now."

"I'm all for that," Billie said.

"Me, too," Des said.

"Where?" Joe asked.

"Out of town," August said. "There's nothing left here anymore."

"To another city?" Des asked.

August tapped the butt of his rifle against the toe of his right foot. "Maybe. There are probably others there. Finding them is another issue altogether. More than likely whoever is still alive is holed up in some makeshift bunker either waiting to die or making some futile effort to wait till this blows over."

"That ain't happening," Billie said.

"It might," August said though Joe detected a hint of doubt in the old man's words. He assumed that whatever trust August had in God might be wavering.

"You said you drove in," Joe told August.

"Yeah, but like I also said, I walked from the TransCanada Highway straight down to here. And it's gridlock, anyway. Traffic is a mess. Unless we find four motorcycles, we can't get around the cars. Anyone here even know how to drive one?"

They all shook their heads.

"Bikes?" Des said. "I mean, regular bikes. The ones you pedal?"

"Hey, if you could find them, you might have a chance. But that's a pretty big 'might.'" August finally stopped tapping the rifle against his shoe.

Des huffed and Joe knew it was because the idea was shot down. Des meant well. He just didn't think before he spoke, more often than not.

Don't be so hard on him, Joe thought. *He's just trying to help.*

"So, what, we're gonna walk out of the city, dodging zombies and hiding in the shadows?" Billie asked.

"Yeah, we'll get killed if we do that," Des said.

Billie shot Des a hot look.

"Was just trying to help."

"I know but like August said, there's probably hundreds right outside the building. Come to think of it, there could be way more than that. We're just focusing on outside the Richardson building never mind the rest of the buildings that connect to the Square. The whole underground structure could be surrounded."

Smart thinking, Des, Joe thought. If there was any one thing he had learned over the past year being a zombie hunter, it was planning for the worst.

The low drumming from above grew louder. The creatures outside were getting antsy.

"We need options, people," Joe said. "August, you know this place best. You were here before us. You saw what things looked like coming into town."

"But it was pretty much a ghost town when I first entered."

"But that's changed. That racket upstairs says it has. Even when we got here things were getting pretty hairy. Wait." He couldn't believe he had forgotten about it. He attributed his forgetfulness to lack of sleep. "There's still also that creature in the building."

"I was about to say that," Billie said.

"Why didn't you mention it?" Joe asked August. "The other one in the building, when we first got here? Why didn't you tell them and only me?"

"I didn't want to scare them."

Joe stepped right up to him. "You think you *could* scare them? Remember what they went through getting into this place? You have no idea all that happened even just getting downtown never mind all the stuff's that gone down in the past year in each of our lives."

"Yeah!" Des said. "Wait. So there's a zombie in the building?"

"So what would you have done, had I told them?" August snapped at Joe. "Lead an army of two young adults on a mad search for the undead? How do you know there's just one?"

He had him there. So far they'd been operating under the idea that only a solitary zombie was roaming the Square, sticking to the shadows. There could very well be a couple working together, perhaps ones not as slow to think as their comrades outside.

"Just because you carry that gun of yours, Joe, it doesn't make you unstoppable. And they're without firearms." August pointed at Des and Billie.

You just don't get it, do you, old man? Joe thought. But August did have a point. It was easy to think of himself as a one-man army, some hero with a gun. However, if one thing had been proven since he hooked up with Des and Billie, it was that he needed help, too, just like everyone else. "When was the last you heard him? Them?"

"Same as you. When we were upstairs."

"Nothing since?" Billie asked.

"No."

The beat from upstairs was joined by another, one seeming to come from somewhere much closer.

"They've made their move," August said.

"Then let's go!" Des said.

Joe turned away and counted on his fingers: "No cars. No bikes. No motorcycles. No walking." He spun around and held out his arms. "What're we supposed to do? Fly?"

August grinned.

32
LOCK AND LOAD

Joe turned to Billie. "Ready?"

She nodded. "Yeah. I think so."

"This is it."

"I know."

His green eyes softened and his gaze penetrated her. For the first time in a long while, his gruff exterior melted and it seemed she caught a glimpse of the man he once was, the one who knew how to love, how to appreciate the little things. Then his eyes changed and the warrior came forth. He cocked his gun, brought it shoulder height, barrel up, and told the others, "Let's roll."

Billie hefted the nail gun they had found sitting on the top shelf above the workbench in the maintenance room. *It's now or never,* she thought and double checked her pockets for the four long packets of nails she carried, two in the front, two in the back.

The four of them lined up in front of the maintenance room door in the predetermined order: August first, to lead the way, she second, then Des, then Joe, bringing up the rear.

"We head straight to the roof. No stops. As discussed, we encounter any trouble, we stick together. Should we get separated, try to stay in pairs, if possible. Get on your own, keep an eye out for someone and scream for help. We're all in this together," August said. He jiggled a box of .22s. The bullets rattled against the cardboard. He stuffed it in his pocket.

"You said this place is empty, right, except for the one on the loose?" Des asked.

"So far as I know."

Des bit his lower lip. "What about the rats?"

"What?"

"Big buildings always have rats and I'm sure since the rain hit and everyone left, they've multiplied. They're changed now, too, you know."

"Changed?"

"Into them," Billie said. "We had a run in at Des's place before we left."

August faced forward. "Then they go, too." He unlocked the door. "Okay, folks, say your prayers and let's go." The old man allowed a moment of silence. His lips moved but Billie couldn't hear what he was saying.

"Want to—" *Want to say that out loud,* Billie was going to say but before she could, August opened the door and led them out.

Joe closed the door behind them as they entered the hallway and remained facing the rear, gun at the ready, walking backwards as the other three kept their ears opened and eyes peeled for anything that might be lurking in the dark.

August had found a new flashlight, but promised to only turn it on once they reached the stairwell. He didn't want its beam to tip off anything that might be looking on.

The low thumping of the undead beating against the windows upstairs hadn't abated. It made it difficult for Billie to hear anything else, even their own footfalls on the tiled floor.

Her heart beat quickly and her breathing became shallow. She alternated between wrapping her index finger around the nail gun's handle and its trigger just to keep her mind occupied and hands busy.

As they walked, she searched the shadows for any indication of movement. Before they left, August said they may or may not hear the zombie on the loose in the building. If any of them saw anything, the plan was to say, "Dead man walking," and simply shoot it down. The purpose of speaking first was to warn the others that a shot was about to be fired and not to unnecessarily startle anybody. Billie wondered if she'd remember to even say those three words let alone hammer down on the trigger. She could easily see herself locking up. Despite having survived so much thus far, she wasn't entirely sure she'd live much longer. Maybe another few days. Maybe a few weeks. Anything further than that didn't seem all that feasible.

The four hit the stairwell and went in.

August flicked on the flashlight. Its lens had been wrapped in an old thin rag, something to mute the beam so it wasn't so bright. He didn't want to prematurely alert anything that might be hiding on the steps.

By the time they reached the ninth floor, Des muttered, "Can't see why we couldn't take the elevator."

"The power's out, remember," Joe whispered.

"No kidding. I can barely see."

190

"Me neither," Billie said.

"Quiet!" August snapped.

The low light shining through the gray rag cast the stairwell in a foggy glow, one that faded into nothing by the time it got to Joe.

Billie wondered how Joe could even see anything. She also admired him for being willing to cover their backs. She didn't know how good his night vision was but hoped it was good enough to help them out should it come to it.

The higher they climbed, the quieter the beating of dead hands against glass became.

As silence slowly settled in, Billie's own heartbeat burst into her ears.

I could die today. How is that different from any other day? Because, we're in a confined space and I'm with two guys with guns. Anything could go wrong.

Though she was skeptical about August's earlier assertion about God's reality, a part of her wished he had prayed that prayer so the rest of them could hear it even if it was only for the sake of comfort and nothing more.

They climbed on.

She considered saying a quick prayer of her own but didn't know how to start. Was she supposed to say it out loud or did God read minds? Could she just think it?

"If You're up there," she whispered. "Keep us safe." It was all she could think of to say.

"Hm?" Des said from behind.

"Nothing," she whispered. She looked up at the back of August's head to see if the old man would give any indication he had heard her. Nothing said that he did. He just trudged up the stairs, rifle gripped tightly with both hands, the hand holding the barrel also holding the flashlight against it.

A low moan came from one of the floors above.

Des lost his footing on one of the steps the moment his ears picked up the noise. Joe backed into him and nearly stumbled himself.

"Watch it," Joe whispered.

"Sorry," Des said.

Billie cocked her head over her shoulder. "You okay?"

"Yeah, fine. Keep going."

"Keep sharp," August said after another low moan came.

The sound of the undead trying to get in from the outside ceased. Whether it was Des and the others' distance from them or if they had finally given up, he didn't know. But he was relieved. It would be brutal if they got caught in this stairwell as a legion of the dead started swarming up.

"Mmmrrrggrrooaann."

It came from one floor up.

"How much further, August?" Des asked.

"Nearly there." The old man adjusted the rag and shone the flashlight up in between the railings. "Four floors, it looks like. Maybe another."

"Good." Des swallowed the dry skin that had formed at the back his throat. He should have had some water before they left.

If they played their cards right, they could just walk on past the floor with the zombie, hit the roof and, like August made them believe, get out of here.

"Hhrrrmmmggrrnn."

"Shhhhhh," August whispered and adjusted the rag over the light again.

All were careful to be gentle with their steps as they began climbing past the twenty-ninth floor.

Des held his breath and got his iron pipe ready. *I didn't come this far to get mangled*, he thought.

They passed the twenty-ninth floor. The zombie groaned again. It seemed to come from just on the other side of the door.

BRDOOM! The low, metallic sound echoed throughout the stairwell.

"Faster," Joe said.

August picked up his pace and Des picked up his the second Billie started to jog up the stairs.

BRDOOM!

The light squeak of a handle turning sent Des's heart racing. They were already two flights past the twenty-ninth floor when he heard the door open.

Footsteps, low, heavy ones.

The thing was inside the stairwell.

A loud bang echoed from far below and drifted up. So did more footsteps.

Lots more.

33

ZOMBIES!

It didn't take long for the foul stench of the dead to waft all the way up to the stairs next to the rooftop entrance. As much as he thought he would have been used to it by now, Joe still had to cover his nose and mouth to keep from gagging. The others did the same, Des going so far as to tuck his nose and mouth inside the front collar of his shirt like Bazooka Joe.

Joe glanced at the pile of office furniture in front of the door. "I'm assuming you did this," he said to August.

"Had to. I got the door open but the roof is cluttered with hordes of those things."

"Why did you wait till now to tell us?"

August gazed at the door. "You'll have to forgive me, but I thought that if I told you, you wouldn't come up here with me and we'd risk our only means of escape."

"Well, that's just great!" Billie snapped, slapping her hands on her sides. "You drag us up here, promising us a way out and then forget to tell us a tiny little detail like there's an army of zombies on the roof? This is also coming from the same guy who thought *not* telling Des and I there was a zombie somewhere in the building was a good idea?" She peered over the railing. "We should toss you to them right now and get out of here on our own."

"You're welcome to try," August said. She moved toward him, about to grab him. "But if you do, I can guarantee you won't leave this place alive."

"And walking into a crowd of zombies will ensure that we do?" Des asked.

A low and guttural groan shook the four to their cores and Joe got the X-09 ready. He kissed the barrel and silently counted to three.

The heavy footfalls of the creature who had evaded them for so long were drawing nearer. Any second now Joe'd be able to see its undead form coming up the stairs. "We haven't much time."

"Then first things first," August said. "Des, gimme a hand. Billie, come up beside me. Joe, you too."

Joe stepped backward up the stairs until all four were crowded together next to the barricade of office equipment.

"It knows we're here so no sense in keeping quiet," August said and lifted one of the chairs he had placed there and handed it to Joe. "Toss 'er down."

Joe took the heavy chair and dumped it over the railing. The legs broke when they smashed against the edge of a stair two flights below. August handed him another and Joe threw that one over as well, aiming for just in front of the broken one. This one broke, too, its seat ripped from its back, landing partly in front and partly on the chair already down there, creating a path that would be very difficult to climb over even for a live person never mind one that was already dead and had stumbling feet.

"Filing cabinets next," August said and had to put his rifle and flashlight down on the desk in front of the door so he could waddle the heavy cabinet across the floor. "Billie, stay back." She pressed herself up against the wall.

The footfalls of the zombie were getting closer as were the countless others coming from the floors below.

"Up and over?" Des asked.

"On three," August said, and the three men grabbed hold of the paper-filled cabinet.

Joe couldn't get a good grip with the X-09 still in his hand so he holstered it before grabbing on again.

"One," August said.

Joe got down near the bottom and prepared to lift.

"Two."

He ensured his feet were planted and prepared his arms and legs for one big heave of exertion.

"Three."

The boys hoisted the cabinet up onto the railing. It teetered against the metal for a moment before Joe finished pressing his feet into the floor and pushed the thing over the edge. The cabinet sped down onto the stairs and landed with a thunderous *BOOM*. The drawers flew open and thousands of sheets of paper spilled out, creating an absolute mess on the stairway.

"Again," August said.

The three repeated the procedure and dumped the remaining cabinet over the edge. It crashed in front of the other, filling the stairs with broken and dented metal drawers and a host of paper.

Cloom, cloom, dradoom. The rooftop door banged against the desk in front of it and opened an inch. Gray, scaly fingers with cracked fingernails poked through and the growls of the undead filled the top of the stairwell.

Joe ran at the desk and rammed it against the door, slamming it shut, sending a spray of fingers and black blood onto the desk's top.

"Grrrrrrnnnn." The voice was deep and raspy.

August shone the flashlight over the railing.

Joe peered over it and felt his mouth drop at the sight of an undead man. This one wasn't like the others and he didn't need to be right up close to him to see that. This creature was different. Its shoulders were wide and well-muscled, with arms as long as pool cues. The thing had to duck as it poked its head out from underneath the floor above it. The creature wore a torn yellowed collar shirt and ripped brown dress pants, his entire outfit laced with crusty dried blood, ligaments and entrails.

Joe scrambled for the X-09 as the zombie began to step its long, thick legs over the chairs at the bottom of the steps.

Gun drawn, Joe lined up his shot and aimed it at the top of the dead man's balding head. As if sensing the bullet about to be fired into its skull, the enormous zombie clamped a set of meaty fingers onto one of the broken chairs and hurled it up toward Joe. The edge of the seat caught Joe in the wrist, sending a shockwave of pain through his forearm. The X-09 went off and punctured a hole in the ceiling. Billie and Des let out a yelp.

August shoved himself beside Joe and pointed his rifle downward. No sooner was the barrel of the rifle in position did a large, gray hand grab hold of it and pull, yanking the rifle from August's fingers.

"No!" the old man shouted.

The rooftop door broke open again, slamming into the desk with a loud bang. Des shoved the desk against the door, closing it.

The massive zombie continued its climb, stepping over the smashed filing cabinets like a normal person would negotiate climbing a rocky hill.

It was at the base of the stairs in no time.

Joe cocked the hammer, ready to take this thing down, but a long leg ending in a size-fourteen shoe plowed him in the chest, sending him onto his back. Ribs aching, his lower back wracked with pain from slamming into the sharp edge of a stair, he couldn't get up. Billie was behind him almost immediately, her hands under his armpits, trying to help him to his feet.

At the top of the stairs, the rooftop door opened again, this time more than an inch.

"Des! The door!" she screamed.

Des pushed the desk into the door. The door moved a little, but not much. Too many bodies were on the other side, trying to force their way in.

"It's stuck!" he yelled.

August shoved past him and told him to help him push against the desk. They did. The door closed.

Billie helped Joe to his feet. Joe snapped his legs back just as the giant zombie tried to grab him. Its haunting white gaze stole his breath. He'd never seen someone so huge in his entire life. Judging by its oversized cheekbones and forehead, the thing must have suffered from gigantism in its former life.

The door opened again and August and Des pressed against it.

"They're coming through!" August said. "We can't hold it."

"This was a bad idea," Billie said and joined the two men at the top of the stairs, helping them keep the zombies on the roof at bay.

What was Billie thinking? She had just left Joe to defend himself against this massive, walking robot of death.

He brought up the X-09, aimed and just as his finger squeezed the trigger, a huge hand swatted at the gun. The shot went off and tagged the zombie in the shoulder. It didn't even flinch.

Suddenly, low growls and groans filled the stairwell and Joe didn't need to look over the railing to know that the mass of the undead from below had finally ascended almost to the top floor. The zombies were getting faster. The rolling over of broken chairs and repositioning of metal filing cabinets echoed throughout the stairwell, the sound so loud he could barely hear himself think.

They had to get onto the roof. Up and over the desk and . . .

"Joe!" August shouted.

A pair of large fingers wrapped themselves around Joe's throat, picked him up off his feet. Before he could cock the hammer on the X-09, he was already flying backward through the air. His body crashed into the drywall at the top of the stairs, just next to where Des, Billie and August pressed against the desk to keep the door closed. The back of his head hit the wall with a resounding smack and a bizarre black flash scattered across his vision. He didn't even feel himself hit the floor. Head spinning, the stairwell he was in feeling like a world that was a million miles away, he tried to get to his feet. His legs wouldn't move.

Through blurry vision, he watched as the massive zombie stepped up the stairs and reached for him.

Two shots fired and a pair of nails appeared beneath the dead man's eyes, embedded in the bruised flesh of his cheekbones.

Billie.

He wanted to say thank you, wanted to wrap his arms around her and thank her for saving his life, but all went dark.

Joe's head drooped to the side and Des thought the trench coat-wearing gunslinger was dead.

The giant zombie on the stairs stumbled back a step and reached for the nails protruding from under its eyes.

"Shoot it again!" he shouted.

Hands shaky, Billie raised the nail gun and Des hoped against hope she was aiming between the creature's eyes.

"Des, I can't hold it," August said, now sitting with his back up against the desk, his feet digging into the floor.

A sudden push from behind sent him and August skidding forward. Des pushed back with a grunt, hoping the effort was enough to slide the desk into the door and close it. The sound of dead fingers and hands slapping against the wall behind them said otherwise.

The giant zombie stomped up the steps just as a half dozen more appeared behind him.

"Joe, wake up!" Des screamed.

Billie fired the nail gun and a nail appeared in the giant zombie's forehead. It just wasn't deep enough to take it down. She quickly turned and got on top of Joe, slapping him in the face and chest, trying to rouse him.

The dead man grabbed Billie around the waist and yanked her off, bringing her to himself.

She shrieked.

No . . . Des thought. "Billie!" He got to his feet and the desk skidded along the tiled floor. He didn't care. This thing couldn't have her. No how and no way.

The zombie opened its mouth wide, about to take a chunk out of Billie's neck.

Rage consuming him, Des dove off the top stair and swung the iron pipe into the zombie's jaw, snapping its head and neck to the side. The thing dropped Billie and she hit the floor with a thud.

August, now on his feet, pulled her up.

"Joe!" the old man shouted.

The desk slid further across the floor and hit Joe in the leg. The door was open a good foot and the undead began to come through.

Others piled up the stairs.

Billie had the X-09 and for a second Des thought she was going to shoot Joe. Instead, the drywall beside his head exploded, the sudden bang causing him to open his eyes.

"Let's go!" she screamed and pulled on him to get him up.

August helped her.

Big arms pulled at Des and forced him down the stairs.

Time slowed and the weight of the heavy iron pipe in Des's hand made him realize what it was he had to do.

At the top of the stairs, August pulled on the desk and helped Joe and Billie get on top of it. A handful of the dead began to come through. August punched one and kicked another. Billie shot one with the nail gun and handed the X-09 back to Joe, who took down the rest.

Strong arms squeezed against Des's chest and his lungs began to close. A rib popped. It was on the same side he had injured before.

August's eyes bore into him. The old man knew something but Des didn't know what.

Billie turned and tears filled her eyes when she saw him. She ran toward him but Des kicked her away.

"Run . . ." he rasped. "Go. Please." He wrestled against the zombie and stomp-kicked backward against the thing's legs.

It tumbled back just as it reached out to grab Billie by her shirt. Its fingers missed and as Des went flying back down the stairs and he and the giant undead landed against a dozen more, he mouthed to her three words: "I love you."

198

34
THE ROOF

"No! Des!" Billie screamed, her voice thick with tears.

Joe grabbed her from behind and tossed her onto the desk. August grabbed her by the shoulders and shoved her out the rooftop door. He followed behind. Joe jumped onto the desk, slid and fell onto the other side. When he hit the ground the X-09 went off, the bullet taking down the nearest zombie.

Billie didn't know what happened. Through teary-eyed vision, the scene changed from being just inside the stairwell to part way down the expanse of the roof, the rooftop door still open, Joe now on his feet and running out. Joe kicked the door closed and socked a zombie in the face.

Her world crashing down, she shrieked and screamed, her voice choked by her own tears.

Des was gone.

"Keep moving," August said, giving her another shove. "You have to."

Screaming, she cursed at him and slapped the old man then kicked him in the gut. August stumbled back a couple of steps; Joe ran up to them.

"No! Billie, stop!" He held her back as she was about to pummel the old man again for taking away her friend.

Her best friend.

Joe took her face in his hands. "Billie, look at me. Look at me!"

Crying, she tried to focus but all she could hear were her own screams.

"Get it together," Joe said.

"Joe!" August yelled, running, waving them along.

Joe spun and took out a couple of zombies edging closer to them.

Billie surveyed the rooftop. Against a backdrop of hazy, gray clouds, over twenty undead began moving toward them.

And there was something else up there with them. Something that took a moment to register as to what it was: a helicopter.

"You got to be kidding me," Joe said as he pulled Billie along to meet up with August.

The helicopter sat just on the other side of a walking wall of corpses, black and unmoving, one of its skis propped up against a series of vents on the roof.

August eyed the flying machine coolly then nodded toward it. "Let's go."

Joe pegged off a couple of the undead moving toward them and cocked the hammer again. Billie followed his example and shot a nail into the face of one and another into a different zombie's shoulder. She grimaced at having missed the head.

"Sorry," she said.

The old man shoved his way through the deceased, paying no mind to the chance that one might grab him and take him down.

"Keep running," Joe said.

Billie glanced back toward the door.

"There's nothing you can do for him," Joe told her. "Des is gone."

"Stop it! Don't say that!"

He stopped her, looked her square in the eye and said, "I'm saying it."

Tears leaked from the corners of her eyes anew and she slapped him one good on his right cheek. The hot zing from her swat made Joe's skin sting. He may have deserved it, he may have not. Either way, Billie needed to wait till she grieved over Des.

All of them did.

The undead formed a semicircle and drew in closer, the circle getting smaller and smaller until Joe and Billie were on its inside, August on the other, running for the helicopter.

Dead hands pawed at them. One grabbed Joe by the shoulder. He shoved it off, delivered a swift hook to the side of the zombie's head, then kicked at another before firing off a clean shot to the face of one straight ahead of him. The dead man dropped and blood pooled around Joe's boots.

Billie yelped as a pair of hands tugged her back and to the side. A couple zombies had grabbed her in a bear hug, her arms pinned to her body, forbidding her from raising the nail gun and taking them out.

Joe spun on his heels and blasted one of the zombies that held her. He cocked the hammer and took out the other. Arms free, Billie ran ahead and got some distance before turning and firing off nail after nail in quick succession. Joe had to dive to the side to get out of the way of the spray of spikes.

She's running off pure adrenaline now. All emotion. Unwise. He got to his feet and headed for the chopper. "Billie, come on!"

She turned, clocked a zombie in the face with the butt of the nail gun, then ran toward the black helicopter.

Joe stopped, fired off a few more shots, then followed her, bringing up the rear.

The rooftop door blew open and that giant zombie filled the doorframe. It eyed the scene with a dead, white-eyed stare, its blood-caked lips grimacing.

It ran after them.

Joe's heart went into a beating frenzy. He'd never seen one of these zombies run before. And this thing wasn't just running. It was moving at an all-out sprint. The creature bowled through his comrades as if they weren't even there. Behind the enormous dead man, a plethora of the undead poured out of the rooftop door, quickly coating the roof in a throng of moving, deceased flesh.

Joe turned toward the helicopter and gave it all he had, running with all-out abandon.

The propellers fired up; slowly at first, but soon they were moving at a blur. August leaned from the pilot seat, waving Billie in through the side door. He was saying something but Joe couldn't make out what above the roar of the propeller blades.

Billie turned as she ran, arm outstretched, nail gun firing in all directions, she evidently not caring what or who she hit. Joe wondered if she even remembered he was there.

He kept to the side as much as he could to avoid inadvertently getting blasted by one of the nails.

The giant zombie was right behind him, its panting groans crawling up his spine and sending goosebumps across his flesh.

Don't look back. Don't! But if walking the streets alone in search of eradicating the undead had taught him anything, looking over your own shoulder was what was needed to survive.

Joe glanced back. Large gray hands reached for him and grabbed him by the face. His feet left the ground and he was dragged over to the building's ledge.

"Joe." The voice was somewhere behind the dark of the dead man's palm, somewhere above the din of spinning helicopter blades, somewhere underneath the constant moans and growls of dead men and women.

August? The voice was faint, almost a whisper.

It was female.

Billie?

He raised the X-09 and fired the two shots it could handle, hoping he'd hit his target in the head. Two low grunts, one for each bullet fired. The hand remained on his face.

Out of necessity, Joe let go of the dead man's wrist and let his head support his body weight. He felt around for the holster and slid the X-09 into it. Then he reached up and clawed at the dead man's fingers, hoping to release them just enough to see what was going on. He managed to pry them loose enough so that his left eye was uncovered.

An empty street lay thirty-some stories beneath his boots.

Pain from the iron claw-like grip around his head spiked through his temples.

Blood oozed from the undead giant's lips. From the little Joe could see, it appeared the X-09 had slugged the creature twice in the chest. Black blood trickled out of the wounds, but it wasn't enough to stop it.

He couldn't see the helicopter.

Go ahead. Drop me. They're gone. I'm ready to go, too. Time to see April.

"Joseph." There was that voice again. "Joe." It sounded pleading, begging him not to give up. "I need you."

Billie?

No. Not Billie. She wouldn't call him "Joseph."

April?

I'm coming, sweetheart. He just needs to let go and soon I'll be there.

Then another voice, this One strong and sure: "If you let yourself die, you will not see her. Not without Me."

Who? Who's "Me"?

The undead giant shook his arm and Joe's body wagged like a rag doll's.

The voice again: "I have called you by name. You now have a choice: listen or perish. Make your decision."

Unsure what to do or if his mind was playing tricks on him, Joe thought about April. She had changed everything. She was why he was here now. If she hadn't died, he would never have taken it upon himself to make war with the undead. He would never have met Billie or Des or August. He wouldn't be here now, hanging by a thread over a rooftop's ledge.

Wouldn't be questioning his sanity at hearing a voice that was not his own.

Have I slipped? Have I finally gone—Just one more chance. Please.

The giant tossed him into the air. Joe went up, tipped forward, and began a swan dive for the street below. Suddenly, a gust of wind stronger than anything he'd ever felt shoved him forward and sent him back onto the rooftop. His forearms hit the ground and he skidded a few feet before finally coming to a stop.

Impossi—

The giant zombie turned and stomped toward him. The crowd of the other zombies came in from the other side.

Behind the giant zombie, the black helicopter rose close to the roof, Billie standing in the side door, waving at him to get in.

Thank you. It was more feeling than thought, but Joe got to his feet, pulled out the X-09 and sent a bullet home between the giant's eyes. The creature stopped its stride, eyes wide, then dropped to its knees as black blood and brain matter gushed from its head.

Joe ran toward the helicopter. Almost at the ledge, about to negotiate how he was going to step off the edge and into the chopper, a multitude of hands pulled at him from behind.

Billie fired the nail gun, sending a barrage of nails into those holding him back.

The zombies wailed.

Joe lurched forward, ran to the edge and jumped.

His foot slipped on the helicopter's ski and he lost his balance. Gravity swept in and he fell. A rush of pain spiked through his underarms and it took him a second to realize he had managed to catch himself on the ski instead of plummeting to the street below.

Four zombies jumped off the roof. Two grabbed onto each of his legs. The third grabbed onto the ski, the fourth missed completely and plunged to the ground. The helicopter tipped to the side.

Through the open door, Joe heard August mutter something as he tried to right the thing.

"Shoot them! Shoot them!" he screamed at Billie.

She aimed the nail gun at the ones by his legs. "Can't get a clear shot."

"Then shoot the other one!"

She aimed at the one hanging onto the ski with one hand. A nail to its throat was enough to force it to let go and drop the thirty-something stories to the street.

The zombies tugged at Joe's legs. He slipped, fell, then caught the ski with his left hand. His *weak* hand. The other still clutched the X-09. There was no way he was going to drop the gun.

Even at the expense of his own life.

Without it . . . . The gun symbolized everything. It was who he was without April.

Gripping the bar as tight as he could, he slowly aimed the X-09 at the head of the zombie clawing at his right leg. He shot; the creature's face exploded. Its body fell.

The other dug into his skin with its sharp nails. Joe's hand began to slip.

Fingers aching, he wasn't sure how much longer he could hold on.

The zombie bit into his boot and was greeted with a mouth full of steel.

Pa-toompf!

A nail appeared dead center of the zombie's forehead. Its mouth dropped open. Joe kicked it in the face and the thing tumbled to the ground.

The weight of the undead suddenly gone, Joe thought he could pull himself up. The moment he tried, his sweaty fingers slipped on the metal of the ski.

He fell.

35
GRIEF

A pair of small hands locked around his wrist and clung on with everything they had. Joe looked up. Billie was squatting at the edge of the side door of the helicopter, a smile on her face, her glasses slipping down her nose.

Joe tried pulling himself up with his left hand, but couldn't lest he risk pulling too hard and yank Billie out of the chopper. Still holding the X-09 in his right hand, he carefully pulled that arm up and tossed the weapon into the helicopter. Hand now empty, he latched onto the helicopter's ski and simultaneously pulled himself up with that one while using the hand Billie held for support. Once he was no longer dangling from the ski, he searched for a better place to put his hands.

"Let go," he told her, eyeing the edge of the side door.

Hesitancy flashed across her face.

"I need my other hand," he said.

There seemed to be a debate going on behind those big blue eyes of hers.

"I'm serious. Let go!"

Behind the roar of the helicopter blades, he heard August yell, "Help him in. Hurry!"

Billie pulled up on his arm. Her grip was slipping and his body's position was awkward. Her fingers suddenly went from being around his wrist to clasping onto the cuffs of his sleeves till all that she held was leather between thumbs and forefingers.

The weight was too much and her hands snapped back when she released the fabric and tumbled back onto her behind inside the helicopter.

Gravity swept in and Joe dropped. His left hand caught the edge of the ski, but his arm and shoulder took most of the blow and the muscles strained from the sudden jerk against them.

"Joe!" August shouted from within.

Billie was at the side door's edge, leaning over, panic written across her face.

Joe dangled there, wind whipping at his legs and blowing him toward the back of the chopper.

Grunting, he leaned into the wind, trying to straighten himself, and got hold of the ski with both hands. The helicopter slowed a little, but it was still moving up and forward at a good clip.

The weight was too much and Joe's arms straightened.

Taking heavy, deep breaths, he tried to calm himself. To slow down. He closed his eyes and purposefully ignored that his body was slowly being pushed by the wind toward the back of the helicopter again.

Growling, he held the ski tight and tried pulling himself up again.

For April, he thought.

"Puuuulllll . . ." His voice gurgled at the end and his head dipped. The city streets were a maze of rooftops and ruler-straight lines far below.

Something grabbed the back of his coat and began pulling him up and forward.

Up. Go. Pull!

Grunting, he slowly worked his hands up off the ski and onto the side edge of the helicopter. He then grabbed hold of something plush and leathery. A seat. Then something bony. A leg? Billie!

The tug against the back of his coat persisted until finally he was inside the chopper, lying on his stomach, up to his knees, feet hanging out.

He lay there panting, the icy wind whipping against his legs sending sweet shivers up his body, cooling down his sweat-soaked skin.

Throat dry, he forced himself to swallow, then used the rest of his strength to finish the job and get himself fully into the helicopter.

Billie grabbed him and helped him into the seat next to hers.

"Thanks," he said.

"You okay?" August asked over his shoulder from the pilot seat.

Joe waved at him, signaling he was fine.

Billie looked at him with glazed eyes.

"Thanks," he whispered, still out of breath.

She bit her lower lip, nodded, then turned and faced the window.

Through tear-covered eyes, Billie watched the roof of the Richardson building drift away, the moving bodies of the undead milling about its top seeming less and less dangerous as the helicopter ascended.

Des was down there, somewhere inside that rooftop entrance, broken, bloody, beaten. She had to fight to keep the mental image of his blood-soaked face and torn flesh from invading her mind. Was he completely gone or was he one of them now? She would never know.

August hadn't said anything since she had pulled Joe inside the chopper. Instead the old man sat in the pilot seat, hands on the cyclic and collective, eyes fixed forward. Joe sat in the seat beside her, hunched over his legs, forearms resting on his knees, head down. She didn't have to see his face to know he was grieving, too, and that a million thoughts of failure were piercing his heart.

Des. The goofy kid with brown hair and a skinny frame.

Des. The young man she had known the longest throughout all this mess, the one person she could count on if she ever needed an ear, a terrible joke or just a cup of milk.

Des. Self-proclaimed zombie wrangler, at first only in video games but then in real life.

Des. Her hero.

He had been there for her in the early days, back when the rain first poured and the world went to hell. They had met online, both frequenting the same message board, each leaving messages like "Is anybody out there?" or "Who else is left?"

ZW1. Zombie wrangler.

Yeah, you are, she thought. She wiped the tears from her eyes and buried her face in her hands. She half-expected Joe to reach over and offer some sort of condolence, but instead she was left to sit there alone and think about the one who had laid down his life for her.

Des had been the only person she had really confided in after the rain.

One night, he had come over to her place to help her install some extra RAM into her PC. Once the task was completed, he was about to go but she had asked him to stay. She didn't know why, at first. Perhaps because the weeks of lonely nights were finally getting to her. Perhaps it was because she was getting tired of no longer being able to *hear* a human voice and only *read* them on a computer screen.

Perhaps because all she needed was a friend.

He stayed. She'd never forget the way he sat on her couch, legs drawn up, hands folded around his shins, thumbs twiddling. She wasn't surprised when later, during the one and only night they got drunk together, he told her that he thought she had wanted him to stay over for sex. It had been the last thing on her mind, at the time, but she couldn't blame the poor kid. It was a lonely world and the gentle caress of human touch was something folks hardly came by. Chat on the message boards had it that none of the girls wanted to risk the chance of getting pregnant and bringing a baby into this mess. As far as everyone was concerned, they were the last generation.

But it had been on that night, as he sat there on her couch, expecting her to come on to him, that she had poured out her heart and told him the story of how she lost her family. The haunting images of her sister, her blood-soaked face and rain-slicked skin. She had been standing across the room at the time, pacing, sobbing, hands shaking. She'd never forget the way he stood from the couch and slowly came over to her, extended his arms and drew her in. His embrace had been warm and sweet and for that night she found shelter in his small frame.

He only said two words that whole night: "I understand." That was it. He never went into detail about how he lost his own family or what happened to them. Even the next day when she asked him if he wanted to talk about it, he simply sat there at her kitchen table, smiled, shook his head and said, "It's okay."

For a time she worried about him, thought that he was bottling it all up inside and that one day, given the right trigger, he'd explode and break down. That never happened. But she could see it though, the pain, lurking there behind his green eyes. Even after the few times she prodded him and asked him to open up, Des resolutely refused. Said that he missed them but had accepted they were gone. His only regret, he said, was that he was unable to join them. That, despite his gratefulness at still being alive, a part of him wished the undead had taken him away from a life of always falling short, of being the brunt of jokes, of utterly low self-esteem. Billie supposed that was why he often said the wrong thing or made inopportune jokes. It was his way of dealing with the pain whether he knew it or not.

Billie glanced out the window. Downtown Winnipeg was far away, a mere blur on the horizon against a misty gray and brown sky that hung over the earth like a blanket of death.

36

THE STORM

It was happening all over again: the aftermath of having to make a choice.

Loss or gain.

Sentiment or judgment.

Life or death.

August chose life.

But Des was still gone. If he or even Joe and Billie had stayed, none of them would be flying now, high and away from the city. There hadn't been time to stop and try and save Des. Sure, an effort could have been made. Perhaps even a heroic effort. But no one would have been left to remember them. Heroes were nothing without the memories of those who were there and lived to tell about it.

As he flew, August's heart ached and his mind drifted back to that night when he pulled the gun on his family. A choice had to be made then just like now.

Good or evil.

Life or death.

August couldn't let evil have its way. Not then, not now.

But You still let it happen, didn't You? Yeah, yeah, I know. You're in control. You know everything. We're supposed to just simply trust You and call it good. Well, I'm sorry. That's fine in sermons and in commentaries, but this is real life. How can You possibly expect a human being—and, yeah, believe me, I know where I stand— how can You possibly expect a human being to look at a world ravaged by the depths of hell and simply say, "God is in control?" Grimacing, he squeezed the cyclic and collective. "Nonsense," he whispered. *I can talk the talk, that's for sure. But walking it out is easier said than done. You even said as much about that Yourself.*

He had promised himself that, for now, he'd keep God at arms length. Let Him come to him. Still, he couldn't help but vent it out mentally. There was no other way to try and come to terms with what just happened, and there was no way Joe or Billie would understand

210

where he was coming from. To them, life was life. No God. No devil. Just life.

An ache swept through his heart. *Now I wish I knew differently.*

The way Des looked at him after he glanced over his shoulder that one final time, that look of fear and shocked abandonment behind the grim expression of determination—it reminded him of Eleanor, the one who was dead even before he squeezed that trigger back at the cabin. Her blood-caked lips opened up and her gaunt cheeks seemed to sink into her face beneath white eyes that, for an instant, seemed to recognize him. There had been pleading in those eyes, a simple begging for one last chance before he let her go. Eyes that read nothing but bewilderment at the man who had forty-one years before swore to love her in sickness and in health, for richer or for poorer, till death would they part. Who could have known death would come like it did?

No, not death, August thought. *Death is when your body can no longer endure what's been handed to it. Doesn't matter how it comes. An accident, cancer, heart attack or simple old age. Death is when you finally raise your hands, let go, and say, "I've had enough."*

He punched the side of his seat. He felt the two in the rear seats stir, their eyes resting on him, but he didn't care. He knew they knew what was going on. Though he hadn't known the lad all that long, Des had begun to grow on him.

You just let him die, no problem. And where is he now? Did he know You? Or did he descend to the depths of the earth? Or is he one of them?

Eleanor. The kids. Jon junior, Bella, Finch, Katie and Stewart. All gone.

Just like Des.

How much longer until Joe and Billie would be gone, too, and he'd be alone once again? To care for them . . . . He didn't want that responsibility. Not now. He already had a family. And they were dead.

There was a tap on his shoulder. It was Joe.

Clenching his teeth, he simply whispered, "I'll deal with You later."

August tilted his head back, giving him his attention.

"Call me ungrateful," Joe said, "but do you know what you're doing?"

"What do you mean?"

"I just find it amazing that you know how to fly this thing."

"I was in 'Nam." Then, with a smirk, "Would you like to talk about it?"

Joe sank back into his seat.

"Hm, that's . . . that's interesting," August said.

"What?" Billie asked, leaning in.

"I should have checked it before, but I didn't. Too busy just wanting to get out of there."

"What?"

"The fuel gauge is on empty."

Joe leaned forward in his seat. "Then how are we . . ."

A sharp dagger pierced August's heart. He checked the gauge again. Sure enough, it was on empty. "Looks like Somebody is on our side."

They flew on.

Joe sat in his seat, arms crossed, wondering where this bird would take them.

The tank had been on E.

And they were still flying.

Could the gauge be wrong? Broken?

Doesn't matter, he concluded. *As long as we find safe ground and have a chance to regroup, we can figure out what our next move is.*

He glanced over at Billie. She sat with one leg up on the seat, bended at the knee, her forehead resting against the palm of her hand. She was no doubt thinking about Des.

I should have saved him. But there were just too many of them. I didn't really know him, but that doesn't matter. Never knew anyone else I helped get away from those things. His heart sank. *April would hate me right now.* He wasn't quite sure what he meant by that, but April always had a way of bringing out the best in him, helping him reach deep down and dig out his full potential. It was one of the things that he loved about her: her ability to make him feel like he mattered. And now he felt he had let her down. That, wherever she was, she was somehow counting on him to make right the wrong that had been her death by preserving the lives of as many as he encountered.

"I miss you," he whispered.

He imagined her saying the same thing to him. Even though their relationship had been left up in the air and she had gone back to Dan, he knew he had impacted her, had pulled her out of the drudgery of "just another day."

If I could do things over again, April, I would. I would have called. Would have gone back to your apartment. Would have found you somehow. Maybe then we could have faced this together instead of . . . Her blood-soaked face filled his mind. He glanced out the window to banish it from view and stroked the X-09, which was now back in its holster, through his coat.

Nothing but gray clouds with coffee-brown.

Joe peered further out the window. The world below was gone.

He quickly leaned forward in his seat and tapped August on the shoulder. The old man was checking the gauges.

"Why are we flying so high?" he asked him.

"We're not. At least, according to this thing." August tapped his index finger against the altimeter. They were only at about five thousand feet.

"Then where's this cloud coming from?"

"Hey, where did everything go?" Billie asked, dropping her foot off the seat and sitting up straight.

"I don't know," August said. "We were just flying along and the air started to get hazy. I didn't think anything of it. Maybe a really low-hanging cloud or something. But it got thicker."

"Go lower," Joe said.

August worked the controls and Joe felt the helicopter begin to descend.

But the cloud wasn't going anywhere. Its light gray began to dim and soon deep gray washed over with a light charcoal embraced them.

The altimeter read three thousand feet.

"Try again," Joe said.

August repeated the maneuver.

Two thousand. The gray grew even darker.

One thousand.

It was impossible to see anything through the glass. Just dark cloud.

It had been so long since Joe had seen anything like it. For the past year, the sky had been washed over in misty gray dotted with brown.

These clouds were different. These were storm clouds.

And the altimeter read only five hundred feet.

"I don't want to take her down anymore. Too dangerous. Might hit something," August said.

"We need to land," Joe said.

Billie tugged on August's sleeve. "What's happening?"

"Not sure. We're—" A crack of thunder cut him off. Its sudden low boom sent a shockwave through Joe's chest.

Billie yelped. August's brown eyes went wide.

A bolt of off-white lightning crackled in the sky beside the helicopter. Ahead, an enormous ghostly skull flashed in the clouds, taking up the whole windshield.

Joe gasped along with the others.

BOOM! The thunder shook the helicopter and August's hands strained against the controls.

Suddenly, his face screwed up and he squinted his eyes.

"What?" Joe said.

"I—"

KRA-BANG!

Joe flew back in his seat. Billie fell into him. Before he could help her back into her seat, another boom of thunder rocked the chopper and another pale, jagged skull flashed against the sky.

Whispers invaded the helicopter. Low, distant. The words incomprehensible, but if Joe didn't know any better, he'd say they sounded foreign, middle eastern. The rhythm of the words were hypnotic enough that, for a moment, worry over what just flashed in the sky seemed to fade.

Another skull. Then another quickly to the right.

KRA-BOOM!

Joe and Billie bounced to the other seat as the helicopter suddenly angled upward.

"This isn't your world!" August yelled. "This is not your time! This isn't—"

Lightning streaked across the sky and thunder rocked the chopper, sending August up then back down again in his seat so violently his headset bounced off and landed beside him.

Low static drifted from the earmuffs. So did voices.

"There's someone out there!" Billie screeched, pointing to the headset.

Joe leaned forward, grabbed the headset, then brought one of the muffs to his ear.

Voices clamored for attention above the static:

"Raven Two, this is Raven Three, over."

"Roger that, Raven Three."

"Found a way out yet?"

"None. It—"

CRACK!

"Ténébreux nuages. Grand nombre!"

"Check votre écartement."

"Ils—"

CRACK!

"Kann nicht eine Sache sehen!"

"Hast du jene Schädel gesehen?"

"Ja. Vier. Nein. Dort! Fünf!"

"Versuchst zum—"

CRACK!

The line went dead.

The whispers surrounding the helicopter grew louder. Joe wished he could understand them.

"What's going on, Joe?" Billie asked, hanging tightly onto the sleeve of his coat. "Who's talking?"

The thunder roared.

"It's Aramaic!" August shouted over the thunder's echo. "At least I think it is."

The old man tried to speak but seemed at a loss for words. They all were. The old timer's thoughts raced behind his eyes and Joe feared the guy might have a heart attack.

A jagged skull with an open, grinning mouth flashed right beside their window.

The whispers grew louder.

BOOM!

CRACK! White lightning intermixed with bright gray snapped in six jagged streaks in front of them.

August tried turning the helicopter, attempting to avoid them.

Heart pounding, Joe fell against the side window from the inertia.

Another skull.

Another burst of thunder.

Static from August's headset the only constant in the turbulence.

KRA-BANG!

The helicopter bounced up then dropped down.

A series of skulls spackled the sky.

Lightning flashed.

The whispers ripped through the air like razors. Their rhythmic words sent shivers up Joe's spine. Whatever comfort they once had was gone.

KA-BANG!

Lightning ripped from a dense cloud that had appeared before them, streaking straight at them, driving into the chopper.

They all covered their heads, expecting to be showered in a rain of glass. Instead, the inside of the helicopter lit up. The light was so bright that when it flashed down, Joe could hardly see, just a multitude of black stars blanketing his vision.

Gravity took over and they were all leaning forward.

The clouds grew thicker and thicker.

Slick, gray muck from the clouds' mist coated the windshield, blocking the flashing skulls from view.

KRA-BANG!

SNAP!

BOOM!

August yelped.

Billie screamed.

Joe called out to April for help.

The helicopter jerked backward and Joe's back was slammed against his seat.

"ARRGGGHHH!" August growled, clutching the controls.

The whispers stopped.

So did the static on the headset.

Watery gray gunk coated the glass, making it impossible to see outside.

"August, did we—" Joe began but was cut off by a sudden *WHAM* as something hard slammed up against the bottom of the helicopter.

Everyone lurched forward as they suddenly came to a stop, the vibration from the impact still reverberating through every bone in Joe's body.

They all sat there, unmoving, their bodies too busy registering that they appeared to be on the ground. What saved them, Joe didn't know.

"Joe?" Billie said, her voice small and far away.

He looked over at her. She sat in a crash position, head pressed tightly to her thighs, hands folded against the back of her head, elbows hugging her knees.

August just sat there, jaw hanging open. Was he—

Joe was about to say his name but the old man jerked in his seat, shut the chopper off and scrambled to open the cockpit door.

When he did, warm sunlight streamed in.

216

37
INTANGIBLE

August stepped out of the helicopter, half expecting to set foot on the gold streets of heaven. If God didn't hold against him his challenging Him, that was. And if the helicopter being able to fly on empty was any indicator, so far God was being merciful not only to him but to Joe and Billie as well.

But it wasn't heaven August set foot on. It was the gray, cracked pavement of a parking lot, one partly filled with cars off a busy street.

Joe and Billie hopped out of the helicopter, shielding their eyes from the sun's bright glare.

"What . . ." Billie said.

It didn't make sense. None of it did.

One minute they were in the sky, the next somehow safely on the ground in the parking lot of a . . . bank?

Brow furrowed, August scanned the street running alongside the bank. This was Henderson Highway. Henderson Highway as it was before the days of gray clouds. Before it became the Haven.

I got to be dreaming, August thought. *I have to be.* He'd had dreams like this before. The kind where something deep within told him that, despite the realism, actual reality was waiting for him on the other side of the veil of sleep. Yet right now, that feeling—that *knowing*—that this was a dream failed him.

This was *real*.

Joe came up beside him; Billie, too.

"Where are we?" Joe asked quietly.

August swallowed the lump in his dry throat. "I don't know." He glanced back at the helicopter. The black flying machine sat there in the middle of the parking lot, propeller unmoving, its hull covered in a pasty gray residue, most likely the goopy, leftover mist from the storm clouds. He didn't know what was more odd: the simple sight of a helicopter sitting in a bank's parking lot or that no one seemed to notice it *was* sitting there.

The cars whipped by on the highway to the left, all seeming oblivious to their presence. One car coming down the street slowed, right blinker flashing, and turned into the parking, heading straight for the chopper.

It wasn't slowing down. Didn't the driver see it?

"Look out!" August said and got behind Joe and Billie and pushed them to the side just as the car collided with the helicopter. Instead of a loud crash and a brilliant display of metal ripping apart metal, the car sailed through the helicopter as if it wasn't there. It pulled into an empty stall and the driver, a young woman with too much makeup, got out and headed toward the bank's doors, her high heels clacking against the pavement. She didn't pay them any mind.

"What's going on?" August breathed.

"Did you see that?" Billie said as Joe walked around the vehicle, his eyes searching it up and down as if for any damage. "It just passed right through it! Just straight on through!"

"I saw it, Billie, but I don't believe it," August said.

Joe joined with them again. He seemed at a loss for words.

August's mind went blank. He had seen a lot in his lifetime. He had thought that after he witnessed the dead rise and walk around, he'd finally seen the unbelievable. Even that couldn't have prepared him for what just happened.

"Hey! Hey!" Billie screeched as she ran to the edge where the parking lot met the road.

"Billie, get back here!" Joe shouted after her and ran to her side.

She waved frantically at the cars passing by. No one slowed. No one stopped. An older black woman with a flower-patterned kerchief made her way down the sidewalk alongside the bank.

Billie ran up to her.

"Help! We need help!" she yelled, pointing back at August and the helicopter.

The woman continued on her way, eyes fixed forward, seeming completely unaware that Billie was there.

"Hey, I'm talking to you! Aren't you listening to—" She moved to grab the woman by the shoulders and her hands passed through her. Billie shrieked and recoiled. A moment later her legs gave out from under her and she fell to the sidewalk. Her hands passed through the cement as she went to break her fall and she looked as if she would continue toppling forward into the ground had Joe not caught her and hauled her back to her feet.

She fought against him, screaming and crying inconsolably.

218

August jogged up to them. "Hold her!"

"I am!" Joe snapped.

Billie fought in his arms and wouldn't calm down.

"Billie," August said. "Billie, listen to me."

She kept screaming. "I'm dead! I'mdeadI'mdeadI'mdead!"

"No, you're not!" August shouted above her voice though he wasn't entirely sure he was telling the truth.

Maybe this was what happened after you died? Maybe you *did* co-exist with the living on a plane of existence unbeknownst to the rest of the world? *If that's true*, he thought, *then everything I've believed about God and about life has been a lie.* He clenched his teeth together. *The dead rising, the world ending in a way not foretold—what if I was wrong?* He shook his head. *No, don't think that. The helicopter flew on empty. It flew on empty. Remember that. Where are You!*

Billie kept shrieking, totally breaking down. "Help! I'm dead! Des! Mom! Dad! Audrey!"

August shoved Joe away from her and grabbed her flailing arms. "Billie, look at me. Look at me!"

Her eyes wouldn't meet his. Instead she thrashed about. Without thinking, his aged palm snapped up and swatted her across the cheek.

"Hey!" Joe said and grabbed his hand just as he was about to do it again.

Billie's shocked blue eyes met August's.

Joe moved to grab him; August snapped out his hand and held him back. "One sec." Still holding one of her hands, he turned to Billie and said as sternly yet as comfortingly as he could muster, "You are not dead. Please, calm down."

Tears dripped from her eyes and fear lit up her gaze.

"Something strange has happened. That's all. Just, please, calm down."

Joe's chest pressed against his palm; August knew he only had Billie's best interest at heart.

"I'm not going to hit her again, Joe," he said. "I'm sorry for that. Billie, I'm sorry. I just needed to get your attention."

She pulled away from him and turned around and buried her face in her hands. Joe came beside her and attempted to put an arm around her shoulder. She quickly drew away.

Placing his hands on his hips, August turned, squinted against the sun, and stared at the bank. "What's going on?"

30

THE MAN IN THE WHITE COAT

While August stared off at the bank, Joe paced beside Billie, giving her a moment.

Heart racing, legs jittery, his mind raced with a million thoughts, all images: the bright sun, the car driving *through* the helicopter, Billie's hands passing through that woman's shoulders, August hitting her, the storm clouds, the undead, Des, the X-09, April and her gorgeous black hair and brilliant gray eyes, that woman with too much makeup not seeing them, the cars that continued to drive by without pausing to look at the chopper in the bank's parking lot, the sun, the storm, Billie falling, her hands passing through the pavement, him catching her, April, their cries gone unheard, August flying the helicopter on empty—Over and over they played. The past, the present. His head hurt.

He reached for the X-09 inside his coat and gripped its handle. The power he normally felt from holding it brought little comfort and very little sense of control. Who was he kidding? This was an uncontrollable situation! There was no explanation. This was impossible. This couldn't be happening.

He'd always thought he'd be able to handle anything, that nothing would surprise him anymore. There was nothing left to lose after April. His life, what little left of it there was, counted for nothing. If he died at the hands of the undead, so be it. If the storm had taken him, so be it. If now, if he was dead and was a ghost among the living in a world where the undead didn't exist, so be it.

"They're not here," he said quietly. Then he shouted at August: "They're not here!"

August turned around to face him. "What?"

Billie kept to herself, some ten feet away on the grass bordering the bank's property.

"The dead," Joe said. "They're not here."

The old man glanced around, as if reevaluating his surroundings for the first time. "They're gone," he said, if only to himself.

220

Joe put a hand above his eyes. "The sky's clear, too. Just a few clouds. White ones."

"It's summer, just like before the rain came," August said.

"Where are we?" Joe asked. A strange idea popped into his head but he wanted to see if August would say it first before he did.

"Home. At least, what it used to be."

"The way I see it," Joe said, "we're either dead and the 'other side' is just a pleasant carbon copy of real life, or we're—"

August arched an eyebrow.

He couldn't say it. To do so would sound, well, just plain crazy.

Mouth clamped shut, old lips pressed together, August didn't reply but instead seemed to be waiting for him to finish.

"We're in the past, before the rain came." Joe's heart skipped a beat and he felt his cheeks flush at the absurdity of the notion. "Or in the future after the dead are gone," he quickly added, as if that would make it better.

It didn't.

"I don't know where or even when we are," August said.

Another car pulled into the parking lot and passed through the helicopter. Joe couldn't help but stare as the car continued on its way just like the other, as if nothing had happened.

A man with a big belly in a plaid shirt exited the bank, went to his rusting brown pickup, and backed out of his spot. He, too, passed through the chopper and joined the traffic on the road.

"Billie, did you see—"

She wasn't on the lawn beside the building anymore. Instead, she stood by the front door to the bank, poking at it with her hand. The closer Joe got to her, the more he was able to see what she was doing. Slowly, she pressed her fingers against the glass. They passed through the door as if through air. She pulled her hand back and did it again. And again. And again.

"Careful, Joe," August said from behind him as he approached Billie.

But before he could talk to her to try and figure out what was going on, Billie passed through the door and went in.

Head aching, eyes stinging from her outburst, Billie slowly made her way through the bank. People milled about, others sat in the waiting area; while others stood at the tills, speaking with the tellers while fishing in their purses or wallets.

The woman with too much makeup snapped her gum as she walked toward her. The woman's shoulder passed through hers as she walked by, heading for the doors. The woman stopped before the doors, adjusted her purse over her shoulder, then opened the door just as it appeared Joe and August were about to pass through the door like she had.

The two men entered.

The old man and Joe searched the people, obviously looking for her.

She didn't want to talk to them. Not right now. She ducked out of view behind a table with a bunch of brochures on it and a for-customers-only coffee machine.

Wondering if Joe would shout her name, if he truly believed no one could see them or hear them, she waited, just needing some space.

Sure enough, Joe called out: "Billie!"

"Argh. Not now," she whispered and got in behind the legs of someone who had come to grab themselves a free coffee.

She searched the bank, looking for a place to take a breather. It was all relatively open area, the only hiding places being either behind the tills or in the vault, which had its door open. As if that could stop her even if the door was closed. She could pass through solid objects!

Then the memory came. Her fall. The sidewalk. Her arms passing through the cement. The sensation of gravity taking her and about to suck her to the center of the earth or beyond.

What happened out there?

She peered over the table. Joe and August had split up, each wandering around the bank, eyes searching above the heads of the people. A little boy no more than four ran through August's legs to catch up with his father on the other side of the old man. An elderly lady passed through Joe as she went to inquire about something at the help desk.

Billie eyed the vault, and when she was certain Joe and August weren't looking, she made a break for it and ran, her body passing through the waist-high gate separating the area behind the tills from the bank floor. About to run into the vault, she caught sight of two stalls for those opening safety deposit boxes on the other side of it. She headed for one of those instead.

When she emerged through the fake-marble-covered door, she stopped and took a deep breath.

Finally, she was alone.

Joe searched the people, hoping to catch a glimpse of Billie. How hard was it to find a small girl with bright pink hair? Especially one who could pass through solid objects?

He couldn't see her. He knew she probably wanted to be alone after what happened outside, but now was hardly the time to leave him and August.

He scanned the bank for the old man. August stood in the far corner, next to a stairwell, seeming to already be waiting for him to make eye contact. Once Joe did, August signaled that he was going to go downstairs to look for her. Joe nodded and August turned and headed down the steps.

A bank of offices bordered the place's interior so Joe decided to check them out, one by one.

Out of habit, he dodged a middle-aged man with thinning brown hair who was coming toward him. Another shorter fellow with spiked blond hair who he didn't see was right behind the man and Joe hit him straight on. The blond fellow's body met his and Joe merged with him, feeling as if he was slowly sinking into a pool of Jell-O. Then the sensation passed and Joe was on the other side, the blond guy still walking forward, not missing a beat.

Joe gave himself a shake and turned into the office with the open mahogany door on his left. A fifty-some-odd-year-old with male-pattern baldness and a moustache sat behind a desk, one hand tapping the keys of his keyboard, the other supporting his chin as he stared at the monitor.

No Billie.

Just in case this whole "no one seeing him" wasn't real, Joe said, "Excuse me, sir?"

The man didn't look up.

Joe stepped up to the desk and waved a hand in front of the guy's face. No response.

He couldn't help but chuckle. *Well, how 'bout that?* He recoiled at his own humor. *Don't turn back. That's not you anymore.*

On the white wall to his right was a black-framed picture of a well-muscled runner hopping over a series of hurdles, and below was the supposed-to-be-motivating slogan that read FORWARD.

"All right," Joe said and approached the wall.

He put his fingers against it and they passed through and, like before, there was a slight resistance, like slipping your hand into a pool of cool, soft mud. He withdrew his fingers, took a deep breath, walked toward the wall, instinctively bracing himself for the dull thunk of impact as his head met drywall. Instead, coolness and darkness embraced him and it felt as if he were slowly sinking in the deep end of a swimming pool albeit with something under his feet for support. The darkness then melted away and he found himself in the closed-door office of two women, one with short brown hair behind a desk, slouched in her chair with hands folded across her lap, the other across from her leaning against the desk, bright blonde hair hanging in her face.

"I'm not going to judge you either way," the woman sitting down said.

"I know. I just don't know what to do."

The woman sitting down leaned forward. "You're gonna have to make a decision, though. Frankly, I'm getting tired of hearing about it. Either make your move with the guy or not."

Joe stepped closer. The woman with the blonde hair stepped back from the desk.

"It's been bugging me for weeks," she said.

"You said that," the other woman said.

"He asked me out this morning. For tonight. Wants dinner and then, well, you know. He didn't say that, but I can tell."

"What guy doesn't want that?"

"But I *really* like him."

"You're married."

"Don't remind me. But that's been cold for a few months now. I mean, *really* cold."

"I'm not going to suggest you break up your marriage."

"Who says I'm breaking it up? Why not a little fun on the side? Doesn't have to last forever."

"These things never end right."

"That's not true. A friend of mine found somebody while she was still attached. She got divorced and they both lived happily ever after."

"One in a million."

"Could be me."

"Could be."

Joe shook his head. He couldn't believe he was hearing this.

"It's not like I'm getting any at home," the blonde woman said.

Okay, I'm done, Joe thought.

"You've been telling me," the other woman said.

"I don't know." The blonde woman began to pace. Joe avoided her on purpose. "Just tired of being torn, you know?"

Joe merely leaned in close to her ear and said, "Don't do it." And he moved toward the far wall, sinking through it and emerging into an empty office, the door open.

Like the other with the two women, no Billie.

He went through the remaining offices, all of their occupants unaware of his presence. Billie wasn't in any of them.

By the time he exited out the door of the office nearest the tills, passing through solid objects was becoming normal and he didn't mind it when a short Asian man carrying too many papers passed through him.

The door at the front of the bank opened and a man wearing an expensive-looking long, white overcoat and white velvet fedora walked in. He paused a moment at the door, surveyed the room, then went to the heavyset woman sitting at the help desk. The woman picked up her phone after he spoke to her, dialed a number, said something, then set the phone back down. A moment later, an office door opened and out came the woman whom the blonde was confessing to. She greeted the man in the white coat with a handshake then directed him toward the vault on the other side of the tills. He waited for her by the vault door while she went in, and when she emerged with a small, silver long box, he went with her to somewhere on the other side of the vault.

Joe's focus changed when August came up the stairwell, hands open, palms up. Nothing.

Joe signaled to the offices he'd just been in and signed that Billie wasn't in those either. Sighing, he glanced out the far window to the helicopter in the parking lot.

Was it his imagination or did the misty residue on its hull suddenly seem a lighter gray than before?

Billie paced the tiny stall, hands steepled together beneath her chin. There wasn't much room to move—at least, without passing through the stall's walls or door and risking bumping into Joe or August outside— and was getting tired of being cramped up in there. Worse, she was just tired of being tired. And tired of being a woman. It was stupid and cliché but she was having a hard time keeping up with everything. The guys seemed to have no trouble, at least from her view of things. Joe rarely showed emotion. August, though warmer than Joe, felt like a grandpa that she only saw on special occasions. And Des . . . . If he was here, he'd be the one to talk to. He'd probably be having a blast walking through solid objects once the shock and newness of it wore off.

But she was just tired. Tired of trying to survive. Tired of being pushed to death's edge then suddenly being tugged back. Tired of weirdness and conflicting emotions. Sick to her stomach over losing her family. Sick of the undead. Her only comfort came from them not being around anymore.

She still didn't know where she, Joe and August were. Des would probably say they were in some parallel universe. He was big into stuff like that: spaceships, aliens, time travel, parallel dimensions. Your regular run-of-the-mill comic geek.

Never got to say good-bye, Billie thought. A sharp pang pricked her heart. Maybe, just maybe, if they somehow returned to—what, their world? — maybe then she'd be able to find Des's body and give it a proper burial. If he wasn't a zombie, that was.

She wiped her eyes and thought maybe now she should rejoin the others.

A muffled female voice interrupted her thoughts: "Right this way, sir."

"Thank you," a man said, his voice low and sure.

The door of the stall next to hers opened.

"Let me know if you need anything," the woman said.

"Thank you."

The door closed and it sounded like something was placed on the small shelf sticking out of the wall, assuming the stall next to hers was laid out the same.

Knowing full well she shouldn't pry and give the guy his privacy, she thought it wouldn't matter if she snuck a peek at what the man had in his safety deposit box. She always thought it'd be cool to have one of those, to have a secret stash of private possessions that no one could get to no matter what, only you and you alone. And living at home with her folks where her mom did regular sweeps of her room to see if she was hiding anything never afforded her that luxury.

"Why not?" she said and put her hands up against the wall dividing her stall and the one next to it.

Just take a peek then go. Won't hurt nobody if I don't stay and linger, she thought, easing her guilt.

Billie walked through the wall, the slow *pressing through* now familiar. She emerged just behind the man.

He wore a long, white overcoat and a white velvet fedora.

Suddenly the man spun around and his blue eyes ignited in bright flame.

39

IN THE BOWELS OF THE EARTH

"Didn't find her, huh?" Joe said when August walked up to him. The old man's presence was comforting in light of him being the only one aware of his being there.

"Nothing. Not a pink hair."

"Any trouble on the stairs?"

August smirked, obviously getting what Joe was driving at. "My feet slipped through a couple of times. Actually, one time significantly. I went through one flight and landed on another."

"Landed on an—How did you stop yourself from going through?"

The old man furrowed his brow, as if to recall the memory. "I don't know. Something along the lines of 'Help!' ran through my mind. That's all I remember. I landed on the stairs. A couple of people were coming up them and they stepped right into me and passed me by. Anyway, I checked the rooms downstairs, the maintenance room, the lunchroom and all that. She's not here. At least from what we can see."

An idea struck him. "Since we can't touch anything and since we're invisible, do you think this is the first step in something bigger? Like, we're slowly fading from existence?"

August shook his head. "I don't know. Maybe. But I think God has something else in mind for us."

It was only a matter of time before August brought up the G-word again. But Joe had to admit that in light of all that he'd experienced, the possibility of God was a strong one. "Okay, I'll go with you on this for a second. If God's placed us here, what's the point? What're we supposed to do?"

The old man didn't reply.

"See, that's it. There's *nothing* we can do. Noth-ing. Can't touch anything. Except, well, maybe the floor, depending, right? Billie nearly went through the sidewalk out there. You went through the stairs. But you also stopped yourself, somehow. And I've got my feet planted."

Then as if saying so was a trigger, something grabbed his ankles and tugged him into the tiled flooring.

"Joe!" August yelled and reached for him.

Just before the old man's hands touched his, another violent tug yanked him downward. The bank and August slipped from view and he was looking up at a ceiling.

Something had him. When he checked his feet, there was nothing but air. The tan tiled flooring of the room below rushed up to meet him and, like above, he was sucked straight through this level as well.

Darkness surrounded him.

Shock shook Billie's innards and she tumbled back. Just as she began to pass through the stall's door, a strong hand grabbed her by the shirt collar and yanked her upright, bringing her face to face with the man with the fiery eyes.

"You're not supposed to be here, Billie Friday," he said. His tone was firm and carried an authority that seemed almost otherworldly.

The words never really formed in her mind but more so did in her heart, and she wondered how he knew her name.

The man let go and left her to stand on rubbery legs.

The flames dancing in his eyes sparkled and she felt compelled to slowly sink to her knees before him. As she began to lower herself, he drew her back onto her feet.

"Don't do that," he said, withdrawing his hand from her. The flames faded, bright and beautiful blue eyes shining forth.

"I don't . . . I don't know why I . . ." She knew what she was trying to say but her tongue suddenly felt five inches thick. She wanted to know what he was and why she felt so small—so insignificant—in his presence.

The man's face was hard and he didn't appear the type to have ever cracked a smile in his whole life.

"You can . . . you can . . ." she started.

"Yes, I can see you," he said. "I can see a lot of things."

Her fingers trailed the collar of her shirt. *He touched me.* "You touched . . ."

He nodded.

"You know my name, too." Her voice sounded far away even to herself.

"I do." He glanced back to the silver box on the table. "Billie, listen to me. I want you to turn around and leave this place. You may never speak of meeting me." He eyed the silver box again.

She wanted to listen to him, to obey instantly, but her curiosity was getting the better of her. "What's in there?"

"None of your concern, but it is of vital importance that I see to it." Then, very sharply, "Alone."

She averted her eyes from his, once more the feeling of being so worthless enveloping her. Who was this guy?

"Time is short. There's—" The man cocked his head. "Oh no . . ." And spun around and grabbed what appeared to be an old, gold-plated antique watch from the safety deposit box. He held the watch up and examined it.

"What is that?" she asked.

His eyes lit up again when he spun around. The frown on his face made her recoil.

"The end of all things," he said.

In the absence of light, Joe was pulled further and further downward, the darkness so thick, so hopeless, that even his own screams were sucked up by its depth.

The darkness was so penetrating his bones began to ache, as if each one was bruised through and through.

The violent pull on his legs ripped him through the dark like a millstone sinking down to the bottom of a lake.

He fell forever. He fell for a moment.

Time had no meaning.

Heart slamming against his ribcage, he cried out into the abyss, calling for help. No one answered and no one came.

April . . . he thought.

Sound brewed below and the further he dropped, the louder it became. High-pitched and filled with fear, he quickly realized it as the desperate screams of those being tormented. He'd heard similar screams before, ones when the undead overcame the living and began to devour their flesh while they were still alive. But this was so much more than that. Those screams had been those of a few. These ones were those of thousands. Of millions.

The sound enveloped him and encased him like a swarm of locusts. No way out. No reprieve from their ear-piercing noise.

Ears ringing from the deafening shrieks and screeches, barely able to concentrate, brain about to explode, Joe fell further into the dark.

The air grew warm, thick and dry. Then it grew warmer still, like that of a sauna. The heat intensified and the image of a red hot burner on a stove flashed before his mind. A sudden sense of permanence invaded his whole being and he found himself resigning to the reality there was no escape from this place.

He was alone and he knew it. Billie and August and the world above were fading quickly into distant memory. His life with April before the rise of the undead seemed so far away it was as if it had never happened at all.

The idea of being forgotten by all who knew him stole his breath away.

The acrid stench of sharp smoke and burnt meat pierced his nostrils, immediately locking up his stomach, making him want to throw up.

He couldn't.

The air burst into flame but there was no fire and Joe screamed from the pain ravaging through his system.

The heels of his boots hit rocky ground and he fell to his hands and knees.

Skin burning against the stone even through his trench coat, he bolted to his feet, panic racing through him.

The sweat coating every inch of him only made it worse, like scalding water on the skin.

"Garrrgh . . ." he breathed, his body throbbing in hot pulses, stinging, dying.

The pale glow of flame brewed in the distance, its expanse as far as his eyes could see to either side. The shrieks and screams rose from the fire and filled the air. Even where he stood, shaking, he could barely hear his own thoughts above their shouts of terror.

Whispers in the dark, somewhere behind him.

He turned around to face them and with a trembling hand tried to pull out the X-09. The hot metal of its handle bit into his palm when he tried to grab it and he had no choice but to leave it in its holster.

"Where . . . am I?" he barely managed. Even the breaths needed to speak were near unbearable as the intense heat on the air invaded his lungs, scorching the inside of his chest.

Coughing, he tried to make out the source of the whispers in the faint glow cast by the flames now behind him.

It was strange he could even hear these whispers above the calls and shouts of what sounded like countless people being burned alive.

Knees aching, he wanted to collapse but couldn't find the will to do so. It was as if something was forcing him to stand there and endure.

A scaled foot appeared out of the shadows, then another then another until four creatures with long, bulbous arachnid bodies, their skin coated in dark green and black scales, appeared out of the dark. Long sinewy arms and legs ran off their torsos, ending with a pair of hands and feet with slender fingers and toes, each digit sporting a long dark claw. Black, leathery wings, each one tipped with a lead-like spike, draped over their muscled shoulders like capes.

Their eyes, rimmed with flaky skin, pale gray with blue irises, bore into him with hate, their glare enough to make him take several steps back.

He stepped on something and when he turned, standing before him were legions of these things, all lined up like a massive army, waiting to strike. Each one watched him.

The strength ran from his legs and whatever force had been holding him upright released. His knees smacked the hot stone floor with a resounding *whack* that echoed throughout his bones.

Palms sizzling against the hot floor, the stench of burning flesh filling his nose all the way to the back of his throat, he couldn't find the strength to pull his hands up.

He was forced to let them burn.

Screaming, Joe tried calling out for help.

He couldn't speak.

The creatures worked their way toward him, long, sinewy fingers outstretched, their claws tickling the air, as if already tasting the kill.

August didn't know how long he'd been on his hands and knees, shouting into the floor, calling for Joe.

Shaking, he got to his feet and took off for the stairs, hoping that Joe had just merely fallen through the main level and was lying on his back in one of the rooms below.

August searched every one of the rooms once he was downstairs.

Joe was nowhere to be found.

Screaming for Billie, August ran back to the stairwell and bounded up the steps.

"It has begun," the man in the white coat said.

"What?" Billie asked.

He took the watch, stuffed it in his coat pocket and grabbed her by the arm. With a violent push, he shoved her *through* the stall's door, his body passing through it along with hers.

No one seemed to notice them as they emerged on the other side and Billie could only guess he had just somehow made himself invisible like her.

The ground shook, each vibration sending a shockwave of fear up Billie's spine. The man in the coat squinted his eyes, flames licking their edges, his grip on her arm increasing.

"What's—"

But he cut her off with a quick, "Shoosh."

The man peered around the bank.

"Billie! Billie!"

She spun in the direction of the voice and was relieved to see August running through the people toward her.

The old man stopped short when he seemed to take note that the man in the white coat wasn't just somebody she was standing beside but rather someone with flaming eyes who held her arm.

The man's eyes darted in August's direction. "August Norton," the man said.

The old man's eyes went wide and his jaw dropped.

The man with flaming eyes said, "You know who I am, don't you?"

It took a moment, but August responded with a nod of the head. Like Billie had, the old man began to sink to his knees.

"Get up," the man in the coat said and August instantly obeyed.

When August spoke, he could barely say the words. "I'm . . . I'm sorry. I didn't mean to." He gazed upward. "It wasn't my fault!"

The building's quake finally ceased. A moment later, a loud rumble shook the place, but only Billie and August lost their footing. The man in the white coat stood there calmly, as if he had been expecting it. Everyone else was oblivious to it.

"My name is Nathaniel," the man said.

August didn't reply.

Nathaniel finally let go of Billie's arm, the aftermath of his tight grip making her biceps ache.

Face white, August's eyes glazed over.

"August?" Billie said.

The old man's lower lip trembled.

Nathaniel's eyes suddenly darted to the floor. A second later, it split apart.

Billie's heart jumped at what began to come through.

40
THE ESCAPE

Nathaniel tossed Billie to August and the old man caught her as she collapsed in his arms. He pushed her up onto her feet and looked to the man in the bright white coat for a clue as to what to do next.

Nathaniel turned to him. "Go!" Then turned his attention back to the creatures climbing out of the tiled floor, their scaly limbs latching onto the floor and hauling themselves up like spiders trying to regain their footing. Otherworldly heat poured up from the floor, the tiles glowing red, the heat tingling through the bottoms of August's shoes.

The sharp stench of sulfur reigned.

Ankles weak, legs void of strength, August stumbled as he tried to push Billie toward the parking lot.

Through the glass at the far end, the helicopter appeared different. The dark gray goop that had coated its hull was now light, nearly white, and though from this distance August couldn't be sure, it appeared as if he could partially see through the helicopter to the cars parked on the other side of the lot.

Growls and roars filled the bank.

The building shook.

Screams roared from somewhere deep below.

Those who were solid and tangible went about their business as usual and August marveled that no one could sense the sudden presence of evil in this place.

That no one noticed the creatures with insectile bodies and leathery wings.

He urged Billie toward the window. They'd run through, emerge in the parking lot and see what was happening with the helicopter.

"Joe!" Billie shrieked and started to turn back but suddenly stopped and slammed into August.

He turned around.

The creatures poured out of the floor like wasps escaping their nest. They clung to the walls, dove on top of tables and chairs; they buzzed around the place like flies around a corpse.

Cackles and cries drowned out the sound of everyday talking.

Nathaniel was gone.

The creatures surrounding Joe had begun to ascend just moments ago. Relief washed over him because it appeared he wouldn't be their prey.

More and more of the things emerged from the dark, their putrid stench of rotten fish and sour eggs twisting his stomach into a knot. He wanted to puke, but everything was locked inside, as if he wasn't allowed even a moment's rest.

The heat scorched his skin and the reality that this place was to be his permanent home terrified him somewhere deep inside.

His spirit.

Most of the creatures slinking out of the dark spread their black, leathery wings and ascended upward, but a few came toward him.

Long, bony fingers grabbed him from behind, their claws digging into his flesh through the thick fabric of his leather trench coat, hauling him backward, closer and closer to the lake of fire in the distance.

Unable to fight against them, unable to scream or do much of anything, the sudden sense that he failed something—someone—invaded him.

Pain soaked through his body; every molecule saturated in torment. He so desperately wanted to scream to help cope with the pain.

He couldn't.

He had to endure.

Suddenly, he was tossed into the air and the bony fist of one of the creatures socked him in the face as he came back down. Green stars burst before his vision and before he even had a chance to clear his head and straighten his legs, another fist came and clocked him on the side of the head. He dropped to the hot ground and fell backward. A long and disjointed foot slammed down onto his ribcage, winding him. His ribs blazed in agony and another foot kicked him in the side of the head. Face numb, brain so dizzy he almost felt like a spectator to the massacre of his own body, he was suddenly jolted back to reality when sharp claws ripped into his thighs, digging in so deep they had enough of a hold on him that he was lifted into the air and thrown across the ground.

Screams shaking the air, he looked up and through hazy vision could make out light coming from somewhere above. White, beautiful light.

Suddenly, the light was eclipsed by the dark and disgusting forms of the creatures. Each one of their pale gray eyes pierced him, their harsh gaze filled with so much malice it made him cringe, the feeling of defeat overwhelming him.

Bony fingers with long, black claws reached for him.

Joe squeezed his eyes shut, preparing to be torn to pieces. *April . . .*

Light blinded his eyes and he couldn't help but keep them closed, its radiance was so brilliant, like staring into the sun. He forced himself to roll onto his side. It was enough to dim the light just a little so he could open them.

White was everywhere.

As his eyes began to focus, the blurred image of a man in a white overcoat ripping into the creatures danced before him.

The man threw one to the side, kicked another and ripped the wing off yet another.

"Joseph Bailey," the man said.

Joe curled up in a fetal position and covered his head. Shaking, adrenaline and fear wreaked havoc on his system. Dizziness and a dreamlike consciousness embraced his mind.

He called me 'Joseph.'

Two strong bars of iron swept under his body and the sweet smell of clean air filled his nostrils. He opened his eyes. The smell wafted off the man like a fresh breeze.

The comfort lingered a moment but soon fled when he noticed the man's eyes: bright and brilliant and aflame.

"This is what you deserve!" the man said and held out Joe, who was cradled in his arms, to the creatures advancing toward them like raptors about to pounce on their prey.

Then, gently, the man said, "But this is not your time."

The man grew bright, shining like a star. The creatures quickly covered their haunting eyes with their leathery wings.

The man's feet left the ground and they rose into the dark sky.

"We have to find him! We have to!" Billie screamed at August.

"No!" he shouted and pushed her toward the window. "We have to leave. Right now!"

The building shook and brilliant white light filled the bank. The creatures flying around shrieked at the sudden light. Some fell from their places in the air.

Then the light faded and Nathaniel emerged through the floor, Joe in his arms.

"Joe!" Billie yelled and ran toward him.

Nathaniel set Joe down on rubbery legs and touched a hand to his forehead. "Go," he said, "and remember what you saw, what you had experienced, but not until you have left this place."

Suddenly Joe was able to stand on his own two feet. He looked at Nathaniel with childlike wonder.

The creatures' shrill shrieks filled the room and the place shook again.

More poured out of the ground. There were so many it was difficult to see anything.

So relieved Joe was here and so afraid to stay a moment longer, Billie pulled Joe by the hand.

"Come on!" she shouted at him.

Joe just stood there, frozen.

Nathaniel turned to him once more. "Go, Joseph. And may the Lord be with you."

He and Billie just stood there.

"GO!" Nathaniel shoved them toward August.

As they ran toward the window, Billie glanced over her shoulder.

A throng of creatures flew toward them.

Nathaniel spun, threw off his hat and coat, revealing himself for what he really was. Though she had never believed in them before, Billie believed in them now.

Angels.

Nathaniel's long robe with a thousand folds was bronze like flame, a gold belt around his middle. Strapped across his back was an ornate silver shield inscribed with a language Billie didn't understand. The man's hair was a pillar of fire, his feet coated in bronze. White light burst from his eyes. His strong hand clasped the bronze hand guard of a sword hanging off his belt. He withdrew his sword and an electric tingle swept through the air, one dripping with authority and power. He brought the bright sliver blade high into the air. The blade burst into flame and he cut into the creatures without reserve.

August waved them forward as they ran toward him. "Come on, come on!"

He took Billie by the hand and the three of them ran through the people in a lineup in front of the ATMs by the door. They passed through the window and emerged in the parking lot beyond.

They came to a stop just in front of the helicopter. Panting for breath, Billie found herself unable to breathe when she saw the helicopter was only partly there, most of it transparent.

Growls filled the air behind them.

The creatures passed through the wall of the bank.

They were outside.

41
THE RETURN

The creatures poured out of the building, flying straight toward them.

The three turned and ran for the helicopter, which was quickly fading from view.

Joe ran to the side door and when he took hold of it, he found it difficult to get a sound grip. Grabbing the handle was like trying to tightly grab a water balloon. It took two hands to latch onto it properly and it took Billie's help once he couldn't open the door on his own to slide it ajar along its tracks.

August got inside no problem, he having had left the cockpit door open.

They scrambled into the helicopter.

"Close it, close it!" Billie shouted and the two grabbed the inside door handle and slid the thing shut just as the creatures came for them.

"Take us up, August!" Joe said.

August tried working the controls. His fingers seemed to be passing through the buttons, but each time he touched them, Joe noticed, his fingers dematerialized on contact.

The creatures flew through the helicopter doors, invading the tiny space, swarming all around.

One grabbed hold of Joe.

Billie screamed somewhere on the other side of the creature.

"Lord, help us!" August screamed.

Just then a flaming sword appeared and sliced through the air, cutting the creatures in two. Their scaly bodies fell to the ground and began to melt until they faded completely from existence.

Catching his breath, Joe peered out the window to see the man with fiery eyes standing next to the helicopter, sword ablaze.

Then the man faded from view, as did the bank, the parking lot and the brightness of the midday sun.

Darkness swelled inside the tiny cabin and Billie took Joe by the hand, squeezing his fingers in fear.

240

The air went cool and the world changed on the other side of the glass.

Gray clouds returned, filling the sky, bringing with them the sickening sense that they were back where they started: in an undead world.

The sky lingered before them then gravity took over and the helicopter dropped.

Joe's stomach flew into his throat and all three of their backsides lifted from their seats.

August pawed at the controls and a few moments later the low droning whir of helicopter blades came from above.

"Hang on!" the old man said and tugged at the collective.

Billie shrieked.

Joe screamed and suddenly the man with the fiery eyes' words from before came to him: *But this is not your time.*

"Is it now?" Joe said.

"What?" Billie shouted.

He shook his head.

After all that, after all that happened, was this how it was to end? To die in a helicopter crash in a world of gray skies and walking dead?

"Arrrrrggghhhhh!" August screamed.

The helicopter lurched forward and the roof of a building occupied the windshield.

"Pull up!" Joe shouted.

"I'm trying!" August snapped.

The helicopter angled back a little, the sky filling the top half of the windshield, the rooftop filling the bottom.

The whistling of the wind streaked by on either side of the chopper's hull.

WHOOM—Crachoonkcrachoonkcrachoonk!

The roof's pavement sprayed toward them as the blades made contact and chewed it up. They lurched forward from their seats and Joe could hear August's body plow into the controls even as his own slammed into the back of the pilot seat. Metal groaned against concrete and Joe covered his head as a barrage of cement sped toward the glass, shattered it and sprayed into the cabin.

The roar of the blades biting into the cement pierced his ears.

One of the blades snapped off the helicopter. The chopper rocked back and the three slammed into their chairs as gravity partly righted the thing, freeing the remaining slowing blades from the cement.

A loud bang resounded within the cabin as the skis hit home against the rooftop.

Covered in glass, Joe waited, listening for any movement from outside. As the helicopter settled, silence came in and his ears began to ring.

"Billie?" he said softly.

She groaned. She was alive.

"August?" he said.

Labored breaths came from the other side of the seat in front of him. "I'm here."

They were alive.

Joe's stiff and achy body shook, and he wept.

Billie could scarcely move. She had to consciously remind herself to sit up slowly lest she strain her aching muscles, which had locked up completely during the crash, something, she was sure, would cause her trouble later.

Joe stirred in his seat beside her and in her peripheral she watched as he sat up, slowly, then turned to her.

"Are you okay?" he asked.

"Yeah," she whispered as she carefully turned her neck from side to side. The muscles on either side of her neck and all the way into her shoulders screamed as she tried to look from left to right. "Sorta."

"Oh, thank God," he breathed.

August groaned.

"You okay, August?" Billie asked, a hand to her neck.

"Yeah," he rasped. "Maybe. I don't know."

From where she sat, she didn't have a good look at him but from what she could see, his face was covered in blood and one of his eyes was already beginning to swell shut.

They sat there for a few minutes, just settling, making sure that the helicopter wasn't going to move or tip or do anything that might forbid them from getting out. Once satisfied everything was as fine as it could be given the crash, Joe slowly moved from his seat and tried opening the side door. It wouldn't budge. He slammed his body against it, trying to rock it open.

"Jammed," he said.

He scanned the floor of the helicopter, as if looking for something. Then, pulling the X-09 from the holster inside his trench coat, he turned to Billie.

"Watch out." He slammed the weapon against the cracked glass of the side door. The glass spider-webbed. He smacked it again and this time it shattered. "Let's go." He put the gun away and tucked his hands into the cuffs of his jacket to protect them from the shards of glass bordering the window frame.

After he climbed out, he held out his arms and Billie eased herself out of the window. Each wriggling movement was enough to make her want to cry.

But she had shed enough tears already. It was time to swallow it and be as strong as she could.

Joe's hands held her firmly beneath the arms as he lowered her to her feet, his face wincing as he tried to control her weight.

"Oh come on. I'm not *that* fat," she said.

Joe smiled. "No, it wasn't that. Just really sore."

"I was joking."

"Oh. I meant . . ."

She turned to the cockpit door. The entire front end of the helicopter was smashed in. The blades above it were bent and twisted, one of them hanging askew over the shattered windshield, making it impossible to get August out from the front.

"How do we get him out?" she asked.

Joe approached the crumpled door and tried to pull it open. It rocked a little on its hinges but not enough to open it.

He stepped back from the door. "I guess the same way you and I got out." He got close to the glass. "August?"

The old man turned his bloody face toward him.

"I'm gonna pop the glass. Can you lower your head?"

August nodded.

"Okay, here we go."

August disappeared from view.

Joe pulled out his gun, took aim, then stopped. "What the—"

"What?" Billie asked.

He rotated the gun, examining it. "It's different."

"Different?"

"This isn't my gun, Billie." Sleek and black, this wasn't the gun he knew. The rotating chamber was gone, as was the enormous hammer he had grown so fond of. It was light, too, easier to hold. The only similarity was the sight at the end of the barrel.

"Then who's is it? No one else had a gun at the bank, Joe."

He shot her a hot glare. "I don't know whose gun it is, but this isn't mine!" And he took aim at the cockpit window and cracked off a shot.

The glass shattered.

"Take it easy!" she yelled.

Grimacing, Joe checked the gun, furrowed his brow, then stormed toward the cockpit door and peered in. "He's pretty banged up. You just gonna stand there or are you gonna help me?"

Supported on either side by Joe and Billie, August stepped slowly toward the rooftop entrance. He hadn't looked around enough to be sure, but from what he could gather, they were back on top of the Richardson building. Whatever happened to all of the undead up here, he didn't know. Maybe they had seen the helicopter coming for the roof and, in their own way, had gotten scared and stumbled off the roof's ledge? Or maybe he and the others weren't back where they started? It didn't matter. He was just thankful the dead were gone.

But that awful gray-and-brown sky. He'd recognize it anywhere.

They were home.

"Easy, man. One step at a time," Joe said.

"I'm trying. Just find me a place to sit. And make sure the roof entrance is secure. I don't want any of those things coming up here and finding us."

"We'll have to figure out a way to get down," Joe said.

"I know. We will."

They found him a spot to the side, against one of the large air vents. His body objected to being lowered down from a standing to sitting position, especially his neck and lower back.

"Here." Joe tore off the bottom of his already-torn shirt from beneath his trench coat. "Use this to wipe your face."

244

August took the fabric. "Thanks." He patted at the blood. Each dab against the wounds stung like flame.

But he was thankful he was alive.

Billie put her hands on her hips and turned to Joe. "How come you didn't notice the gun was different inside the helicopter?"

"I don't know. Wasn't paying attention. I knew it felt different but I thought that was because my hands were sore because of the crash."

"Weird."

"You're telling me."

"I'm going to take a quick look around," Billie said.

"The door," August rasped and weakly pointed to the roof's entrance. The door was ajar and looked pretty much like how Joe remembered it.

"I'll get it," Joe said.

As he neared it, he stopped when he heard footfalls within. He pulled out the X-09 and got it ready.

The footsteps drew closer. Faster.

He took a step back and called to the others, "Guys, we got company!"

August slowly turned his head toward him and looked at him with weak eyes. Billie just stood at the roof's edge, a hand covering her mouth.

The footsteps faded.

"Billie? Did you hear me?" he yelled across the roof.

She turned and faced him. Even from this distance, the look across her face was unmistakable. Something was wrong.

The footsteps didn't return.

Keeping his gun trained on the door, Joe quickly jogged over to her. "What's going on? Why didn't you—"

Her big blue eyes pleaded with his.

"What?" he said.

She pointed down to the street below.

Joe looked over the edge. The muscles in his legs lost their strength and he teetered back a step then fell onto his haunches. He inched forward and looked again. "No way."

The dead were enormous.

Below, they walked the streets. Ten of them, all giants, each at least fifteen stories tall, with wide shoulders, well-muscled jaws and razor sharp yellow teeth.

"We're dead," Billie said.

Joe couldn't help himself but nod.

From across the roof: "Joe, the door! Something's coming!"

Joe stood and, with weak legs, spun in the direction of the door and ran toward it. His thumb moved to cock the X-09's hammer, ready to blast the head off anything that came through. There was no hammer. He forgot.

What do I do? he thought. He hoped the thing was ready to roll just like before.

Closer now. The footfalls were back, growing louder.

Take it out, fast and swift. No time for games. Not with those . . . giants . . . moving around down there.

He stopped several paces from the door. He took one quick look over his shoulder to make sure Billie and August were far enough behind him and out of harm's way. Billie was at August's side, her arms around him, helping him to his feet, seemingly getting ready to run if need be.

The footfalls stopped and a humanoid shape filled the frame of the door.

Joe's heart jumped into his throat when the person emerged.

It was Des. Alive.

"What?" Joe said.

"Guys!" Des shouted and ran out to meet them, all smiles.

"Des!" Billie screamed, let go of August and ran to embrace him. The two collided in a big hug.

August teetered on his feet as he slowly came toward them. Joe moved to help him.

They made their way over. Billie still had Des in her arms.

"I can't believe this! How—" she said with a voice sopped with tears.

"What? I'm fine. You guys left without me," Des said.

"Huh?" She let go and gave him a playful shove. "Those things came after you—after us—and they . . . they . . ."

"They got you, Des," Joe finished.

Billie nodded and wiped the tears from her eyes.

Silence hung on the air.

Joe didn't know what to say. Des was alive, somehow. And there was no way he would have been able to stand against so many of the creatures alone.

A low drumbeat filled the air. Then another. And another.

Joe, August and Billie froze.

The creatures below were getting closer. Joe wasn't sure if he should do it now or wait a few more minutes to tell August about the change in the zombies' appearance.

Then again, in a few more minutes they could all be dead.

August eyed Des up and down.

"What?" Des said.

The old man arched an eyebrow, as if he knew something the others didn't. "What's going on, Des? I'm thankful you're alive, that you survived somehow, but you haven't asked about the crash or even why I'm cut up."

Joe felt himself straighten. The old man had a point. No matter who you were, you asked how someone was if you saw them bleeding. You asked if anyone was hurt if there was a crash. Joe quickly drew the X-09. "You got three seconds to answer, Des."

"Joe?" Billie said, eyeing the gun.

"One."

Des opened his hands. "Guys, come on. Everything's fine. I don't know what—"

"Two."

"Joe!" Billie snapped.

The drumbeats grew louder.

"Answer the question," August said.

Des squinted his eyes, as if at a loss for words.

Then he snarled and his peachy-white skin faded, revealing a sickening gray epidermis with chunks of flesh missing. His green eyes lit up an awful white.

He lunged for them.

"Three."

ABOUT THE AUTHOR

A.P. Fuchs is the author of many novels and short stories, most of which have been published.

He is also known for his superhero series, *The Axiom-man Saga*. The most recent installment, *Axiom-man Episode No. 1: The Dead Land*, pits Axiom-man against the undead.

Fuchs lives and writes in Winnipeg, Manitoba, with his wife, Roxanne, and two sons, Gabriel and Lewis.

Visit A.P. Fuchs on the Web at:

www.apfuchs.com and www.undeadworldtrilogy.com

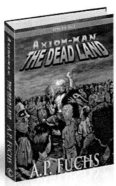

COSCOM ENTERTAINMENT

Where Imagination is Truth

www.coscomentertainment.com

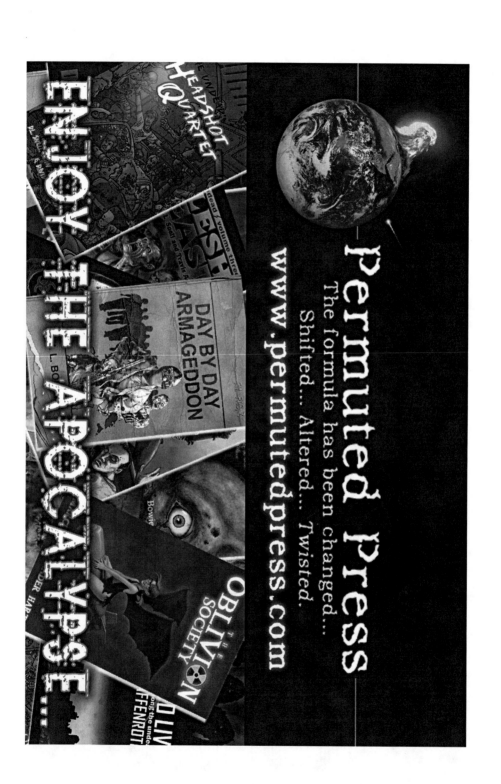

LaVergne, TN USA
24 April 2010
180356LV00002B/1/P